ZEROVILLE

Steve Erickson

ZEROVILLE

Europa
editions

Europa Editions
116 East 16th Street
New York, N.Y. 10003
www.europaeditions.com
info@europaeditions.com

Library of Congress Cataloging in Publication Data is available
ISBN 978-1-933372-39-6

Erickson, Steve
Zeroville

Book design by Emanuele Ragnisco
www.mekkanografici.com

Printed in Canada

CONTENTS

ZEROVILLE - 13

ACKNOWLEDGMENTS - 331

ABOUT THE AUTHOR - 333

*I believe that cinema was here
from the beginning of the world.*
JOSEF VON STERNBERG

ZEROVILLE

1.

On Vikar's shaved head is tattooed the right and left lobes of his brain. One lobe is occupied by an extreme close-up of Elizabeth Taylor and the other by Montgomery Clift, their faces barely apart, lips barely apart, in each other's arms on a terrace, the two most beautiful people in the history of the movies, she the female version of him, and he the male version of her.

2.

This is the summer of 1969, two days after Vikar's twenty-fourth birthday, when everyone's hair is long and no one shaves his head unless he's a Buddhist monk, and no one has tattoos unless he's a biker or in a circus.

He's been in Los Angeles an hour. He's just gotten off a six-day bus trip from Philadelphia, riding day and night, and eating a French dip sandwich at Philippe's a few blocks up from Olvera Street, the oldest road in the city.

3.

There in Philippe's, a hippie nods at Vikar's head and says, "Dig it, man. My favorite movie."

Vikar nods. "I believe it's a very good movie."

"Love that scene at the end, man. There at the Planetarium."

Vikar stands and in one motion brings the food tray flying up, roast beef and au jus spraying the restaurant—

—and brings the tray crashing down on the blasphemer across the table from him. He manages to catch the napkin floating down like a parachute, in time to wipe his mouth.

Oh, mother, he thinks. "*A Place in the Sun*, George Stevens," he says to the fallen man, pointing at his own head, "NOT *Rebel Without a Cause*," and strides out.

4.

Tattooed under Vikar's left eye is a red teardrop.

5.

Is it possible he's traveled three thousand miles to the Movie Capital of the World only to find people who don't know the difference between Montgomery Clift and James Dean, who don't know the difference between Elizabeth Taylor and Natalie Wood? A few blocks north of Philippe's, the city starts to run out and Vikar turns back. He asks a girl with straight blond hair in a diaphanous granny dress where Hollywood is. Soon he notices that all the girls in Los Angeles have straight blond hair and diaphanous granny dresses.

6.

She gives him a ride, staring at his head. She seems odd to him; he wants her to watch the road. I believe perhaps she's been taking illicit narcotics, he thinks to himself.

"Uh," she finally starts to say, and he can see it right there in her eyes: James Dean, Natalie Wood . . . What will he do? She's driving and, besides, she's a girl. You can't smash a girl over the head with a food tray.

"Montgomery Clift," he heads off her blunder, "Elizabeth Taylor."

"Elizabeth Taylor," she nods. "I've heard of her . . ." pondering it a moment. "Far out."

He realizes she has no idea who Montgomery Clift is. "You can let me off here," he says, and she drops him where Sunset and Hollywood Boulevards fork, at a small theater—

7.

—where he goes to the movies.

A silent European film from the late twenties, it's the worst print Vikar has seen—less a movie than a patchwork of celluloid—but he's spellbound. In the late Middle Ages a young woman, identified in the credits only as "Mlle Falconetti," is interrogated and hounded by a room of monks. The woman doesn't give a performance, as such; Vikar has never seen acting that seemed less to be acting. It's more an inhabitation. The movie is shot completely in close-ups, including the unbearable ending, when the young woman is burned at the stake.

8.

Afterward, he makes his way farther west along Sunset before cutting up to Hollywood Boulevard. Where once was the Moulin Rouge nightclub at the corner of Vine is now a psychedelic club called the Kaleidoscope. Vikar really has no idea what a psychedelic club is. Along Hollywood Boulevard are shabby old jewelry shops, used bookstores, souvenir stands, porn theaters. He's startled there are no movie stars walking down the street. Still hungry from having sacrificed his French dip sandwich at Philippe's, he orders a chicken pot pie at Musso & Frank, where Billy Wilder used to lunch with Raymond Chandler while they were writing *Double Indemnity*, both drinking heavily because they couldn't stand each other.

9.

He spends a few minutes looking at the footprints outside the Chinese Theatre. He can find neither Elizabeth Taylor nor Montgomery Clift. At the box office he buys a ticket and goes inside to watch the movie.

As Vikar traveled on what seemed an endless bus to Hollywood, the Traveler hurtles through space toward infinity. Dimensions fall away from the Traveler faster and faster until, by the end of the movie, he's an old man in a white room where a black monolith appears to him at the moment of death. He becomes an embryonic, perhaps divine Starchild. Vikar has come to Los Angeles as a kind of starchild as well, a product of no parentage he acknowledges, vestiges of an earlier childhood falling away from him like dimensions. Vikar tells himself, I've found a place where God does not kill children but is a Child Himself.

He's now seen two movies, one of the Middle Ages and one of the future, in his first seven hours in Los Angeles. Vikar crosses Hollywood Boulevard to the Roosevelt Hotel, built by Louis B. Mayer, Douglas Fairbanks and Mary Pickford in the year the movies discovered sound.

10.

Vikar walks through the Roosevelt lobby, which has a statue of Charlie Chaplin. With its stone arches and palm fronds, it's slightly seedy; the first Academy Awards were held here forty years before. At the front desk, he asks for room 928.

The young clerk behind the front desk says, "That room's not available." His long hair is tucked into his collar beneath his coat and tie.

"Are you certain?"

"Yes."

"Seventeen years ago," Vikar says, "Montgomery Clift lived in that room."

"Who?"

Vikar restrains the urge to pick up the small bell from the desk and lodge it in the philistine's forehead. For a moment he considers the image of the clerk having a bell for a third eye, like a cyclops. People could walk up and ring it, and every time they did, this infidel would remember Montgomery Clift. "Montgomery Clift," Vikar says, "lived here after making *A Place in the Sun*, when he was filming *From Here to Eternity*."

11.

The clerk says, "Hey, man, have you seen *Easy Rider*? I usually don't go to movies. I'm into the Music."

"What?"

"The Music." The clerk turns up the radio. There's a song playing about a train to Marrakesh: "All aboard the train," the singer sings. It's horrible; they've forgotten *A Place in the Sun* for this? Vikar also suspects there's something narcotics-related about the song.

"Montgomery Clift's ghost lives in this hotel," Vikar says.

"No," the clerk answers, "that's that D.W. guy."

"D.W.?"

"It's in the brochure. He died here or something, busted." He adds, "I don't mean busted like by the cops—I mean broke. His ghost rides up and down the elevators trying to figure out where to go."

"D.W. Griffith?"

"I think that's him," the clerk nods, impressed, "yeah, D. W. Griffin." He looks at the register. "Room 939 is available, that's in the other corner at the other end of the hall, so it's like Room 928 except backward."

"All right."

"By now," the clerk shrugs, "they may have changed around all the numbers anyway."

"The ninth floor is probably still the ninth floor," says Vikar.

The clerk seems slightly stunned by this. "Yeah," he allows, a sense of revelation sweeping over him, "the ninth floor *is* probably still the ninth floor." In the register Vikar signs *Ike Jerome*, which is not an alias. No one, including himself, calls him Vikar yet. He pays cash; the clerk gives him the key and Vikar heads to the elevator. "That was heavy, man," the clerk calls after him, "that thing about the ninth floor."

12.

When Vikar steps in the elevator and pushes the button for the ninth floor, one by one all of the other floors light up too.

At each floor, the door slides open. Vikar feels someone brushing past him, leaning out and peering just long enough to determine it's the wrong floor, before continuing on to the next.

13.

Vikar can't see the Chinese Theatre from the window of room 939, but he can see the Hollywood Hills and the Magic Castle above Franklin Avenue. Houses topple down the hills in adobe and high-tech, some rounded like space ships. Leaning far to the right and staring west toward Laurel Canyon Vikar could also see, if he looked for it, the speck of the house that he'll live in nine years from now. The morning after his first night in the Roosevelt, he walks down the hallway and finds, as the clerk advised, room 928 at the other end, and peers in as the maid makes it up. From its window overlooking Orange Street, Montgomery Clift couldn't see the Chinese Theatre either.

14.

That first night in the Roosevelt, Vikar has the same dream he always has after every movie he sees, the same dream he's had since the first movie he ever saw. In his dream there's a horizontal-shaped rock and someone lying on the rock very still. The side of the rock seems to open, beckoning to Vikar, like a door or chasm.

15.

Vikar stays at the Roosevelt three nights. When he checks out, he asks the clerk where Sunset Boulevard is. The clerk directs him south on Orange. "When you get to Sunset," he says, "see if you can hitch a ride west." He motions with his thumb. "That will be to your right, man."

"I know which direction is west."

"That's where the Music is."

"Thank you," Vikar says, leaving quickly, still inclined to lodge the desk bell in the clerk's head.

16.

He sees phosphorescent cars and vans painted with Cinema-Scopic women with stars in their hair and legs apart and the cosmos coming out of the center of them, bearing travelers and starchildren. At Crescent Heights, Sunset winds down into the Strip's gorge, and Vikar stands as if at the mouth of wonderland, gazing at Schwab's Drugstore . . . .

. . . he knows the story about Lana Turner being discovered there isn't true, but he also knows that Harold Arlen wrote "Over the Rainbow" there and that F. Scott Fitzgerald had a heart attack there. Vikar is unclear whether F. Scott Fitzgerald actually died there; he lived somewhere around the block. Actually, he's unclear about F. Scott Fitzgerald, beyond the fact he was a writer whose work included *The Women*, starring Joan Crawford, although he didn't get a screen credit.

17.

Across the street, on an island in the middle of the intersection, is a club called the Peppermint Lounge. Another kid with long hair points Vikar north, up the boulevard into the canyon. "Check it out," he advises, staring at Vikar's head, "about half way up you'll come on this old fucked-up house where people crash." The hippie adds, in a manner at once conspiratorial and breezy, "Lots of chicks up there who don't wear anything, man."

18.

An hour later, halfway up Laurel Canyon Boulevard, grand stone steps swirl into the trees, to a ruin a little like Gloria Swanson's mansion in *Sunset Boulevard*. William Holden's role in *Sunset Boulevard* was written for Montgomery Clift, who turned it down because he was afraid the character of a younger man kept by an older actress was too much like him; at the time Clift was seeing an older actress, one of the rare romantic relationships with a woman he had. Someone at the country store in the belly of the canyon tells Vikar the house is where Harry Houdini lived while trying to become a movie star in the twenties, making movies with titles like *The Man From Beyond, Terror Island, The Grim . . . The Grim . . . The Grim* what . . . ?

19.

The only chick Vikar finds who doesn't wear anything is three years old. Standing in the clearing of what was once the house's great living room, she has dark curls and a preternatural gaze.

She looks at Vikar, the pictures of the man and woman on his head, the tattooed teardrop beneath his left eye. She's undecided whether to laugh or cry. A paternal distress at the vulnerability of the little girl standing alone before him sweeps through Vikar, and he feels a surge of rage at whoever could have abandoned her here. For a few minutes the man and girl study each other there under the cover of the canyon's trees.

"Zazi."

20.

Vikar turns to look over his shoulder at the voice behind him.

The most beautiful woman he's ever seen off a movie screen calls to the little girl. With long auburn hair and a tiny perfect cleft in her chin, in the same gossamer dress that all of the young women in Los Angeles wear, she smiles at the tattooed man a cool, almost otherworldly smile he's never seen, its source a secret amusement. At the same time, he's relieved to sense in the woman the same concern for the girl's safety that he feels. The woman's eyes lock his; he smiles back. But she's not smiling at him, rather she's smiling at her power to enchant him—and it's like a stab to his heart for him to realize that he is the reason for her concern, that she would believe for a moment he could hurt a child. When the woman's eyes fix on his and she softly says the girl's name again, it's as if trying not to provoke a wild animal only feet away.

"Zazi." This time the young woman glides slowly to the middle of the ruins to take her daughter and back away from Vikar slowly, clutching the girl to her. Neither the woman nor the girl takes her eyes off him. The woman looks at Vikar a moment longer as if to make certain the spell will hold long enough to get the girl to safety.

Then she turns and carries the child across the boulevard to a house on the opposite corner, the small girl watching Vikar over her mother's shoulder.

21.

Like the wild animal the woman believed he was, Vikar stalks the grounds of the Houdini House in the dark, pounding on the walls, trying to remember. *The Grim . . . ?*

Houdini was related to one of the Three Stooges by marriage. I'll bet I'm the only one in this Heretic City who knows that.

22.

Vikar later learns that the Houdini House has secret passages leading to all parts of the canyon, although he never finds one. The house across the boulevard on the corner, where the young woman took her daughter, once belonged to Tom Mix. Now it's occupied by an extended family of hippies led by a musician with a Groucho Marx mustache. Hippies and musicians everywhere . . .

23.

. . . but something has happened, it's become a ghost canyon.

Above the ruins of the house, Vikar sees caves in the hillside. A fire burns in one and he makes his way to it, climbing through the trees. The cave has two entrances, forming a small tunnel. Inside the cave, a young couple huddles around the fire.

24.

Vikar stands in the mouth of the cave. The young man and woman look at Vikar, at his bald illustrated dome, and spring from the fire lurching for the cave's other opening.

Vikar watches them run off the hillside into the night air, then plummet the rest of the way down into the trees and the stone ruins of the house below.

25.

In the August heat, the lights of small houses in the canyon shimmer like stars while the stars in the sky hide in the light and smog of the city, as though outside has turned upside down.

In the tattoo on Vikar's head, Montgomery Clift looks away slightly. It's as if he's not only rapt with Elizabeth Taylor but hiding from everyone the face that would be so disfigured later upon smashing his Chevy into a tree, when it would be Taylor who first reached the site of the crash and held him in her arms.

26.

When Vikar wakes in the cave the next morning, the campfire is out. Standing in the cave's mouth he looks out over the canyon; he sees houses and the small country store below, but not a soul. The canyon is abandoned and still. "Hello?" he calls to the trees.

27.

As the minutes pass, there's not a sign of life for as far as he can see . . . .

. . . until in the distance, at the end of the canyon boulevard, a police car appears and then another behind it, and another, stealthily winding their way up through the hills, sirens silent but coming fast, determined in their approach.

Vikar watches the police as they grow nearer. They stop below at the foot of the stone steps that lead up to the house, a dozen cops emptying from four cars and fanning out at Vikar's feet . . . .

. . . then one looks up and spots him. Then they all stop to look. They draw their guns and charge the hillside.

28.

Below, the closest cop points his gun up at Vikar and tells him to raise his arms. In the mouth of the cave, overlooking the canyon, Vikar is too stunned to move. "Arms in the air!" the cop repeats. Other cops emerge from the trees at the foot of the hill, their guns also pointed. Vikar raises his arms. "Get on your knees!" says the first cop.

"I have to pee," Vikar says.

The cop says, "Get. Down. On. Your. Fucking. Knees." Vikar lowers himself to his knees. Looking around, he can see hippies come out of their houses all over the canyon to watch, he can see in the doorway of the house across the street the beautiful woman with the small girl. The cop tells Vikar to lie on his stomach and keep his arms away from his sides, then slide slowly down the hillside on his stomach.

"Slowly?" Vikar says, apparently to no one as he comes hurtling down the mountain, face skimming dirt and rock all the way. When he finally stops at the base of the hill, one cop lands hard on Vikar's back and another cuffs his hands behind him. Another tells him he's under arrest and has the right to remain silent and to a lawyer. "Can I pee?" Vikar says as they shove him in the back of the patrol car.

29.

The Grim Game.

30.

At the police station they draw a sample of his blood. For three hours he waits in a holding cell before he's brought to an interrogation room.

This is for hitting that man with my food tray, he believes. Or perhaps for the others, the ones before Los Angeles. *It's the end of righteousness.* But he decided long ago that if righteousness means no movies, he would rather be damned.

Three white men and a black man and a white woman wait for Vikar in the interrogation room. All the men wear suits. A graying man, distinguished looking, like the chief of detectives in a movie, appears in charge. The woman, who never says anything, seems to be a kind of doctor.

31.

Vikar is seated at a table with the woman on the other side and the men standing around him. "Is Jerome," the chief asks, "your first name or last?"

"Someone asked me that before," says Vikar.

"Well, now I'm asking you," the chief says.

"It's my last name."

"Ike is your first name?"

"Someone asked that as well."

"Well, if you had some sort of identification, Mr. Jerome, like a driver's license, we wouldn't have to ask."

"I don't know how to drive."

"Ike is short for . . . . "

Vikar shakes his head: *It's not short for anything.* "It's just Ike," he says.

"You say you're from Ohio?"

"It's not short for anything," Vikar says.

"O.K.," the chief says, "it's not short for anything. Where in Ohio you from, Ike? Cincinnati?"

"I didn't say Ohio. I said Pennsylvania." He knows I didn't say Ohio.

"How long you been in town?"

They asked this before as well. "Four days. Five."

"Is it four or is it five?"

"It depends."

"Not really, Ike. It's either four or it's five."

"No," Vikar says, "it depends. Do you count the first day I got here as the first day, or after the first twenty-four hours—?"

The good-looking movie-star chief brings the back of his hand crashing across the side of Vikar's head, catching Elizabeth Taylor just under the chin. Vikar flies off his chair across the room and crumples against the wall.

32.

The chief comes over and kneels beside him. "Don't be cute."

"I'm not," Vikar says.

"I think you're being cute."

"No."

"What did you come to L.A. for?" says the chief.

"I came to Hollywood."

"O.K., Ike. What did you come to Hollywood for? Score some weed? You have some sort of big transaction in the works?"

"Weed?"

"Our blood work shows you have marijuana in your system."

"That's not true," Vikar says calmly.

"We know about you. We know about the scores up in the canyon."

"Scores?"

"People are spooked in the canyon these days. Maybe you noticed."

"No."

"No more happy hippie wonderland since a few days ago." The chief acts as though he's pondering something. "About the time you came to town, now that I think of it," as though thinking of it for the first time, but he's not thinking of it for the first time, and Vikar realizes none of this is about any "weed" or "score." The chief says, "What did you say you came to L.A. for?"

"Hollywood."

"O.K.," irritated, "Hollywood."

"To work in the movies."

"Are you an actor?"

"No."

"What is it you do in the movies?"

"I don't do anything yet." He adds, "I just got here. Four days ago. Or five."

"Let me show you something," says the chief, "here, let me help you to your feet."

"It's all right," Vikar says.

"No, let me help you." The chief pulls Vikar to his feet and picks up the chair. Vikar sits again at the table. "Better, Ike?"

Vikar nods.

"Sorry I lost my temper there. I apologize."

Vikar looks at the others standing around.

"Let me show you something," says the movie-star chief, and one of the other men hands him an envelope.

33.

The chief opens the envelope and pulls out seven black-and-white photos and lays them out on the table.

Vikar sees them for only a second, it's all he can look. "Oh mother!" he screams, and topples from the chair as if struck again.

The chief comes back over to Vikar on the floor and, as before, kneels next to him. "This one," he says, holding up one photo, "was the eight-month-old fetus cut out of this one," holding up another photo with the other hand. Vikar turns away, sobbing. "Pretty much slaughtered, wouldn't you say, Ike? Pretty much butchered. This last one," the chief holds up the seventh photo, "this one of the writing on the door, this business about the pigs . . . what does it say?" he turns the photo around as though looking at it for the first time, but he's not looking at it for the first time. "This one about the pigs. Written on the door of the house in the blood of," waving one photo, "the mother of," waving the other, "this one. Am I supposed to take it personally, Ike? Was this for me, this about the pigs?" but Vikar sobs, wishing he never had seen it.

34.

Five minutes later Vikar is still on the floor and the police are trying to get him to stop crying. "O.K.," the chief says. "O.K., God damn it."

"Oh mother, oh mother . . . . "

"Stop it." The chief hands the photos back to the black detective who gave them to him. Vikar begins to calm down. "You O.K.?"

Vikar says nothing.

"You O.K.?"

Vikar shakes his head. The chief studies him, disappointed.

The woman and the other men now leave the room, one by one. Vikar is still. "So," the chief finally says, nodding at

Vikar's head, "what's with the James Dean and Natalie Wood?"

35.

They leave him in the interrogation room—

—but through the open door he can hear a couple of voices. " . . . couldn't even look at the photos," one of the voices sounds like the chief's, "how could he have done that to those people?"

"He's a freak," the other voice says.

"That's awfully astute, Barnes. But the city is full of freaks and by itself it doesn't put him on Cielo Drive with five butchered bodies."

"I think I like them better when their hair's down to their asses. Never thought I'd say *that* . . . . " The voice lowers. "Chief, I can't say this when Peters is around, but I'm telling you it's the coloreds on this one."

"Don't say that when Peters is around," sternly.

A pause. "Odd about the name thing. That he would lie about that, of all things—that business about 'Ike' not being short for . . . . "

"It doesn't," the chief interrupts, "put him up there in the canyon hacking up five people including a pregnant woman."

"Fucking Hollywood degenerates. Live freaky, die freaky."

"For God's sakes, don't go around saying that either." Another pause. "You know when we located his father, he wouldn't admit having a son."

"Well, chief, would you? What's with the fucking head, that's what I want to know. I like all the hair better, never thought I'd say it. The hair down to their asses. Live freaky, die freaky, I'm telling you."

36.

Forty-five minutes later, a patrol car deposits Vikar at Hill and Third in downtown Los Angeles. "I'd stay out of those canyons if I were you," one of the cops tells him. "There's something going on up there."

"Tell the chief my father was right," Vikar answers. "He doesn't have a son."

37.

That night Vikar slips into the Chinese Theatre through a back door and sleeps on the stage behind the screen. All night, images from the movie fly over him, as though he's lying at the end of a runway, below an endless stream of jetliners landing.

For four months after arriving in Los Angeles, he works as a handyman at the Roosevelt, riding the elevator with the ghost of D. W. Griffith, who died there twenty years earlier. On his days off, he walks the two miles down Vine to the edge of Hancock Park and the old Ravenswood apartments and the baroque El Royale where Mae West lives, and the orphanage where Norma Jean Baker once could see from her window, a half mile east on Melrose, Paramount Studios and its arched wrought-iron gates just beyond the fountain at Bronson Avenue. When he gets a job at the studio building sets, he rents a $120 second-story apartment on Pauline Boulevard, a secret street in the Hollywood Hills entered only on foot by a long flight of stone steps.

38.

Vikar sees an Italian movie in which a father's bicycle, on which his job depends, is stolen. The father and his small son search the city for the stolen bicycle. When they don't find it, in desperation the father steals another bicycle and is caught, threatened and humiliated by an angry mob. The father loves his son so much he's willing to defy God's laws for him. But for this transgression he's punished and abased, and the boy learns that it's a sin for fathers to love their sons too much.

39.

Vikar still had his hair when he was a twenty-year-old studying architecture at Mather Divinity and saw his first movie. Actually, having finally summoned the courage to defy his father, he saw his first two movies on the same day, back to back.

One, about a London photographer who discovers a murder in a photo of what otherwise appears to be a serene park, made sense to Vikar like nothing else had. The second movie was about a family of sirens living in snowy mountains, pursued by police and leaving a trail of malevolent music. Some months after arriving in Los Angeles and after his own experience with the police, Vikar thinks of this movie when another singing family is arrested for the murders of five people, including a woman eight months pregnant, that took place in the canyons on Vikar's first night in the city. Gazing at the ravines from the window of his apartment on the secret Pauline Boulevard, Vikar can't shake, no matter how hard he tries, the movie's refrain, going around in his head. *The hills are alive*, he shudders, *with the sound of music.*

40.

When Montgomery Clift was living at the Roosevelt Hotel in room 928, Ike Jerome was seven years old in eastern

Pennsylvania. One night he heard come into his room his Calvinist father who allowed in the house no books except the Bible, no magazines, newspapers, radio or the then new invention of television. The little boy pretended to be asleep as his father knelt next to him in the dark.

"Our God the Father," the father whispered in the boy's ear, "had one hour of weakness for which He has spent eternity paying, and that was the moment He stopped Abraham from proving to Him his true faith and devotion. Children are the manifestation of the sin that soiled the world with pleasure's seed, and the Bible teaches us that sanctification lies in the deliverance of children from this life and from the sin of their birth and existence. Our God the Father learned His lesson. When He punished the Pharaoh for his pride and disobedience, did He smite the Pharaoh? No, shrewdly and without further weakness He smote the Pharaoh's child, as He smote all the Egyptian children. Down through all the Book of Books He has smote the children until in the end he smote His own child, and had He not stopped Abraham in a moment of heedless mercy then perhaps our God the Father would not have had to kill His own child later. Remember that you are bound to transcend the sin of your childhood by finally setting aside the things of childhood for the things of manhood so that you might live down all your days of sin before delivering your soul to Him, unless by some fantastic glory the God our Father should decide to deliver you from this life now, while still in your wretched state of childishness, you . . . you . . . " breathing heavily, "you manifestation you, of all men's sins."

"Wallace?" The voice of his mother in the doorway. Ike continued to feign sleep. There was a trembling in his mother's voice he had never heard.

"Go to bed," his father said to her without turning from the boy.

"Wallace." Her voice more firm. This was a moment,

though Ike didn't realize it for years, when anything might have happened.

"As all sons are marked by the destiny of righteous sacrifice," the father hissed, "so all righteous fathers would be Abraham again, to guide our God the Father's hand in His hour of weakness."

"*Wallace,*" his mother again, insistent in a way the boy hadn't heard before, and wouldn't again.

41.

At Paramount, Vikar works for a while on the set of a Vincente Minnelli musical about reincarnation. Then he works on an Otto Preminger movie about a burned woman who happens to be played by Vincente Minnelli's daughter. He can't believe his luck to be working on movies by Vincente Minnelli and Otto Preminger. But no one else seems impressed.

In the evenings Vikar takes the bus to the Vista, the theater at the fork of Sunset and Hollywood Boulevards where he saw his first movie upon arriving in Los Angeles. More than sixty years before, the Babylon set for D. W. Griffith's *Intolerance* was built on this spot, so monumental that it could be seen for miles around. Vikar catches revival screenings of *Scarlet Street*, *Forty Guns*, *Humoresque* with John Garfield as a concert violinist and Joan Crawford as the woman who loves him. In *Written on the Wind*, the Four Aces croon a love theme over a drunken Robert Stack careening his roadster through town, haunted by the conviction he's sterile, as nymphomaniacal Dorothy Malone sits in a mansion stroking the small gold replica of an oil derrick.

42.

Vikar buys a small black-and-white television that he carries home on the bus. He even buys a radio. On the television he watches old movies and the news. Asian jungles aflame, a spaceship on the way to the moon malfunctioning, a very famous rock band breaking up . . . when four students are shot by soldiers on a Midwestern campus, it reminds Vikar of his father, and he turns the news off. Amid the rest of the music on the radio, occasionally he hears something beautiful.

> *Now I'm ready to feel your hand*
> *And lose my heart on the burning sand*
> *Now I want to be your dog*

He's only been living in the Hollywood Hills six or seven weeks when one night around 12:30, as he's in bed about to fall asleep, he hears the footsteps of someone on the stairs outside that lead to his door.

43.

Vikar gets up from bed, unplugs the radio, glides into the dark of the kitchen and waits behind the door.

The knob turns slowly back and forth. *From now on I should remember to lock the door.* When the door opens and someone steps through it, Vikar smashes the radio on the intruder's head.

I like that song about the dog, he thinks, the unconscious burglar at his feet.

44.

Vikar ties the burglar to a chair and calls the police. He sits on the couch waiting, wondering if the movie-star chief will come. The black man with a large afro slumps in the chair.

Still waiting twenty minutes later, Vikar turns on the television to a Bette Davis movie. Paul Henreid puts two cigarettes in his mouth and lights them both, handing one to Davis.

45.

The burglar comes to. He gazes around, disoriented; it's a moment before he realizes he's bound to a chair.

"I called the police," Vikar tells him. The burglar just grunts. "What are you breaking into my house for?"

The burglar doesn't answer at first. Vikar stares at his hair. The burglar finally says, "What are you staring at?"

"Your hair."

"You're staring at my hair?" the burglar says, nodding at Vikar's head. "You want to see some strange shit maybe you should look in the mirror sometime." He studies the ropes around his chest and squirms, grumbling to himself. "Elizabeth Taylor and Montgomery Clift in the terrace scene from George Stevens' *A Place in the Sun* tattooed on this white motherfucker's head, and he's staring at *my* hair."

46.

Vikar sits up on the couch. "That's right," he says. "It *is* Elizabeth Taylor and Montgomery Clift from *A Place in the Sun*."

"Yeah, I know that, fool," the burglar looks back at him, "isn't that what I just said?"

"Most people believe it's Natalie Wood and James Dean from *Rebel Without a Cause*."

"*Rebel Without a Cause*?" the burglar says in disbelief. "Well, my fresco-crowned, tinsel-towned friend, you're hanging with a distinctly uncultured class of folks if they don't know James Dean from Montgomery Clift." He settles in the chair and stares at the television.

"He died five years ago," Vikar says.

"What?" says the burglar.

"Montgomery Clift died five years ago." It was seven months after Vikar saw his first movie. He read Clift's obituary in the newspaper and saw *A Place in the Sun* at a revival house in Philadelphia, one of half a dozen people in the theater. "He was forty-five."

"Hmpf," says the burglar.

"I'm in the Movie Capital of the World," Vikar says, "and nobody knows anything about the movies."

Fixed on the TV, the burglar mutters, "I'll tell you one thing, Dean wasn't in Clift's class as any actor. I'll tell you that."

"All anyone talks about in this city is music."

"Best thing that little fag did was smear that faggy little Porsche Spyder of his clean across the highway. But of course he went and stole all Clift's thunder when he did that . . . . " The burglar squirms more in the chair. "Clift was a homo too," he allows, "he just didn't have the good sense to die in *his* car accident. Fucked up his face—would have been better off dying."

"It's horrible."

"What?"

"The music."

"White hippie bullshit."

"A lot of it is about illicit narcotics."

"I'm not into that hippie jive bullshit," says the burglar.

"Well, Sly is a hippie, but he's a brother. 'I Want to Take You Higher.'"

"That sounds like it's about illicit narcotics."

"Bebop man, myself. Bird, Mingus, Miles. *In a Silent Way*. Some of the old cats too. Ben Webster. Johnny Hodges."

"I heard a good song about a dog," says Vikar. "Right before I smashed my radio on your head."

"I don't want to hear about any song like that."

"Sorry about the rope. The police will be here soon."

The burglar shrugs. "No rush on my account."

"You weren't going to kill me and write 'pig' on the door in my blood, were you?"

"Are you being funny, jackass?" the burglar glares at Vikar. "Don't you read the papers? That was some fucked-up white hippies did that business, no matter how hard they tried to pin it on black folks."

A silence falls between the two men as they wait for the police. For about ten minutes they watch Bette Davis on TV.

47.

The burglar says, "Here's the scene. I love this part. The looks on their faces when she goes from being the frump to the fox. Or as foxy as Bette got, anyway."

"*Now, Voyager*," says Vikar.

"Yeah, I know it's *Now, Voyager*, man. You think I don't know that? The apotheosis of the forties studio system's so-called 'women's picture'? Like I don't know it's *Now, Voyager*."

"I like the music in *Now, Voyager*. The music in *Now, Voyager* and the song about the dog."

"I told you I don't want to hear about any song like that."

"John Garfield playing the violin when he walks into the sea in *Humoresque*, I like that as well."

"Joan Crawford walks into the sea in *Humoresque*," says the bound burglar.

Vikar says, "Are you sure?"

"Course I'm sure."

"I saw it not long ago."

"Well, you didn't see it very well."

"I believe it was Joan Garfield who walks into the sea. I mean John."

"You can't even keep your Joans and Johns straight. Why would John Garfield walk into the sea? How is John Garfield going to play the violin if he walks into the sea? You ever seen anybody trying to play the violin while walking into the sea?"

"He could. He could play the violin while walking into the sea."

"No, man," the burglar shakes his head.

Vikar says, "I guess I'm not sure, to be honest."

"It's Joan Crawford who walks into the sea, take my word for it."

48.

Watching more of *Now, Voyager*, the burglar continues, "Garfield's violin parts in *Humoresque* were by Isaac Stern, though Franz Waxman did the score." The burglar nods at the TV. "The music for *Now, Voyager* here is by Max Steiner. Waxman and Steiner were both of the German/Austrian persuasion but Waxman came over right before the War while Steiner was here earlier. Waxman also scored your *Place in the Sun*," nodding at Vikar's head, "copped himself an Oscar for it, while Steiner composed the music for that racist *Gone With the Wind* jive. Maybe if Steiner had Hitler on *his* ass like Waxman, he'd have had a different outlook on things."

"I don't believe *Gone With the Wind* is a very good movie."

"So aren't you enlightened," the burglar says. He lapses into silence. "Bette didn't dig it one bit," he says after a moment.

"*Gone With the Wind*?"

"Steiner's score for *Now, Voyager*. She actually bitched to Jack Warner it was upstaging her performance."

"Really?"

"Tried to get the music dropped, that's a stone fact."

"What happened?"

"Well, you're hearing it, aren't you? So they must have used it, right? Got to be the only time in the history of the movies that one of the biggest stars of all time lost a creative power struggle to the composer," the burglar laughs. "Steiner wound up getting *his* Oscar for it, while Bette lost hers that year to Greer Garson—so that must have *really* fried Bette's ass. It's a complete Puccini rip but that's the thing about the movies. If the music was just a little better, it wouldn't be as good, you hear what I'm saying?"

"No."

"I mean that's the whole thing about the movies," says the burglar. "Bigger than the sum of the parts and all that? If the parts are too good, the whole is somehow less. I mean, you can't have, you know, Trane doing the score for *Now, Voyager*."

"Trane."

"I mean, if he had been around then, which of course he wasn't. But if he was, what would Coltrane sound like on *Now, Voyager*? Wouldn't be the same, would have been *too* good. You hear what I'm saying?"

"What movies did he score?"

"How's that?"

"I don't know Trane. What did he score?"

The burglar stares at Vikar evenly. "You're trying to vex me now."

"What do you mean?"

"I know you got me tied up here and shit, but that's cold, trying to vex me that way."

"I'm not trying to vex you."

"Man," the burglar closes his eyes, wincing, "what did you say you hit me with?"

"My radio." Vikar says, "Your hair probably saved your life."

"Don't start in on the hair, O.K.?" The burglar tries to shake his thoughts clear. Turning his attention back to the TV, he says, "*Now, Voyager* was directed by Irving Rapper after Bette got Michael Curtiz thrown off, so dig it," he laughs, "she could kick Curtiz's ass but not Max Steiner's. Course, next picture Curtiz did was *Casablanca*, so he didn't do too badly. Rapper here did *Glass Menagerie* later and has a new movie out right now."

Vikar says, "The director of *Now, Voyager* has a movie out now?"

"In theaters as we speak."

"He must be a hundred years old."

"Well, he's not a hundred, but he's up there."

"What is the movie he has out now?"

"*The Christine Jorgensen Story.*"

"Who?"

"*The Christine Jorgensen Story.*"

"Who's Christine Jorgensen?"

"Christine Jorgensen is Christine Jorgensen."

"Is that a real person?"

"Course it's a real person. It's *The Christine Jorgensen Story*. Have you ever heard of *The So-and-So Story* that wasn't about a real person?"

"Perhaps."

"No, not perhaps," the burglar says in exasperation, "you've got some peculiar notions, even for a white boy. If it's got *The* at the beginning and *Story* at the end, then it's a real person. Is *The Adventures of Robin Hood* called *The Robin*

Hood Story? Is *Gone With the Wind* called *The Scarlett 'White Racist Bitch' O'Hara Story*?"

"So who's Christine Jorgensen?"

"Cat who became a lady, jack."

"What?"

"This cat who became a lady."

Vikar says grimly, "You mean one of those men who wears women's clothes."

"No, son. I mean one of those men who *becomes* a woman."

Vikar's mind races frantically. "What do you mean becomes a woman?"

"I mean he gets his dick cut off. I can't explain the whole thing surgically—"

"Oh, mother."

"—it's sort of out of my area of expertise. But they cut off the dick and balls and—"

"Oh, mother!"

The burglar shrugs. "—just tuck the rest up inside. Make a pussy out of it somehow . . . . "

"Stop."

"I'm just trying to expl—"

Vikar leaps from the couch. "Stop."

49.

He looms over the bound man. Alarm flickers across the burglar's eyes.

"Yeah, solid, man," the burglar says as calmly as possible, "we're cool." Vikar sways where he stands. "I'm just trying to update you," the other man says, as calmly as possible, "on the oeuvre of our boy Irving Rapper here, who directed *Now, Voyager* which, with all due allowances to *Humoresque*, may or may not be the apotheosis of the forties 'women's picture.'"

Vikar relaxes a bit.

"We're mellow now, right?" the other man says. Vikar sits back down on the couch. For a moment they don't say anything. "Dig it," the burglar finally goes on, "Rapper's last movie before *The Christine Jorgensen Story* was about Pontius Pilate. So Rapper's tripping on some extremely intense weirdness or maybe those are just the gigs he's getting."

"Was it called *The Pontius Pilate Story*?"

"No, it wasn't called *The Pontius Pilate Story*. I didn't mean every story about a true person is called that."

"Pontius Pilate was the great Child killer, the descendent of Abraham as God's greatest instrument."

"Uh," the burglar says, "O.K." He watches the movie for a while.

Vikar says, "Why would that man do that?"

"What?"

"Make himself into a woman."

"Now, do we want to have this conversation or not?"

"I just wonder why."

"Cause a bit ago you had some volatile shit going on. So are we going to have this conversation? Because if we are, you have to decide."

"Just why. Not how."

"Check it out," the burglar wearily shakes his head, "who would you rather be," to *Now, Voyager* on the TV, "Bette Davis or Paul Henreid?"

"Paul Henreid," Vikar answers.

"No, man, negatory. You wouldn't. I don't believe you. Not a cat as seriously into the cinematic aesthetic as yourself. I'm not talking about real life or faggy shit here, I'm talking about *the movies*. Dig it, Paul Henreid not only lights Bette's cigarette, he gets it going for her too." The burglar laughs. "The movies, man! Shit that would be downright *silly* in real life, in the movies it's the most out of sight thing ever. Lighting two cigarettes at once! For years after, women were always stopping Henreid in the street asking him to do that. No, man, if you were in *Now, Voyager*, you definitely would rather be Bette Davis."

"Paul Henreid is in *Casablanca*."

"Exactly! Exactly my God damned point! In *Casablanca* Paul Henreid, he's leading the whole Resistance against all those white Nazi motherfuckers, he's got the whole café singing the *Marseillaise* and shit, he's like the noblest stone-righteous cat in the place—and you still would rather be Humphrey Bogart. Check it out," nodding at Henreid on the TV, "Paul Henreid is the most whipped man in the history of movies, jack! Pussy whipped and he's not even getting the pussy! Cause I can assure you positively that Bette is not letting him bang her, he's lucky if he gets to lick her." He laughs at the TV, stomping one foot on the floor. "All whip and no pussy for you, Paul!"

"That's why that man became a woman?" says Vikar.

"I'm just making an empirical observation," the burglar sighs, "that in *Now, Voyager*, anyone would rather be Bette Davis, and some people out there," he says, "maybe they don't know life isn't a movie, they don't know about playing the hand you're dealt."

"Perhaps he became a woman so he can walk into the sea with John Garfield playing the violin in the background."

"There you go! Right on! Now you got it. He wanted to walk into the sea with the violin playing and you got to be a lady for that shit to be glamorous. Can't do it as a man, even if you're wearing a dress, without it being too pathetic. Especially if you're wearing a dress." They hear an approaching siren in the night and stop talking, but then it fades into the distance. *Now, Voyager* reaches the end and Max Steiner's music swells. In unison, Vikar, the burglar and Bette Davis say, "Oh, Jerry, don't let's ask for the moon. We have the stars."

50.

Vikar wakes with a start on the couch. " . . . check it out," he hears a voice, "some wicked shit on the tube tonight."

Vikar's prisoner is still tied to the chair, watching the TV.

"My Darling Clementine," the burglar is saying. Vikar realizes he's fallen asleep, and that in his sleep he's been hearing the other man's voice as though there's been no pause in the conversation, as though the burglar has been talking the entire time. Vikar tries to clear his head and wipes his eyes. "John Ford's greatest movie," says the bound man, "now I know what you're going to say . . . . "

It's four in the morning, hours since Vikar called the police.

" . . . *Stagecoach.* Right? *The Searchers.* Well," the burglar continues, "*Stagecoach* was a distinct landmark in the genre, no getting around it. But that shit hasn't aged well—"

"Uh."

"—though no one wants to cop to it, while *The Searchers* is one wicked bad-ass movie whenever my man the Duke is on screen, evil white racist honky pigfucker though he may be. I mean he may be a racist pigfucker, but he's bad in *The Searchers*, no getting around it."

"Bad?"

"I can see I need to choose my words more carefully," says the burglar. "I mean Duke gives a performance of terrifying intensity and sublime psychological complexity, whether by intent or just natural fucked-up white American mojo. *The Searchers* loses it, though, whenever Jeffrey Hunter and Vera Miles come on—Ford, he couldn't direct the ladies for shit, unlike my man Howard Hawks where all the ladies are fine and kick-ass on top of it, even if they're all versions of the same fox, or as William Demarest puts it down in Preston Sturges' *The Lady Eve*, 'Positively the same dame!'" The burglar stomps his foot and laughs, pleased with himself. "I mean

Lauren Bacall in *To Have and Have Not* actually has some of the same exact lines as Jean Arthur in *Only Angels Have Wings*. But now *My Darling Clementine* here, it's practically noir Western, all moody and shit, Ford's first after the War and all the concentration camps and maybe he wasn't in his usual sentimental rollicking drunk-Irish jive-ass mood. Check out my man Henry Fonda as Wyatt Earp and, dig it, Victor Mature as Doc Holliday and, dig it again, Walter Brennan as Pa Clanton! I don't mean no Grandpa McCoy from TV, I mean in *My Darling Clementine* Walter Brennan is one stone fucked-up killer, you hear what I'm saying? 'When you pull a gun, kill a man!' Damn! *My Darling Clementine,* it's got the inherent mythic resonance of the Western form but in terms post-War white folks understood, figuring they were all worldlier and more sophisticated than before the War. Ford's creation of the archetypal West, laying out codes of conduct that folks either honored or betrayed—and I'm just trying to give the motherfucker due credit, not even holding against him, not too much anyway, the fact that he played a Klansman in that jive *Birth of a Nation* bullshit—anyway Ford's view of the West was so complete by this point that Hawks, Budd Boetticher, Anthony Mann, they could only add to it, you hear what I'm saying? But of course the Western changed along with America's view of itself, from some sort of heroic country, where everybody's free, to the spiritually fucked-up defiled place it really is, and now you got jive Italians, if you can feature that, making the only Westerns worth seeing any-more because white America's just too fucking *confused*, can't figure out whether to embrace the myth or the anti-myth, so in a country where folks always figured you can escape your past, now the word is out that this is the country where you can do no such thing, this is the one place where, like the jive that finally becomes impossible to distinguish from the anti-jive, honor becomes impossible to distinguish from betrayal or just, you know, stone cold murder . . . what are you doing?"

Vikar unties him from the chair. "Don't break into my place again," he says.

The burglar looks almost hurt, but he stands from the chair slowly, a bit painfully, and arches his back and rubs his wrists. "O.K., man," he answers quietly, "solid."

"I'm sorry about your head," Vikar says.

The burglar's eyes return to the movie. "It's cool. Occupational hazard. Hey, uh," there's a slight pleading in his voice, "can I just see the rest of this?"

"Well." Exhausted, Vikar is due on the Paramount lot in five hours.

"There's this scene coming up where Henry Fonda is having a drink in the saloon and," the burglar starts laughing again, "he says to the saloon keeper, 'Mac, you ever been in love?' and Mac answers, 'No, I've been a bartender all my life.' Oh man!" the burglar slaps his thigh.

"I'm tired," says Vikar.

"I've been a bartender all my life!"

"I—"

"Hey, go ahead and get some sleep. It's been a long night."

Vikar looks at the room around him.

"Hey," the burglar says, "on my honor as a foot solder in the armed struggle against the white oppressor, I'm not touching anything. Go ahead and get some sleep. I just want to see the end of *My Darling Clementine*. What do you say."

Vikar returns to the couch. In his sleep, he hears sirens again. When he wakes two hours later to daylight coming through the window, the other man is gone and so is the television.

51.

In Vikar's dream, the horizontal rock, open and gaping, draws him in, while lying across the top of the rock is someone unknown yet utterly known, awaiting a judgment. The bright night of the dream is always dazzled by an unseen full moon, in the light of which Vikar can, with every passing recurrence, read across the top of the rock something carved in a glowing white, ancient language.

52.

After seeing his first film, Vikar forsook divinity school for cinema. He was transfixed by the sight of a beautiful nude woman painted entirely gold; her body was discovered by the spy who seduced and thereby doomed her. It was difficult for Vikar to be certain just how bad the spy felt about this. In another movie, a private eye fell in love with the blonde he was hired to follow. The blonde was haunted by past lives and the memory of once having committed suicide by flinging herself from an Old California mission steeple; when she described the steeple, the private eye recognized it, and told her she had seen it not in any past life but this one. But it was the private eye who didn't know the truth, a truth he could never suspect.

53.

As his graduating thesis at Mather, Vikar designed the model of a small church. He woke one morning seeing the church perfectly in his mind. He saw the church's unusual steeple and its carving of a crowned lion holding a gold axe, with which a beautiful nude woman might be struck and turned to gold herself. Vikar's vision of this church was so perfectly realized in his mind that he worried it was something he had seen and forgotten, as though in a past life.

When the review committee became angry at Vikar's presentation, at first the architecture student believed it was for some sacrilege having to do with the crowned lion and its golden sacrificial axe. In fact the committee chairman's fury had nothing to do with the lion or axe but with the fact that the small model church had no door. "There's no way in!" the chairman thundered, and even as the years passed, by the time Vikar got to Los Angeles he couldn't be sure whether leaving out the door had been inadvertent: "I believe," Vikar had answered in all innocence, "it's more that there's no way out."

54.

For a moment Vikar thought that, in his fury, the committee chairman might hurl the model to the floor and shatter it.

If he had, the committee would have seen that where an altar should be was a tiny blank movie screen, blank because the image that belonged there was from the movie of his dreams, the scene of the mysterious figure lying on the horizontal rock.

55.

That was the night Vikar shaved his head. The tattoos would come later, at a bus stop on the outskirts of Las Vegas, on the road to Hollywood.

56.

After finishing a Jack Lemmon comedy, Vikar is assigned by Paramount to a love story about a rich boy and a poor girl. At the end of the movie, the girl dies. "It's like *A Place in the Sun* except reversed," Vikar whispers one afternoon on the set to a tiny older woman who has about her the smell of bourbon. "In *A Place in the Sun*, he's poor and she's rich and he dies at the end."

"You look stupid and rich," the actress says to the actor in the scene that's shooting.

"Well," the actor answers, "what if I'm smart and poor?"

The older woman next to Vikar smokes a cigarette and looks at him dead-eyed. "Yes, it's like *A Place in the Sun*," she whispers back, "except she," pointing at the actress, "isn't Liz Taylor and he," pointing at the actor, "isn't Monty Clift and," glancing at the director on the other side of the set and dropping her voice even lower, "no disrespect to poor Arthur, but he's definitely not Mr. Stevens."

"*I'm* smart and poor," says the actress.

"Well, what makes you so smart?" says the actor.

"Mr. Stevens?" says Vikar.

The actress answers, "I wouldn't go out for coffee with you, that's what."

"Well," says the actor, "what if I wasn't going to ask you to go out with me?"

"Well, that's what makes you stupid."

On the other side of the set, the director calls for a cut. The woman next to Vikar rolls her eyes. "Still think it's like *A Place in the Sun*?" she says to Vikar.

57.

Vikar says, "You knew George Stevens."

"He's still with us, you know," the woman says. "He's not past-tense yet." She puts out her cigarette on the arm of a stranded chair. "Saw him about eight months ago over at Fox, as a matter of fact, making another picture with Liz. Monty," she says, "Monty's not still with us, of course. It's Warren in the new one. Liz will survive all her men," then, thinking a moment, "except maybe Warren." She reaches her hand out to Vikar. "Dotty Langer," she says, and as they shake hands she reaches up and gently rubs Vikar's bald head like the little old mother she appears to be, before walking off to a nearby trailer and closing the door.

58.

For a week Vikar watches Dotty Langer go in and out of the trailer during and after each day's shoot. The next time they talk, an exterior street scene which Vikar helped build is being shot with the same actor and actress. The actor has so little presence it seems to Vikar as though at any moment he'll disappear into thin air. Vikar is more captivated by the actress, whose brown eyes remind him of a faun.

Dotty stands by the door of her trailer talking to a burly black-bearded man. In red bermuda shorts and an unbuttoned white dress shirt with the sleeves rolled up, he smokes a cigar; his Volkswagen bug is parked in the distance with a surfboard on top. When they finally walk over, Dotty says to Vikar, "*Place in the Sun*, meet *Red River*."

"What do you say, vicar," the bearded man laughs, sticking out his hand. Vikar has no idea why the man calls him this; he's never been called it before. "Viking Man," the bearded man introduces himself.

Dotty rolls her eyes. "The 'Viking Man' here is writing a Western for Huston over at Warners."

"Quiet on the set!" someone yells.

"Quiet!" someone else yells. The set goes quiet. "Action," calls the director.

"I forgot my key," says the actress.

"Jenny," answers the actor, "I'm sorry."

"Don't. Love means never having—"

"Cut," calls the director. He consults with the A.D. in the chair next to him, who consults with the script supervisor in the chair next to him. "You're writing a movie for John Huston?" Vikar says to the black-bearded man.

"Ali," the director says to the actress, "the line is 'not ever.'"

"What?" says the actress.

"You said 'never'. The line is 'not ever.' "Love means not ever.' Let's try it again."

"Quiet on the set!"

Silence, then the cameras begin rolling again. "Jenny, I'm sorry," the actor says.

"Don't," she answers, "love means never—"

"Cut."

The actress glares down the street past her leading man. She becomes less bewitching to Vikar. "I don't believe they're very good," he whispers with some concern to Dotty, who's smoking again. Viking Man next to her smiles broadly at the spectacle. "Make-up!" calls the A.D.

"He's a TV soap-opera star," Dotty explains, "who got the part after five other actors turned it down. She's a fashion model who's sucking the new head of production's cock until his eyes roll so far back in his head they would be looking at his brains if he had any."

"Can we get make-up on Ryan?" the A.D. calls. After a couple of minutes, filming begins again. "I forgot my key," says the actress.

"Jenny, I'm sorry."

"Don't. Love means never having—"

"Cut."

"What the fuck's it matter!" the actress explodes. "Who cares whether it's 'not ever' or 'never'! Doesn't 'never' mean 'not ever'? It's a shit line anyway!"

Viking Man guffaws and people turn to look.

"I don't even understand the fucking line!" says the actress. "Where's Bob?" looking around.

"Bob's the new head of production," Dotty says to Vikar.

"I want to talk to Bob!" the actress demands.

"Bob needs to fuck this broad in the ass a few times," Viking Man chortles loudly. Now everyone turns to look.

"John has a charming perspective," Dotty tells Vikar. "He thinks Vietnam is a good idea, too." She says to Viking Man, "Louder, John. I'm not sure Evans can hear you on the other side of the lot."

"Too much cowgirl for this broad," Viking Man announces merrily, "not enough ass-fucking to put her in her place."

"Jesus," Dotty moans, covering her face.

"Hey, what do I care?" Viking Man shrugs happily. "I don't work for this dinosaur," waving his cigar at the studio. "What junk."

"Come on," Dotty says to the two men, turning toward the trailer.

"Pork her one in that tight little Wellesley ass," Viking Man advises the multitude. "She'll get the line right."

59.

Inside the trailer Dotty turns to Viking Man and says, "Speaking of dinosaurs, I would like to keep this job. I don't know how many more I'm going to have." Behind her on a worktable is a moviola.

"God love you, Dot," snorts Viking Man, "you'll be here when the rest of us are long gone."

"I worked on a Vincente Minnelli movie and an Otto Preminger movie," Vikar says.

Dotty and the Viking regard him for a moment. "Minnelli's a fairy," Viking Man finally answers, "and Preminger is a Nazi."

"I would think," Dotty says, "that puts him right in your pantheon, John, but actually Preminger's a Jew. Can you please go away now? Go shoot someone, as long as it's not me or someone who might hire me in the foreseeable future." She says to Vikar, "The man has an arsenal."

"Not a Stevens man, myself," Viking Man indicates the tattoo on Vikar's head, "*Shane*'s a little rarefied for me. Dot here can tell you about that one."

"I didn't work on *Shane*," Dotty says. "They thought a woman wouldn't know anything about a picture like that. I came back for *Giant*."

"I'm more a Huston/Hawks/Ford/Walsh/Kurosawa man," Viking Man continues.

"If the screen grew balls and a penis, that would be John's idea of the ultimate cinematic experience," says Dotty.

"But I appreciate the concept," Viking Man says, still looking at Vikar's head.

"He senses in you untapped reserves of psychosis. It makes him all moist."

"Dot here will give you my number. Do you surf?"

"No," says Vikar.

"I've got some friends who live out at the beach. Actors, writers, directors—God love them, they're pinkos and hippies, but they're O.K. They'll dig the Liz/Monty trip," pointing at the tattoo, "if it doesn't freak them out."

"Do they listen to horrible music all the time like everyone else in Hollywood?"

"A couple of the girls are into music," Viking Man says at the trailer door, "but the guys pretty much live, breathe, eat and shit movies. See ya, Dot. So long, vicar."

Dotty and Vikar look at each other after he leaves. "At least he cares about movies," Vikar says.

"If he didn't," she says, "he'd be a whack job, all surfing and guns."

"I tell people I've worked for Vincente Minnelli and Otto Preminger," Vikar exclaims, "and nobody cares."

60.

"Well, listen." Dot lights a cigarette and lowers herself slowly in a chair by the moviola. Next to the moviola is a Jack Daniels bottle. "You've got people your age just coming into the business who will be running Paramount in five years, along with Warners and Columbia and Fox and MGM—all of which will be owned by companies that have nothing to do with pictures—who have never heard of Minnelli or Preminger, or just might be erudite enough to think of Liza when you say her father's name. Then you've got people like me who have been around long enough not to have much romance about any of it anymore and are just trying to find some cover because we have no idea what's going on. Biker pictures are winning prizes at Cannes and pictures about cowboy hustlers in New York getting sucked off in the cheap seats are winning Oscars, so the execs upstairs who are old enough to be my grandfather—which means we're talking Dawn of Man here—feel gripped by a kind of cultural dementia. When my mother was in her last years, in her mid-eighties, she would wake at four in the morning and look out the window and wonder why it was so dark at four in the afternoon. The reasoning process by which you realize it can't be four in the afternoon but has to be four in the morning had broken down. That's what's going on with these gentlemen. Minnelli musicals about past lives or whatever that thing was? Here at this studio we've brought in a gigolo to head production and the best we have going for us outside that door is a trite romance with two no-talents who don't know how to say their lines, and a second-rate Mob picture written by a hoodlum and an egomaniac practically just out of film school. And in these groovy times, who's going to see those?"

61.

Vikar says, "I've missed my chance."

"Maybe you have," says Dotty, "or maybe this is your chance and you're not paying attention, or your chance hasn't come yet and you should start getting ready for it. I'm not saying forget about Vincente and Otto—you obviously know enough about pictures to know you can still learn from those guys, which is more than the punk who made that biker picture will ever figure out. I'm just saying don't expect those names to have the magic for most people they have for you. John's crowd," she nods at the trailer door where Viking Man just left, "will get it—writing this thing for Huston, he's as gaga as you are in his own way—but nobody else will. What do you want to do in pictures? I assume not build sets for the rest of your life."

"I don't know."

"Well, that's different. Did you go to school?"

"I was an architect."

"Really." She says, "Maybe we can get you into production design."

"You edited *A Place in the Sun*," Vikar says, looking at the moviola behind her.

"I worked with Billy Hornbeck who edited it. We won the Academy Award. A few years ago they kicked Billy upstairs over at Universal where they're about to give up altogether and concentrate on television. Now he's one of those old men who can't figure out why it's dark at four in the afternoon."

"I had a television," Vikar says. "It was stolen."

Dotty puffs her cigarette. "Did it exactly leave a gaping hole in your life?" Vikar coughs from the smoke; Dotty puts out the cigarette and waves the smoke in the air. "I have to go back out there now," she says, "and face the music for letting John on the set. What an asshole." She pulls from the editing table a scrap of paper and writes on it, then rises from the chair, suddenly seeming even older. She hands the scrap to Vikar. "I don't always hang around a picture I'm cutting, there's not really a need unless it's a massive production on a tight schedule and we have to cut as we go along. But when I know making anything decent of it is going to be impossible, I get this crazy idea that being on the set and seeing dailies will give me some hint how to go about it. You would think I'd be disabused of that notion by now." She nods at the phone number in Vikar's hand. "You might give John a call. He *is* an interesting guy and knows some interesting people."

62.

At the Vista Theater, Vikar sees a black-and-white Japanese gangster movie about a contract killer hired by a mysterious woman to carry out a hit. As the gunman is about to dispatch his target, a butterfly lands on the barrel of the rifle and diverts his aim, resulting in the murder of an innocent bystander. It's also the first movie Vikar has seen that shows people having sex. "We are beasts," the woman moans in the Japanese movie. "Beast needs beast." Vikar leaves the theater with the most unforgiving erection he's ever had. He waits in the shadows of the lobby for sundown and catches a bus.

63.

On the bus, the erection doesn't go away. A pretty girl gets on a few stops after Vikar, and then at the next stop a Latino mother with a small child, and when the bus reaches Vikar's stop and he still has the erection, he's too embarrassed to rise from his seat, so he goes on riding . . . .

64.

. . . into the night—

—west on Hollywood Boulevard and then cutting down La Brea to Sunset, turning right. The mother and child get off and then the pretty girl, but Vikar continues on until he's the only one on the bus and he can see the driver watching him in the rear-view mirror. By the time the bus reaches the Strip, Vikar's erection is finally gone. The driver still stares at him in the rear-view mirror.

65.

The bus winds past the Continental Hyatt where rock musicians throw pianos off the top floor, toward Tower Records and the Whisky-a-Go-Go. The Strip is a corridor of glimmering broadcasts from other times, each corner set on a different channel: intergalactic geisha houses and flophouse chateaux,

Persian flying saucers and supersonic English Tudors. When Vikar departs the bus, the blue-deco Sunset Tower looms above him; he looks up at it awhile because he happens to know George Stevens lives there. Vikar crosses the street and waits until a bus arrives, heading east to take him back into Hollywood. When he gets on, it's the same bus with the same driver.

66.

It's only after several attempts that Vikar gets an answer. "Oh yeah, the vicar!" the voice booms on the other end of the telephone. "George Stevens man! Never was a Stevens man. A bit of a pussy Western, *Shane*, if you don't mind my saying so." They plan to see a foreign movie about Algiers that Viking Man already has seen four times, but on the appointed day he doesn't show.

Two weeks later, at a minute past six in the morning, almost eighteen months to the day since arriving in Los Angeles, Vikar is thrown from his bed by a terrific jolt. He believes a bomb has gone off. The bedroom bends to a new geometry; beyond the windows is the flashing of electrical wires collapsing. Vikar can hear in the kitchen a tremendous crash of dishes flying from their cupboards, and the light he leaves on in the kitchen at night, ever since the burglar broke in, goes out.

67.

Among the rubble flung from shelves and cupboards, Vikar searches for only one thing until he finds it: the small model of the church with no door, with a crowned lion holding a gold axe on the steeple, and a blank movie screen inside where an

altar should be. One of its walls is slightly folded, but otherwise the model survives intact.

Outside Vikar's apartment, people slowly emerge from
their houses to survey the aftermath. After a while Vikar makes
his way gingerly down the outer stairs that are no longer
aligned. He's standing on the lawn watching everything when
a Volkswagen pulls up, a surfboard on top. The window on the
passenger side rolls down. "Vicar!" a voice calls out.

Vikar strolls into the street and peers into the car.

Viking Man's hair is wet and crusted with salt. "My God," he
says, cigar between his teeth, "I was out in the ocean, water like
glass, and there was this . . . " he thinks a moment, ". . . shift,
like someone had pulled the plug at the bottom. And I look
up, vicar, and there's the grandest wave I've ever seen. Hop
in," he says.

"I have to work today," Vikar says.

"Vicar," Viking Man explains patiently, taking the cigar
from his mouth, "nobody's working today. We've just had the
biggest fucking earthquake in forty years. Get in the car. I need
to stop at my place first, if you don't mind."

68.

In Viking Man's apartment, a large closet he's made into a
movie library is strewn with reels of film. The reels have
unspooled into a sargasso of celluloid; a projector stares from
the end of the closet. Outside is the sound of sirens. Viking
Man assesses the destruction calmly; he flicks a switch by the
door but no light comes on. "I would say let's watch a movie,"
he continues flicking the switch, "but we don't seem to have
power."

"Maybe we don't like the same movies anyway," says Vikar.

"Vicar," Viking Man says, "there's five hundred movies

here. If there's not one we both like, one of us is the Antichrist."

69.

Back in the Volkswagen, Viking Man cuts up to Sunset Boulevard which is still dead, until they hit Crescent Heights where traffic becomes more congested with every passing minute. He turns the Bug up Laurel Canyon and now traffic is heavy, particularly coming down the canyon from the other side; they pass the Houdini House where Vikar spent his first night after leaving the Roosevelt Hotel. A fallen eucalyptus partially blocks the boulevard. Brazenly, Viking Man scoots his Beetle around it. At Mulholland Drive, police are turning traffic back; just as brazenly, Viking Man zigzags left and heads west along Mulholland until he finds a place to stop in a vacant patch of dirt overlooking the San Fernando Valley.

70.

The Valley looks like the crater made by a dead star. On the car radio is continuous news about the quake. At one point the broadcaster announces plans to evacuate the Valley west of the 405 freeway, due to a ruptured dam in the north.

"Get this, vicar," Viking Man exclaims. "They're saying an eight-foot wave is going to come roaring through that ravine up there—" he points to the Santa Clarita Pass on the other side of the Valley, "—at a hundred miles an hour. Can you fathom that?" He can hardly contain his excitement.

"Are we all right here?" says Vikar.

"Hey, I'm ready," Viking Man smiles, reaching out his window and slapping the surfboard on top. "I'll just hop my board and you can roll up the windows and float to Redondo Beach."

"You're making a joke," Vikar finally says.

Viking Man looks at him. "Yes, vicar, I'm making a joke," he says quietly. "Eight feet, a hundred miles an hour, it's still not going to reach Mulholland Drive. But it will be righteously holocaustic if it happens," he says wistfully. "What I wouldn't give for a tab of acid right now. This may be as close to the Bomb as we ever get."

Vikar studies the scene.

"You know, vicar," Viking Man says, tossing away his half-devoured cigar, "for some reason I feel like maybe you and you alone would understand this, but God loves two things and that's the Movies and the Bomb. Of all the monuments we've made to God over the last five thousand years, have there been any that so nearly communicate our awe of Him? Have there been any that so nearly approximate His majesty? With the Movies and the Bomb, we've offered gifts that are worthy of Him."

"God hates children."

For a moment Viking Man is too lost in his reverie to have heard, but then he turns to the other man. "Can't say I ever thought of it that way, vicar."

"God is always killing children in the Bible or threatening to," says Vikar. "He kills His own child."

Viking Man nods slowly. "That's a hell of an observation," he says. "Listen, vicar, can you hand me something from the glove compartment?"

Vikar opens the glove compartment. There are maps and an old note pad and pen. There's also a small package of something wrapped in foil.

"Hand me that small bit of tin foil there, will you?" says Viking Man.

Vikar takes the foil from the glove compartment. Under the maps is a gun. "There's a gun," says Vikar.

"Smith & Wesson .38. Go ahead and hold it if you want."

"No, thank you."

"Good for you, vicar," Viking Man says, unfolding the foil and carefully beginning to roll a joint in his lap, "it's not a damned toy. Schrader already would have shot one of us by now, the stupid son of a bitch." He lights it and draws in the smoke and offers it to Vikar.

"No, thank you."

"Good for you again. It's a hippie pinko indulgence, basically fit for fairies with flowers for cocks and spade musicians, for some of whom I have an extraordinarily high regard, I should add. But some sort of mind alteration is called for in these circumstances, and in lieu of the lysergic sacrament or a bottle of half-decent Cuervo, this will have to do."

Viking Man throws the Bug into reverse and backs out of the lot. He continues driving west on Mulholland, crossing the Sepulveda Pass and winding along mountain roads. All of the freeways are closed and the surface streets are clotted with traffic. It takes two and a half hours to reach Malibu Canyon Road and cut over to Pacific Coast Highway.

At the sea, Viking Man turns right and heads north, talking about movies all the way.

71.

Past the Colony and up the highway until they're almost to Zuma—

—where Viking Man finally pulls off PCH, heads up the beach side of the boulevard along a row of water-logged houses until he slides into the drive of one. Pulling the surfboard off the top of the car, without a word to Vikar he strides toward the beach, circling around the house rather than through it.

Vikar sits in the car a moment, until Viking Man is nearly out of sight, before he gets out and follows.

72.

A crowd of about a dozen people, more men than women, are on the beach on the other side of the house. "Viking Man!" one of the guys calls out to him. "Earthquake waves!" All the guys call out to Viking Man and the women ignore him, until one sees Vikar standing alone in the sand. She looks after the other man running toward the ocean with his surfboard. "Uh, John?"

Viking Man stops at the water's edge and turns.

"Is this guy with you?" asks the young woman. She's lying on a towel in the sun; she has dark hair and is naked and has the largest breasts Vikar has ever seen. Two other women, one dark and one blond, wear bikini bottoms and no tops. Two other women, one petite and the other large, are dressed; the petite one says more bad words in five minutes than Vikar has heard a woman say or all the women he's heard combined.

"That's the vicar," Viking Man answers.

The dark-haired woman looks at Vikar. Vikar says, "I'm a friend of Viking Man."

"The vicar and the viking," the woman says, lying back on the towel and closing her eyes, "isn't that too cute for words?"

73.

Vikar stays three days. He can't figure out how to get home. He loses track of when Viking Man is around and when he isn't, and he doesn't want to ask anyone else for a ride into town. The crowd grows smaller and then larger, faces come and then go just as they become familiar; the dark-haired naked woman and the topless blonde are attentive to Vikar, asking now and then if he wants something to eat or drink. He believes no one is paying attention until he turns his gaze fast enough to catch people staring at him. He suspects some of them are taking illicit narcotics.

They seem only vaguely aware there's been an earthquake. This is mostly a subject of concern as it applies to the size of the surf or when someone makes a trip to the local market and finds the beer or wine understocked. Everybody is involved in the movies but they're not like Vikar imagined; none of them looks like a movie star, except perhaps the dark-haired woman and one of the guys who's not particularly handsome but has a big black beard like Viking Man and also a flashing smile and a matinee manner about him. He wears a safari outfit that he seems to consider debonair. Vikar believes he's an actor but in fact he's an aspiring director.

74.

All the guys Vikar believes are actors are directors, and all the guys he believes are directors are actors. The women cook the meals and take care of the guys who, as Viking Man said, care and talk about nothing but movies. "The peak of Hawks' art," one is saying the first afternoon. "Hemingwayesque in its understanding of masculinity's values and rituals."

"Dean Martin is underrated in that movie," Viking Man agrees.

"The opening scene," points out another, "where he's digging the coin out of the spittoon? All wordless. A kind of American kabuki."

"Existential," someone adds, "in its exploration of courage and professionalism even at its most futile."

"Angie Dickinson," Viking Man says, "is the modern incarnation of the quintessential Hawks woman." The conversation continues like this for about half an hour, until there's a pause.

"The Western," Vikar says, "has changed along with America's view of itself from some sort of heroic country where's everybody's free and shit to the spiritually defiled place it really is, and now you have jive Italians, if you can feature that, making the only Westerns worth seeing anymore because white America's just too confused, can't figure out whether to embrace the myth or the anti-myth, so in a country where folks always figured you can escape the past, now the word is out that this is the country where you can do no such thing, this is the one place where, like the jive that finally becomes impossible to distinguish from the anti-jive, honor becomes impossible to distinguish from betrayal or just, you know, stone cold murder."

It's the first thing more than four words long that Vikar has said since arriving. Including the women preparing the meal, the household comes to a stop. After a long silence Viking Man says, "That's a damned interesting perspective, vicar."

"Uh," someone else says, "let's go surfing!" The room immediately clears of everyone except the women. The dark large-breasted one studies Vikar for a moment and returns to the cooking. After that, Vikar doesn't say anything else. The only person who talks as little as Vikar is an intense dark man in his late twenties who sits on the couch staring at him and at his head in particular; he has a strange smile. Five years later Vikar will remember the man, and the way he looked at Vikar's head, when Vikar sees him with a mohawk in a movie about a cab driver who goes crazy and kills everyone.

75.

The beach house is shabby, the plywood walls warped from moisture, the garish shag carpet blotched and worn. There are three bedrooms upstairs, and a balcony circles and overlooks the downstairs, which is organized around a fire pit in the center. Sofas and chairs line the walls. His second day in the house, sitting in the living room and staring at the blue necklace of the sea stretched across the breast of the sky, Vikar turns to see a five-year-old girl standing next to him, looking at his head.

76.

It's only when the girl's mother calls that Vikar realizes it's the same child he saw in the ruins of the Harry Houdini house in Laurel Canyon, after first arriving in Los Angeles.

"Zazi." Vikar turns to the same soft voice and the same beautiful young woman with the auburn hair and the perfect cleft in her chin who hurried the little girl across Laurel Canyon Boulevard that day a year and a half before. Now the beautiful woman wears only a bikini bottom.

The little girl reaches out to Vikar's face, to wipe away the red teardrop tattooed beneath his left eye.

77.

As she did that day in Laurel Canyon, the woman appears to float across the room to take the girl back, just as the girl's finger almost touches Vikar's face. Perhaps there's more urgency in the rescue this time, the hubbub of this house lending itself not so much to the woman's gifts for casting spells. The mother carries Zazi through the sliding doors of the house out onto the deck, looking—as she did in Laurel Canyon—over her shoulder at Vikar.

"Soledad Palladin," Viking Man explains to Vikar later that afternoon.

"I would never hurt a child," says Vikar.

"How did a three-year-old wander across Laurel Canyon Boulevard anyway? Who was Soledad fucking or what drug was she inhaling when she was supposed to be keeping an eye on her kid?" They sit on the deck watching everyone. "They're really not a bad lot, vicar," says Viking Man, "for a bunch of hippies and pussies and over-indulged bohemian brats. The guys all want to be the next John Ford and haven't yet come to grips with the fact that *I'm* the next John Ford, and the only reason I'm the next John Ford is because I'm not the next Howard Hawks, who made the greatest movie of all time, *Red River*, with your Mr. Montgomery Clift. Of course Monty was a fairy. Are you a fairy, vicar?"

"No," says Vikar.

"I wouldn't want to offend you if you were."

"Thank you."

"You got to hand it to Monty. For a little fairy he near pulls it off, you almost accept in *Red River* he actually could hold his own in those fisticuffs at the end with John Wayne, when hard logic tells you it's patently preposterous. He had presence, Clift did, there's no taking that away from him. But I can't be the next Howard Hawks because I could never make a musical or screwball comedy—I know my limits, vicar, you got to give me that. So I have to settle for being the next Ford, and there you have it in a scrotum sac: what all these other pussies would kill for, I'm just *settling* for. You can't blame them for the profound disappointment, vicar. It must be damned disconcerting. The women all want to fuck me, that's obvious, you can't blame them for that either." Looking at the women, Vikar isn't so sure it's obvious. "I'm too overpowering and, after me, where would they go? Marty? Paul?" He points to this guy and that. "Margie Ruth fucks Hitch because he's writing her a horror movie, of all things."

"Margie Ruth?" says Vikar.

"The crazy one with the tits," the Viking gestures his cigar at the dark-haired woman. "My God, vicar. Imagine getting to fuck those tits for a horror movie. What would she let him do for a good movie? Hitch," he points at the bearded man in the dapper safari jacket with the matinee smile, "he's the one who wears the stupid jungle costume all the time—Mr. Big Game Hunter. I call him Hitch because he doesn't want to be the next John Ford, he wants to be the next Alfred Hitchcock. He's got Margie thinking she's going to play Siamese twins in this movie of his," he snorts, "Siamese twins, vicar! Will they be joined at the tits or have four of them?"

"Are they all actresses?"

"Who?"

"The women."

"Well, sure," he shrugs, "that's what I'm trying to tell you, vicar. The guys want to be John Ford and the girls want to be Siamese twins in horror movies joined at the tits, that's the difference. What else are they going to be, the next . . . " he waves his cigar, searching his brain, " . . . *Donna Reed*? What's the point, vicar? That's what I'm saying. These days you've got veteran actresses who once won Academy Awards playing gorillas from the future. It's really not a business for broads. Used to be, of course. But it's not like any of them is going to be the next Garbo—they're not even going to be the next Ava Gardner. Janet over there," he points to one, "had a glory-moment ten years ago, some arty movie about some retarded girl in love with some retarded boy—doesn't that give you a hard-on, vicar? Isn't that something you just have to see? It won some festival somewhere and she hasn't done anything since. Margie was in a Gene Wilder movie a year or two ago, and Jenny, the blonde, is up for some dinky part or other in some movie or other because her dad just won a screenplay Oscar after being blacklisted most of the fifties—so the commies are making a comeback, God love 'em. Not *all* of them want to be actresses—Cass over there," the large woman in a muumuu, "has nothing to do with the movies, she was in a singing group everyone in the world has heard of except you, probably, and made a fortune in the lifespan of a larva and is already washed up at the age of thirty, living in the next house over with Julia," the petite woman with short cropped hair in jean shorts, "who doesn't want to be Garbo or John Ford but the next Jack Warner or Harry Cohn and may just be evil enough to pull it off, now that I think about it. Now that I think about it, Julia's the one who will show us all up, right before she uses the least of us, whoever that is—there's about four candidates within a beer bottle's throw—to pick the rest of us out of her teeth."

78.

"As for Soledad," says Viking Man, "where do you start? It's one crazy story after another. No one is sure how old she is, anywhere between her early twenties and her early thirties, born in Seville to Andalusian gypsies or some damned thing that sounds just silly enough to be true. Legend has it her father is Buñuel illegitimately—if that's so, then she's at least three or four years older than she admits to since Franco ran Buñuel out of Spain in the late forties. She may not know for sure about her father any more than she knows for sure who's the father of little Isadora—Zazi—there. Story has it Sol was dancing flamenco by the time she was eight. Story has it she was in a nuthouse for a while in Oslo, and story has it she was cast as the woman who vanishes on the island in *L'Avventura* and then was dropped at the last minute, for mysterious reasons no one ever has understood or explained. She did some soft-core in Italy or France, came to the States, what? six, seven years ago. Hung around the Strip making the circuit between Ciro's and the Whisky—story has it she's a witch and that on Venice Beach twenty miles down the sand here," he points down the beach, "she gave Jim Morrison the blowjob of all time, channeled from the netherworld. She can be medusa or sweet as candy on pretty much a moment's notice. It's hard to know exactly what she feels about her daughter. For a while they were part of Zappa's commune in the canyon, so of course the story's gotten around that if Morrison isn't Zazi's dad, Zappa is, and if Sol knows, she's not saying, and if she says, she's only guessing. Neither seems likely. By all accounts Morrison can't get it up most of the time and, other than just happening to share the same roof along with thirty other people, Zappa himself is actually a fairly straight arrow about such things, as I understand it. 'Isadora,' well, that's a little elegant, hell, that's practically blue-blood for a guy who names his kids Dweezil."

79.

On his last night at the beach house, Vikar is trying to sleep in one of the bedrooms upstairs and has dreams of Soledad Palladin as Siamese twins, naked and joined not at the breasts but sometimes at the hip, sometimes at the shoulder, sometimes at the place between her legs. Beast needs beast, Soledad keeps whispering in a Spanish that Vikar somehow understands. When Vikar is shaken awake past midnight by one of the quake's persistent aftershocks, he hears voices downstairs.

Four or five of the group are still up talking. After a moment the voices take on some clarity; Vikar gets up from his bed. "—out of your mind," he hears Viking Man, half with laughter and half in disbelief.

"I'm telling you," comes a woman's soft voice.

"One of the Manson Family?" says one of the other male voices.

"He's not one of fucking Manson Family," answers Viking Man, as Vikar moves toward the bedroom door and the upstairs railing beyond. The woman downstairs says, with what Vikar now recognizes as a slight accent, "He was there in Laurel Canyon. I saw him." The floor creaks beneath Vikar; downstairs someone says, "Shhh."

Vikar stops where he stands. There's dead silence beyond the door, then someone whispers. After another pause Viking Man calls out, not too loudly, "Vicar?"

Vikar doesn't answer.

"You awake, vicar?"

80.

Vikar doesn't answer or move.

There's another pause. "He was in Laurel—" the woman starts again.

"*Everybody* was in Laurel Canyon," interrupts Viking Man, "everybody except, I would remind you, the Manson Family. They were in Benedict Canyon. Those longhairs you were living with had more to do with Manson than the vicar does. Odds are better, Sol, that *you're* one of the Manson Family."

"He does seem a bit of a nut job, John," suggests another male voice.

"Oh yeah, and you don't, Paul. The rest of us, we're paragons of stability. Bobby here? He's perfectly *normal*." Viking Man snorts. "The vicar's O.K. He works on sets over at Paramount, I met him through Dotty Langer. She—"

"Is she still around?" someone asks.

"I keep telling her," Viking Man says, with what sounds to Vikar like the only uncertainty in the man's voice he's heard, "she'll survive all of us, God love her. But I don't know—"

"The tattoo-head, John," someone prompts.

"Well, Dot worked on *A Place in the Sun*, you know, with Hornbeck. She thinks maybe she can get the vicar a job in production design . . . he studied architecture somewhere back east . . . . "

"A set builder?" says a male voice—the one Viking Man calls Hitch—with a tone of scorn, and then another female voice that Vikar recognizes as Margie Ruth answers, "Fuck you, Brian—he makes himself *useful*. More than some people in this room can say."

"Take it easy, Margie," Viking Man says, "Hitch here—"

"Don't call me that," says Hitch.

"—is above all that, with his Siamese-twin movie . . . . "

"Fuck you too, John," says Margie.

"I keep meaning to ask you," Viking Man says, "these twins, are they joined at—"

"John," comes the prompt again. "The tattoo-head."

81.

Viking Man says, "We're driving out here a couple of days ago, day before yesterday or whenever it was—day of the quake—and we're talking movies the whole way . . . this guy isn't a cinéaste, he's a *cinéautistic*."

"A what?"

"*Cinéautistic* . . . . "

"It means he's backward," says Hitch.

"Nonsense. I tell you he's got a degree in architecture."

"So he says."

"O.K., let's say he made it up," says Viking Man. "Even just making up a degree in architecture, you can't be that backward. No, I'm telling you it's socially that he's, uh . . . he barely knows who the Beatles are. He barely knows there's a country called Vietnam let alone a war there. I don't know if he was raised in a fucking monastery—he's not into drugs and I'd make a wager of some significant amount the guy's never been laid. But he's nuts about movies, as obsessive as anyone I know, which in this house is saying a lot—"

"He's never been laid?" says Margie.

"—but absolutely unschooled, his knowledge and opinions absolutely unmediated . . . he doesn't know from Pauline Kael let alone Andrew Sarris let alone James Fucking Agee. I'm not sure he knows who D. W. Griffith is, but he could probably run down for you the entire filmography of John Cromwell."

"Who?"

Since You Went Away, Vikar's mind races. *The Prisoner of Zenda. Dead Reckoning* with Humphrey Bogart and Lauren Bacall. "This guy," Viking Man continues, "has never been to USC or UCLA or Columbia or any fancy school . . . . " Not Lauren Bacall. Liz Scott. " . . . for this guy, Film 101 is whatever theater he's randomly walked into that's playing whatever movie is randomly playing. An obsession that's still pure, untouched by cultural cant or preconceptions or—"

Of course I know who D. W. Griffith is. I used to ride the elevator with him at the Roosevelt Hotel.

"You mean he's a virgin?" says Margie.

82.

The next time Vikar wakes, it's in the middle of what he believes is a wet dream. He's hard and it's a moment before he realizes that the hair falling across his belly isn't a dream and that his cock is somewhere it's never been. He starts to sit up.

"Relax," he hears her command in the dark, "lie down," and he lies back down and Margie puts him back in her mouth. He panics when he feels himself begin to come and she sucks all the more furiously. Do all the women on the beach give blowjobs channeled from the netherworld? "O.K., superman," she says a few minutes later, kissing him hard, "just wanted to see what you're made of."

83.

By the third day, everyone calls him vicar. He never liked "Ike" anyway. He'll replace the c with a k around the time people start dropping the k from Amerika.

He gets a ride back into the city only when Margie Ruth talks Soledad into it. Vikar overhears the conversation. "For God's sake, Sol," Margie says, "he's not one of the Manson Family. He's harmless. I promise you," she says knowingly.

"He is not harmless," Vikar hears Soledad answer. "He may not be one of the Manson Family," she concedes, "but he's not harmless."

84.

They leave around eight, driving south on Pacific Coast Highway. The road is eerily empty except for the single figure of a young woman stumbling barefoot along the side in what looks like a hospital gown. From the top of the colony, between the dark gray highway and gun-metal sea, in the twilight Vikar can see the brown thread of the beach, like the string of a gyroscope pulled by God. In the front seat of the car, the little girl says to her mother, "I'm hungry."

"We will eat when we get home," Soledad says quietly. She looks at Vikar in the rear-view mirror.

"I'm really hungry."

"In a bit," Soledad says.

"I'm hungry now."

The woman checks the rear-view mirror again. "We are going to stop and get something to eat."

"All right," says Vikar.

85.

They stop at a taco stand and order fish tacos. They sit at a table outside; although it's February, it's warm. Vikar and Soledad drink sangria in plastic cups and for a while no one talks. "Do they have tacos in Spain?" Vikar finally says.

"Tacos are Mexican," Soledad answers. "They have tacos in Mexico. Mexico is not the same as Spain."

"Have I been to Spain?" asks the five-year-old.

"No," Soledad says.

"Was I born in Spain?"

"You were born here in Los Angeles."

They're on the canyon side of the highway. Although it's not dark yet, they already can see, on the other side of the highway, the moonlight on the ocean. On the other side of the highway, from the direction they came, approaches the barefooted young woman in the hospital gown. An aftershock of the quake is followed by a gust as though it's blown from the earth: and suddenly there's no one else in the world but the three of them eating tacos and the woman in the hospital gown on the other side of the road. No one else sits at the tables, no one is behind the counter of the taco stand, no other cars are on the highway. "I believed they were alike, Spain and Mexico," Vikar says.

"Spain is European," Soledad says.

"Did you make movies there?"

Soledad absently takes her hair and wraps her fist in it. "Yes." It would be rude, Vikar believes, to ask if Buñuel really is her father. "Art films," she says. She glances at her daughter, then says to Vikar, "Lesbian vampires."

"What's that," says Zazi.

"Do you want some of my other taco?" Soledad answers her.

"Can I see your movies?" Zazi says.

"No."

"Can I see them when I'm older?"

"No."

"She can have more of my taco if she wants," says Vikar.

"Can I ever see your movies?" says Zazi.

"No," Soledad says. She says to Vikar: "I'm up for a part in a private-eye film. It doesn't shoot until later this year."

Vikar nods.

"I would play a gangster's girlfriend."

"What's a gangster?" says Zazi.

"A bad man." Soledad says to Vikar, "She gets a soda bottle smashed in her face. It is violent but a good scene."

"Can I see that movie?" says Zazi.

"No. If I don't get that part," Soledad says to Vikar, "they would give me another part."

"I've worked on an Otto Preminger movie and a Vincente Minnelli movie," Vikar says.

"You build sets."

"Yes."

"Someone told me you studied architecture."

"Yes."

"You should work on grand buildings."

"I do work on grand buildings. I worked on an Otto Preminger movie and a Vincente Minnelli movie."

"I wonder if I know what you mean," Soledad says softly, but Vikar wonders if she wonders. Gazing toward the beach, Soledad wraps her fist in her hair as though she's binding herself, like she would if she were tying herself to something or someone. Across the highway, the barefooted woman in the hospital gown has stopped and stands staring at them; it's not clear to Vikar if she's considering crossing the road. Soledad stares back; it's not clear to Vikar if she sees the woman or just watches the sea. "Are you a gangster?" Zazi asks Vikar.

"Zazi," says Soledad.

"No," Vikar says to Zazi.

"Are you a serial killer?" Zazi says.

"Zazi," says Soledad.

Zazi says, "I don't even know what it is. Serial like corn flakes?"

"I'm not a serial killer," says Vikar.

"Did the police take you away that time because you have a picture on your head?"

"Do you remember that?"

"Sort of. Mommy reminded me."

"I'm certain," Vikar says, "the police wouldn't arrest someone for that."

"Did you do something bad?"

"Zazi," Soledad says.

"No. I believe the police thought I was someone else." Two people ran off a hillside, he thinks, but I didn't mean to.

"I saw a movie about gangsters," says Zazi.

"Which one?" says Vikar.

"The man and woman who rob banks and shoot people."

"You saw that movie?"

"I didn't know," Soledad protests feebly.

"The cartoon deer one was worse," says Zazi.

"What deer one?" says Vikar.

"The little deer whose mom gets shot."

"There," says Soledad to Vikar, "you see? That one was worse."

"Did you like the one about the gangsters?" Zazi says to Vikar.

"The man and woman who rob banks?"

"Yes."

"I don't understand comedies," says Vikar.

"What's a comedy?"

"A funny movie."

"That movie was funny?" says Zazi. "I think maybe I don't really like movies that much." She looks at Vikar. "I want a picture on my head."

86.

In the car on the way into the city, Zazi sits in front again. She's turned in her seat studying Vikar. "Zazi," Soledad says, "turn around in the seat." She drives irregularly.

"She should be in the back," Vikar finally says. Soledad looks at him in the rear-view mirror and Vikar can see her cool smile, like the way she smiled the first time he saw her. She says something so quietly he can't understand her. "What?" he says.

"I said, Would you like that?"

"It's not safe in the front for a little girl."

"You would like that, wouldn't you?" Soledad says, nodding. The car comes to a screeching stop. "Get out," she says.

Vikar looks around him. It's ten o'clock and they're on one of the long stretches of Sunset where there's no sidewalk. "Here?" he says. Zazi looks at her mother.

"Do you think I am going to let her sit in back with you?" Soledad says calmly in her accented English. "Get out."

Vikar continues to look around at the dark boulevard and then slowly opens the door and gets out. He watches the dance between the Mustang's white taillights and red brake lights until they've vanished in the distance.

87.

He goes to the movies all the time, new and old. He sees *Performance*, *The French Connection*, Preminger's *Laura* (for the third time), *Murmur of the Heart*, *Gilda*, Disney's *Pinocchio*, *The Battle of Algiers* (with Viking Man, who's seeing it for the sixth time), *Dirty Harry* (for which Viking Man is writing a sequel), an old forties movie called *Criss Cross* where Burt Lancaster and Yvonne De Carlo drive each other mad across what seems to Vikar a fantastical downtown Los Angeles with trolley cars that glide through the air. In Buñuel's *Belle de Jour* Vikar imagines Soledad Palladin, as directed by her father, in Catherine Deneuve's role of the housewife turned prostitute who, in one scene, is splattered with mud. At night he dreams about Margie lying between his legs, her naked breasts pressed against his thighs, and then in the dream she transforms into Soledad—at which point Vikar wakes with a start, unspent.

88.

He buys another television. He almost never reads the newspaper, but one afternoon he sees a headline on the front page of the *Herald-Examiner* that several members of the singing family who murdered the pregnant woman, her unborn child and four others in the canyon have been sentenced to die in the state gas chamber.

89.

Vikar telephones Margie Ruth at the beach house. "Not here," a male voice on the other end of the line says, "she's gone to New York to make Brian's movie. Who's this?" and Vikar hangs up.

90.

Vikar has been working in production and set design at Paramount nearly a year, and is freelancing on a job at United Artists, when the art director of a Don Quixote musical comes to see him.

"I've been looking at some of your sketches," the art director says in a heavily accented English that reminds Vikar of Soledad. He's an Italian in his late forties with a background in opera. "You have mixed several elements in this set," he points at the draft.

"Yes," Vikar agrees.

"It . . . " The art director thinks. "It is an interesting effect but these elements do not go well. They are taken from different time periods."

"Yes."

91.

The art director looks at Vikar. "Do you understand what I am saying?"

"Yes," Vikar says, pointing at the design, "this arch doesn't go with the time period of the façade in back."

"That's it," the other man nods, relieved.

"This arch is from twenty-three years later," Vikar says.

The art director looks at the draft and back at Vikar. "Twenty-three years?"

"Yes."

The two men look at each other. "But you see the problem, yes?" the art director finally asks.

"No."

"You do not see the problem."

"No."

"You do not see the problem with the same building, uh," he gropes for the language, "from different time periods."

"No. This arch is from twenty-three years later, when the character of the prostitute Dulcinea will die here from consumption."

"Excuse?" says the art director.

"The prostitute will die here of consumption in twenty-three years."

Some panic seems to take hold of the art director. "There has been a change in the script?" He grabs a nearby telephone and dials. After a moment he says, "Elvira, it is Luciano. Have I received the, uh, last changes in the *La Mancha* script?"

"It's not in the script," says Vikar.

"Perhaps I should speak with Arthur," Luciano says to Elvira on the other end of the phone.

"It's not in the script," Vikar repeats.

"Excuse," Luciano says to Elvira, then to Vikar, "what?"

"I don't believe it's a very good movie," Vikar says.

"Elvira, I will call you back." Luciano hangs up the phone. "It is not in the script?"

"It's twenty-three years after the script ends," says Vikar, "she dies of consumption . . . " He taps the drawing. " . . . here."

"Who says this?"

"Under this arch."

"Who says she dies of consumption?"

"Every building has a back story and future story," Vikar says. "Like an actor's character."

"This building is in the present."

"The building is in all times. Every building is in all times and all times are in the building."

92.

Dotty Langer says, "I hear you're vexing them in set design over at UA."

"I vex people," Vikar acknowledges. "Have you ever heard of someone named Trane?"

They're in an editing room on the Paramount lot. Dotty has about her a slightly boozy air, and a Jack Daniels bottle sits next to the moviola as before. "Is he in set design?" Dotty says. She opens a canister of film and begins spooling it through the moviola; she starts a cigarette. "Cut the light, will you?"

Vikar reaches over and turns out the light. In a moment, Montgomery Clift is on the small screen of the moviola, standing by the road trying to hitch a ride. Franz Waxman's music rises up behind him over the moviola's rattle.

93.

Montgomery Clift comes to town, the poor relation of a rich family that finds him a job at the local factory, where he meets and sleeps with Shelley Winters despite stern orders not to fraternize with the other workers. At a party he sees Elizabeth Taylor, the most beautiful of the local rich girls.

After twenty minutes, Dotty finally speaks. "Now watch this here," she says. In the scene, Taylor and Clift dance. "Do you know what an editor does on a picture?" she turns to Vikar.

"Puts the scenes in order because they've been shot out of order."

"That's the first thing," says Dotty. She stops the camera, Taylor and Clift mid-dance. "The editor also chooses which shot to use. In this scene here," she waves her cigarette at Taylor and Clift, "something is happening that hasn't happened in this picture until now."

Vikar stares at the image. "A close-up," he says.

"Very good."

"I had to think about it awhile."

She says, "It's not something most people are aware of no matter how long they think about it—when the camera is close and when it's far away. Those are the kinds of choices an editor makes."

"Doesn't the director make them?"

"It depends on the director. Most directors in pictures, up until the last ten or fifteen years, started off as writers or in the theater, so they concentrated on the actors and story. Your Mr. Preminger started in theater, Lubitsch and Welles started in theater. Sturges and Wilder started as writers—they really became directors just so they could protect their scripts from idiots. But Hitchcock was an art director early on, so he knew what he wanted his pictures to look like, and Von Sternberg and David Lean were, guess what, editors, so the same thing. Kubrick was a magazine photographer. Mr. Stevens started as a photographer too—though his parents were actors—then he was a cinematographer. He shot a lot of early Laurel and Hardy, of all things. You see what's unusual here?"

"They're dancing and we're not seeing their bodies."

"I'm impressed. The audience may not know it, but this picture's been keeping them at arm's length all this time. Monty has even slept with Shelley Winters from a distance. But as soon as Monty and Liz lay eyes on each other, the camera is pulling at the leash, it wants to get close. And now they're dancing and we're going crazy with the liquid dissolves, one image dissolving into the next. We're getting tighter and tighter on their faces. No picture ever used close-ups like this one."

"The first movie I saw in Los Angeles was a silent movie that's all close-ups. An actress named Falconetti played Joan who's burned at the stake."

"O.K., smart guy," she rolls her eyes, "no *Hollywood* picture." She looks at him and says, "What happens next here?"

"Elizabeth Taylor stops and says they're being watched."

"And looks right at us when she says it. That's how close we've gotten. The picture has crossed a line it hasn't crossed before now—we've intruded. So Liz and Monty run out onto the terrace to get away from us. But they don't get away from us, do they?"

Taylor and Clift are on the terrace in each other's arms. In the background, all the other dancers and partygoers seem to fall away. The camera moves in so close on the lovers it can't get all of their heads in the frame. "I've loved you since the first moment I saw you," Clift says. "I guess maybe I loved you before I saw you."

"Tell mama," Taylor says. "Tell mama all." Dotty stops the film, freezing it on an image similar to the one on Vikar's head. She stares at it and pours a glass of bourbon, takes a drink and says, "Jesus, is this the sexiest moment in the history of movies?"

94.

Vikar says, "There's hysteria in it."

Dotty puts out the cigarette. "'Vicar,' huh?"

"With a 'k,'" he decides.

"Does any man not fall in love with Elizabeth Taylor when she says that?" She points at Clift on the viewer. "Hell, Monty fell in love with her, and he liked boys, although there are people, people who would know, who insist he and Liz became lovers. Brando, he couldn't have pulled off this scene—'I loved you since before I saw you'? He would have read that dialogue and thrown up. There wasn't another man who could have given himself over to this scene the way Clift does, because Monty *did* love her—he loves her in this scene and he loved her off screen and she loved him. 'Tell mama all'—Liz was, you know, seventeen going on forever when this was shot. Liz didn't want to say the line. She thought it was crazy any girl her age would say a line like that, and you know, she's not wrong. And though most people wouldn't believe it, I'm fairly certain she was still a virgin at the time. She even had made a picture with Mickey Rooney, for Christ's sake, who brought to every picture he worked on a steely dedication to fucking his female lead. So Liz objected to the line but Mr. Stevens, who wrote it the night before, was adamant, because it was the only thing she could say that could match Monty's intensity. Liz is a virgin, and Monty is queer, and you're right, there's hysteria in it, and with any other two actors on the planet, it wouldn't be the same."

95.

Dotty turns the scene back on. "If you watch closely," she says, "you'll notice something else. We're cutting back and forth between Liz and Monty and none of the close-ups match up. We're seeing them from one side, then the other, from one profile to the next, but in terms of sheer continuity it's all fucked up. Mr. Stevens didn't care about that. The D.P., Bill Mellor, is using a six-inch lens no one used until then, and Stevens was making the most of it, he was going for intimacy and rhythm—fuck continuity."

Another half hour passes and neither Dotty nor Vikar says anything until Clift takes Shelley Winters out on a lake in a small rowboat.

"You have to hand it to Shelley," Dotty says. "She was supposed to be a bombshell, that's what the studio was grooming her for—she was going to be Marilyn Monroe, before anyone knew who Marilyn Monroe was. She and Marilyn were roommates when this was made. But she fought for this role, this role of the dowdy little factory mouse who, you know, comes fully alive only when she's terrified, and she plays it right on that edge between pathos and pathetic. Now watch this." Montgomery Clift's eye dissolves into a shot of the rowboat and its passengers in the distance, a faraway glint of light on the dark lake that becomes a glint in Clift's eye before his face fades altogether. "Like with the close-ups, this picture did things with dissolves no one had seen, not in Hollywood pictures anyway. You had two images dissolving at the same time, one coming in and one going out. There have to be more dissolves in this picture than anything since Murnau. Stevens planned all that—we were measuring the dissolves in *feet*, if you can believe that—and the thing is, this picture doesn't look like any of Stevens' others. If anything, Stevens always had been a purist, he liked the idea of stillness, just putting the camera there and watching, especially if he thought, like when Astaire and Rogers dance in *Swing Time*, a cut would just disrupt things. Your boy Preminger is another one like that—no cuts at all, put the camera there and show the audience everything and let them figure out who or what they're supposed to pay attention to." Clift and Winters talk in the boat and the camera turns from one to the other. "You see what's going on here?" she says.

"I'm not sure."

"Every time we turn to Shelley, she's right in the middle of the frame. She's pregnant with Monty's baby, she's both threatening and pleading with him to marry her, and when we see her, she almost seems to loom. Overbearing, frantic, somehow she's not only shrill to the ear but to the eye—hell, shrill to the *soul*. Then every time the camera turns to Monty—"

"—he's hunched down in the boat," says Vikar, "at the end—"

"—the far end of the boat. The far, *far* end. Like he wants to crawl out of it. Like he wants to crawl out of not just the boat but the fucking movie. Like he can't get far enough away."

"The whole world," nods Vikar, "is coming down."

"Half the frame is the dark lake, the dark woods, dark sky behind him, everything dark hovering over him, enveloping him, bearing down on him. Back to Shelley, she almost seems to be growing closer, even though the camera isn't closing in at all. That's editing, if I may say so. Choosing the shot. It's telling us everything. It's telling us things we don't even know it's telling us. It's not just telling us what these characters think, it's telling us what we think. It's manipulative as hell, there's no getting around it, but then all movies are manipulative. When people complain about a picture that's 'manipulative,' what they really mean is it's not very good at its manipulations, its manipulation is too obvious. A few minutes ago we thought Monty was going to take Shelley out on the lake and throw her overboard and drown her—and we're horrified, we're thinking you can't do that, she's pregnant with your child, you have to do right by her. Then in the boat he seems to have changed his mind—hard to know whether it's conscience or failure of nerve, but he seems to be reconciling himself to a life with her, his dream of Liz slipping farther away, and now we're thinking, even if we don't realize it, Jesus, will you please throw this broad in the lake already? Liz is waiting for you! The most beautiful woman in the world is naked in bed, waiting for you to come to her *right now*! Life with Shelley Winters? You would be better off dead—at which point we've doomed him, we've doomed all of them. The picture's even gotten the *women* in the audience half-thinking this, which has got to be the mindfuck of all time. Now, the truth is I'm not sure Stevens understood any of it. I think he thought he was making some sociological thing about class in America or something. But everything about the way this picture is shot and cut says this is a dream. This is a dream where you're guilty not just for what you do but for what you think and feel, where you're guilty not just for acting on your fantasies but having them in the first place. I mean, this picture couldn't be more morally absurd. But in some way that we don't understand, it makes sense. So when you get to the end of the picture and he's going off to the execution chamber and Liz is going into a *convent*—a complete cliché—giving her life to God because there's no one left after you've fallen in love with Montgomery Clift, that makes sense, too."

Vikar reaches over and turns on the light, even though the movie isn't over. "God," he says, "doesn't deserve her."

96.

Each scene is in all times, Vikar tells himself, and all times are in each scene. Each shot, each set-up, each sequence is in all times, all times are in each shot, each set-up, each sequence. The scenes of a movie can be shot out of sequence not because it's more convenient, but because all the scenes of a movie are really happening at the same time. No scene really leads to the next, all scenes lead to each other. No scene is really shot "out of order." It's a false concern that a scene must anticipate another that follows, even if it's not been shot yet, or that a scene must reflect a scene that precedes it, even if it's not been shot yet, because all scenes anticipate and reflect each other. Scenes reflect what has not yet happened, scenes anticipate what already has happened. Scenes that have not yet happened, have. "Continuity" is one of the myths of film; in film, time is round, like a reel. Fuck, as Dotty would say, continuity.

97.

Seven years after coming to Los Angeles, Vikar will meet at a party in Laurel Canyon, not far from the cave where he slept that morning the police came for him, a famously renegade director trying to get another feature off the ground. His previous movie was something of a hit and the director was nominated for an Academy Award, along with the star of the movie who's his wife—but now he's back to struggling again. His new movie is ostensibly about a strip-club owner trying to protect his establishment and his dancers from gangsters. Really it's about the director protecting his dreams from Hollywood.

The director will stare at Vikar's head with a wild lopsided grin and tell him about the time he was a young actor just out of the army in the early fifties, about to enroll in the Academy of Dramatic Arts in New York City, and he went to see *A Place in the Sun* in a theater downtown. God I hate this movie, the young actor thought when the lights came up. The next afternoon he went back to see it again. He went back to see it again the next afternoon and the next and the next, the theater getting emptier around him, each time telling himself, God I hate this movie, until finally, halfway through the eighth consecutive time seeing it, he whispered to himself in the dark: God I love this movie.

98.

One night Vikar cheats on Elizabeth Taylor. He finds the air around her too thin to breathe anymore, which is to say he finds the air of his own dreams too thin to breathe. Defied and thwarted and driven to distraction by her, he feels no choice but to back away and give her up, and find someone else—the later Elizabeth, perhaps, the Elizabeth of *Cat on a Hot Tin Roof* or *Butterfield 8*. That Elizabeth would lie between his legs and take him in her mouth. But that Elizabeth has no hold on him.

99.

He's captivated by Ann-Margret's sexual malevolence in *Kitten With a Whip*. In a fifties Mob movie called *The Big Combo*, he's fascinated by Jean Wallace coolly performing oral sex on Richard Conte below the camera frame. In the opening shot of a Godard movie at the Fox Venice, the camera pans the length of a nude blonde, next to the Elizabeth Taylor of *A Place in the Sun*, the most beautiful woman Vikar has seen in the movies. She reminds him of the same nude he saw years before in the movie about the spy, except now washed clean of the gold paint and resurrected, glowing with an amber of her own.

But it's with another blonde, less beautiful than Bardot but somehow less resistible as well, that Vikar cheats on Elizabeth. Perhaps Vikar wants the blonde in *Strangers When We Meet* because, in the way that he has added a k to his name, she could have dropped the k from hers, such was the nova of her career. In three years in the mid-fifties, she went from being Miss Deepfreeze—a small-time Midwest beauty queen selling refrigerators—to the world's biggest female star, Marilyn notwithstanding. She bruises as easily as Marilyn but is not felled by the blow, as is Marilyn; surviving what Marilyn could not, she's denied the martyrdom of goddesses. At the end of *Strangers When We Meet*, a sadness lingers about her both enduring and inevitable. Flung from the Old California mission steeple in the earlier movie about the private eye who's obsessed with her, it's as if she somehow peeled herself up off the ground, coolly gathered her dignity, and moved on to another town in another movie, just in time to be devastated anew by Kirk Douglas. Her golden hair in his grip as she lies between his legs, Vikar feels he's cheating not only on Elizabeth Taylor but Soledad Palladin.

100.

As on the night he left the Japanese gangster movie with an erection, Vikar takes to riding the bus. He rides across the whirling grids of Los Angeles, east to west. He rides into the early morning hours until the buses stop running, at which point often he must figure out a way home. For a while, all the bus drivers watch him in their rear-view mirrors. But soon he becomes a familiar passenger and they ignore him.

With each bus Vikar sails farther into a city of neon lily pads floating on an immense black pond. In this city a person can hide from God a long time. He rides past bars and shops, the Frolic Room and the Formosa and the Tiki Ti, Boardner's and the Firefly on Vine, he rides past the Body Shoppe and Seventh Veil and Jumbo Clown strip joints and the Pussycat Theater at Western, and the streetwalkers on Sunset who become younger and prettier the farther west he gets from La Brea. He rides over old bridges and is struck by how many there are in Los Angeles that cross no water whatsoever, arching over rivers of dust. He rides past the hotels where the stars stay, the Roosevelt and the Marquis and the Landmark on Franklin and the Knickerbocker on Ivar; he gazes up at the Chateau

Marmont's tower and wonders who might be on its parapets, gazes up at the spinning lounge on top of the Holiday Inn on Highland and wonders who looks down at his bus at that moment.

101.

At one point, he gets off at Santa Monica Boulevard and Fairfax and walks south. Passing Melrose, he comes to a small wooden theater; at the ticket counter the woman says, "You've missed the first two hours."

"It's all right," Vikar says.

The woman sells Vikar the ticket and he goes inside. He has to wind through narrow wooden passages like a fun house. He gets to his hard seat just as the screen is filled with white hoods, the Klan thundering on horseback. At the front of the theater, before the silent screen, a small round man in his seventies plays the accompanying organ.

102.

The tiny theater around Vikar is half full. He finds himself riveted less by the images than by the sound of the organ, which thunders along with the Klan's horses. He can feel the vibration of the sound in the seat beneath him and in his feet on the floor.

103.

The lights go up and the rest of the audience leaves. The small wooden theater is even less imposing with the lights on. Vikar remains in his seat watching the little old man who played the organ, who smiles at him. "Did you like it?" the old man says.

"I liked the sound," Vikar says.

"You mean me?"

"Yes."

"Well, thank you," he says. He looks at Vikar's head. "Friends of yours?"

"Elizabeth Taylor and Montgomery Clift."

The old man shrugs. "Kids to me. I would have said Janet Gaynor and what's-his-name from *Seventh Heaven*. Didn't he die?"

"Montgomery Clift?"

"I remember something about a car accident."

"He didn't die in the car accident. It was after that. Do you play here all the time?"

"Not all the time. I play out at UCLA a lot when they have screenings." He walks over to where Vikar sits. "I'm Chauncey." He puts out his hand.

"I'm Vikar. Did you play for silent movies?"

"Can you believe I'm that old?"

"Yes," Vikar says. Chauncey laughs. "Did you play for this movie?"

"I don't remember when I first played for this movie." Chauncey lowers himself into one of the seats in the row before Vikar's. "The big pictures had orchestras when they opened."

"I met a man once who didn't like this movie. He broke into my apartment."

"You discussed motion pictures with someone who broke into your apartment?"

"He said it's jive bullshit."

"Well, there's probably something to that, I suppose. Of course I'm from a different era, so maybe not the one to ask— I just see the picture, not the politics. We play it for the kids over at UCLA—you know, long hair," he pantomimes long hair, "they're actually quite respectful but I'm sure they also think it's jive as-you-say. Probably the most sophisticated audiences I've ever played for, though God knows they don't look very sophisticated."

"John Ford played one of the Klansman."

"I didn't know that."

"I used to ride the elevator of the Roosevelt Hotel with D. W. Griffith."

"Is that right?"

"He was a ghost then," Vikar says.

Chauncey laughs. "Well, that makes sense. I think he did die in that hotel."

"He built it with Louis B. Mayer, Mary Pickford and Douglas Fairbanks."

"You sound pretty sophisticated, too."

"I don't know," Vikar says. "But I know things about movies."

104.

It seems to Vikar that Dotty already has made some impact on her Jack Daniels bottle and it's made some impact on her when she suggests they walk up the street from the studio for a drink. On the corner, Nickodell's wearily bleats in the night its electric pastels. The blood-red booths of the cavernous interior are like the cells of a dead beehive.

Almost no one else is in the restaurant. Vikar and Dotty take a booth in which, twenty years before, William Holden and Lucille Ball had lunch; the waiter comes and Dotty orders a Jack Daniels and Vikar asks for a Coke. "Come on," moans Dotty, "don't do this to me. Bring the man a vodka tonic," she says to the waiter, "maybe a little light on the vodka."

For a while they drink in the dark belly of the restaurant saying nothing. Dotty leans against the red upholstered booth with her eyes closed; it occurs to Vikar that she dreads going home, wherever that might be. He wonders how many nights she sleeps in the cutting room. "I was thinking," he says. "What you said about it being a dream."

"Isn't that the cliché about movies, Vikar," her head still against the upholstery, as she peers at him from beneath half shut eyelids, "that they're dreams?"

"I have this dream. I mean the same dream, all the time. Every time I go to the movies, that night I dream and it's the same. There's a rock, it's night and the moon is full, someone lies on top of the rock waiting for something terrible."

"Is it you?" Perhaps there's a slight slur to her words.

"No. At the top of the rock is ancient white writing. The rock is open, like a . . . . " Vikar stops and after a moment says, "I cheated on Elizabeth Taylor."

"There's no such thing," Dotty says, "as cheating when you go to the movies. Don't you know that? Just like there's no such thing as cheating in dreams. In the movies you get to fall in love with who you want, sleep with who you want, live happily ever after as often as you want. Liz," she says, "understands. If anyone understands, it's Liz."

"When you work on a movie like that, do you know what it's going to be?"

She turns in her seat. "Can we have two more? Excuse me?" The bartender in the shadows on the other side of the room looks up. "Two more?"

Vikar hasn't started his first one yet. "When you're making a movie like *A Place in the Sun*?"

"You mean do you know it's going to be great?" She shrugs, "Of course not. You understand you've got a first-rate director, a first-rate cinematographer, a fairly blazing cast . . . ironically, at the time the gamble was Liz, she hadn't done anything grown-up, and Shelley was cast completely against type—but Monty, Monty was the hot young actor in

Hollywood, he already had done *Red River, The Search* with Fred Zinnemann, and, uh . . . " she stops to think, shaking her head groggily, " . . . oh God . . . . "

"Are you all right?"

"The other one. First picture I ever worked on." The drinks come. "Monty and Olivia de Havilland."

"*The Heiress.*"

"*The Heiress.* I wasn't supposed to be on that at all because I wasn't union, always suspected it might have been Monty himself who got me in—he was sweet that way. Up till then I was a messenger girl on the lot running notes back and forth among Billy Wilder and Jean Arthur and Marlene Dietrich, who were making a picture and couldn't abide each other. Cutting was easier than a lot of things for a woman to get into, because in their quaint way Mayer and Warner and Zanuck and Zukor all had this idea that editing was like sewing. Brando was just coming along, shooting *Streetcar* when we were doing *Sun*, still an unknown quantity as far as pictures were concerned—so Monty was *it* and everyone knew except maybe sometimes Monty himself, who always had that thing great artists have, tortured doubt half the time and arrogance the other half . . . or maybe he knew he was It and couldn't stand it. I worked on another picture with him years later, *Suddenly, Last Summer*, after his accident, and it was even more obvious then when you could see what he lost, not just his face but his spirit. At his peak he seemed somehow both modern and classic at the same time . . . so we knew we had the stuff for a good picture. But when you're actually shooting the thing? You don't know the iris of Monty's eye is going to turn into a distant boat on a lake. At the moment you're shooting it, Monty's just another flesh-and-blood entity, right there, right then, before he gets turned into something else. Before he gets *translated*." She says, "I suppose I'm one of the first people who has an idea a picture might be special, because in the editing room that's when it really gets made into what it is."

"Yes."

Dotty lets out a sigh so heavy it startles him. "Young man, most pictures, they stay in the time they're made. A really good picture—say, *Casablanca*—lives beyond the time it's made, and then there are a few perfect pictures, a few sublime pictures—*The Third Man*, *The Shop Around the Corner*, that silent *Joan of Arc* picture of yours—that exist *before* they're made . . . . "

"The movie is in all times," says Vikar, "and all times are in the movie."

" . . . but the making of any movie, it's in the here-and-now, it's in the here-and-now no matter how much you want to be some place else," the bourbon beginning to take over, "any place else. Sometimes you throw yourself into the work just to get out of the here-and-now. When I was working on the Stevens picture, the here-and-now," she blinks heavily, "was the hell-and-gone. I was," she takes another drink, "in love, of course. Ever been in love, of course?"

"No, I've been a bartender all my life."

She blinks at him. "What?"

"It's from *My Darling Clementine*."

"This isn't a joke," she says quietly.

"I'm sorry."

"Fuck it."

"I'm sorry."

She lapses into a deep silence. "Fuck it."

105.

She says, "I was twenty-nine, about to turn thirty, which in those days was like being, well, practically like being the age I am now, ha. He was thirty-nine, an actor—a married actor . . .

you knew that was coming, didn't you? . . . big actor of the day though I don't know how many remember him now . . . couple of Oscar nominations, even some loose talk about him for the Monty role in *Sun*, but Monty was in the middle of his hot streak and this other actor, his hot streak was ending. Boxing picture, Lana Turner picture, crazy Joan Crawford picture where he played, uh . . . a violinist? Or . . . and this big prestige picture about anti-Semitism everyone was talking about . . . So the world saw this guy who seemed on a hot streak when, really, everything was coming apart. A few years before, he and his wife lost their little girl, to a *sore throat*, if you can believe it— so his marriage was falling apart and he and I were sleeping together and it was all very hot hot hot going cold cold cold, dead cold, cadaver cold, and if the public didn't know, well he knew and I knew and Hollywood knew and the House Un-American Activities Committee, they sure well knew. Someone's been drinking my drink," she says suspiciously, holding the bourbon glass up to the dim Nickodell light, then dropping her head back again on the red upholstery behind her and Vikar can't tell if the bourbon is making her memories hazier or bringing them into focus, " . . . all falling apart . . . ran Ingrid out of the country for having a baby by a husband that didn't happen to be hers—well at least he was a husband, hey, Vikar? *somebody's* husband—ran out Orson for having been a loose cannon ever since they wheeled him on deck, ran out Chaplin for his politics or for not paying his taxes or liking his girls too young or take your pick or take the whole lot. The courts made the studios sell off their theater chains, people were hauled in front of Congress for being stupid enough to attend some meeting fifteen years before, then there was television which as far as the studios were concerned was worst of all. Night Jules died, not long after I finished *Sun*, he was in New York and called me here in L.A. and I could tell he was in trouble. I got the next plane out. Never belonged to anything in his life let alone anything political, it wasn't his style—didn't know any names to name but wouldn't have named any if he had, of course, and they knew that, of course, and while the Committee's about to charge him with perjury he's also getting it from the other side, the lefties who're pissed at him for testifying at all, including his wife, she's busting his balls too. Got to the city about one in the morning, let myself in the flat there in Gramercy Park that a friend kept for us in her name, I could smell the liquor and cigarette smoke and I could hear him sleeping and I curled up and went to sleep next to him and sometime in the night I woke and he hadn't moved and I knew he wasn't sleeping anymore. So-called 'confession' on the desk, though nothing was confessed. Paramount got some of the other studios, UA, Zanuck over at Fox, to circulate this story he'd died in bed with, I don't know, a stripper or something, in order to protect me, and in some state of stupefaction—and I do mean stupe, Vik—I let them do it and that's my cross to bear. So when all that's going on, you're not thinking too much about whether *Place in the Sun* is going to make it to Movie Valhalla, and the last thing you're thinking is twenty years later you're going to run into some guy with a scene of it on top of his head."

106.

She looks straight at him and suddenly seems very sober. "A sore throat, Vikar."

"God kills children in many ways," he says.

She covers her face with her hands. "So what does it say?"

"What?"

"The writing."

"The writing?"

"The ancient writing, in your dream. You said on the side of the rock there's writing."

"I don't know. It's ancient."

"I know, but sometimes in dreams you know what things say or mean that you wouldn't otherwise."

"I don't know what it means."

"Maybe it's a movie you're going to make someday," she suggests wearily, "maybe it's one of those movies that's in all times, that exists before it's made."

"The movie is in all times," he agrees, "and all times are in the movie. But this one already has been made."

107.

He sees *Deliverance, The Bride of Frankenstein*, Alan Ladd as a hit man in *This Gun For Hire, Badlands, The Devil in Miss Jones*, Lewton and Tourneur's *Cat People, Sisters*, Minnelli's *Some Came Running, Aguirre the Wrath of God*, Pam Grier in *Coffy, Phantom Lady, La Planète sauvage, Mean Streets, Force of Evil* with John Garfield, the nearly four-hour *Mother and the Whore* and Rivette's four-hour-plus *Out One: Specter* cut down from twelve hours which plays for one night at the Fox Venice on Lincoln Boulevard, Vidor's *Duel in the Sun, Pat Garrett and Billy the Kid*. When the Sheriff goes hunting for the Kid, it's not as the Kid's former friend but as a father who will sacrifice the son to the new god, whose shiny icon in the form of a star the Sheriff wears over his heart. The Sheriff shoots down the Kid in the aftermath of sensual pleasure, the son wandering from the arms of a lover out into a night he doesn't know or care is filled with danger; he comes to the father open and trusting, and the father shoots him down. God despises the innocence of children and answers it with execution.

108.

Vikar has ridden one bus particularly far one night, farther than he's ever gone and for longer than he's ever ridden, and has lost track of where he is when he disembarks. He finds himself on the other side of the Hollywood Hills; before him in the dark seems to be a great park with rolling knolls. Vikar passes a gate and begins climbing the largest hill toward a massive estate, the grounds around it bathed in a shallow light.

He circles to the far end of the building. A security guard is walking out a pair of glass doors just as Vikar rounds the corner; Vikar catches the doors before they close. The building is enormous but there seems to be nothing in it. The hallways are colossal but with little furniture; Vikar can't imagine who lives or works here.

He turns to leave when he sees on the wall in front of him JEAN HARLOW in large chiseled letters. It's like the names on the sidewalks of Hollywood Boulevard, except in walls, until he realizes that in the wall directly behind her name is Jean Harlow's body.

109.

Dead at the age of twenty-six. She became a star in *Red Dust*, "1932," Vikar says out loud, "with Clark Gable," and as he's saying it, he turns to see on the wall CLARK GABLE. Next to him is CAROLE LOMBARD, dead at the age of thirty-three from a plane crash while selling bonds during World War II.

Now Vikar gazes at all the names on the walls around him. HUMPHREY BOGART. MARY PICKFORD. ERROL FLYNN. LON CHANEY. CLARA BOW. THEDA BARA. ALAN LADD. WALT DISNEY. SPENCER TRACY. The movies are in all times, but the people who made them are in the walls.

110.

One night Vikar is removed from a theater for laughing at the movie. It's about the possession of a child by the Devil; her head pivots on her body and she retches something primordial, a reptilian green, and she has sex with a crucifix.

Around Vikar, people in the audience vomit. When they turn to look at him laughing, it's with the same expression as when they watch the child in the movie. The ushers who hold him at each elbow regard Vikar with the same expression. "I don't understand about comedies," he says, "but I believe it's a very funny movie." The audience stares at Vikar—glowing in the ushers' flashlights—as if on his head is the Devil's mark, as if being possessed by the two most beautiful people in the history of movies, with their graven images on his skull, is satanic possession itself. "It's God who takes children," Vikar explains to the ushers, "not the Devil."

111.

When Vikar walks along Sunset Boulevard, he travels with the Music. He's not following the Music and the Music isn't following him, they just happen to travel together, on opposite sides of the street, keeping an eye on each other. Along the Strip to Laurel Canyon and beyond, the Music is all buckaroos in the crossfire of utopia and hedonism, clothes slightly spangled, with guitars over their shoulders; but as Vikar gets farther into Hollywood, the Music gets more primal and the buckaroos give way to space-age drag queens with soft-focus genitals and lightning bolts for eyes. Vikar hears this music on his bus rides at night. It creeps from the east under cover of dark.

He goes to see *Treasure of the Sierra Madre* at the Vista and is mesmerized by Walter Huston's demented jig in the swirling dust and gold. One afternoon a few days later, Vikar is passing Book City on Hollywood Boulevard when he stops to look at a battered paperback in the window; the paperback's cover says it's by the author of *Treasure of the Sierra Madre*. Vikar goes into the bookstore and buys the paperback, which is about a stranded sailor far from home who becomes trapped in the cargo hold of a doomed frigate that sails on and on and on. It's the only novel Vikar has ever read. For the next several nights, he foregoes the movies to stay home and read it.

112.

Not long after being kicked out of the movie about the Devil, Vikar sees a better movie about possession, from the early sixties. "Spoiled, Mama? Spoiled?" Natalie laughs insanely from a bathtub in the thrall of sexual hysteria, at the mother who questions whether she's given her virginity to Warren. It's the most terrifying performance Vikar has seen since Mlle Falconetti as Joan burning at the stake; he shrinks from the screen.

Vikar imagines Natalie lying between his legs, supreme succubus of all, starved on her chastity, drawing him into her mouth until there's nothing left of him. That night he stares at his head in the bathroom mirror, runs his fingers over the features of Elizabeth and imagines her as Natalie, although not the Natalie of *Rebel Without a Cause* for whom everyone mistakes Elizabeth. Rather he imagines her as the Natalie of another movie, an unmade sequel: In this movie, the shattered young lover of *Splendor in the Grass* flees her bathtub to relocate in Europe and become the dead wife of *Last Tango in Paris*, over whose body Brando rages at a love that forgives nothing.

After three years, Vikar replaces his radio. It broadcasts ongoing coverage of a political scandal that he doesn't understand. Although he tries to resist it, he prefers the drag-queen music to that of buckaroos:

> *These cities may change, but there always remains*
> *my obsession*
> *Through silken waters my gondola glides and the bridge,*
> *It sighs*
> *I remember all those moments lost in wonder that we'll*
> *never find again . . . .*
> *Jamais, jamais!*

113.

L.A.'s rare rains come in a torrent. Only the steps that lead from Vikar's secret street make it possible to descend. The intersection of Sunset and Crescent Heights is a lake, as though having risen from a hole in the ground. All the buses run behind schedule, and by the time Vikar makes his connections, he's forty-five minutes late to the studio. A river runs down Melrose; the parked black Mustang isn't familiar to him, he doesn't really remember it when he hears a tapping on the window as he sloshes by.

"Hey!" he hears behind him, and a young girl about eight years old leans out of the car. In the rain Vikar stands looking at her. She opens the door and signals wildly to him to come inside the car; he hesitates. "Come on!" she calls over the roar of the rain and water. "It's me, Zazi—remember?"

114.

He gets in the car on the passenger side. The girl sits behind the wheel; the key to the car is in the ignition, and the tape player is turned up full blast. "You're too young to drive," he shouts over the music. She turns the music down a bit. "Where's your mother?"

"Over there," Zazi says, indicating the Paramount Gate, "trying out for some movie."

"Did she ever get that role in the private-eye film?"

"What?" over the music.

Vikar says, "You mean she leaves you in the car . . . ?"

". . . I saw you walking by and said, 'The guy with the head!'"

He picks up a cassette case and studies it. He believes the person on the front with bright red hair is a man but he's not sure. "He looks like people I see on Hollywood Boulevard."

"No," the eight-year-old points out, "*they* look like *him*." She turns the music back up. They listen to a song about an aging actor and a woman who stands for hours at Sunset and Vine. "Should you be listening to this kind of song?" Vikar says.

"Oh, I know all about that stuff," the girl says.

"I liked this song I heard once about a dog."

"That doesn't sound like a very good song."

115.

Vikar says, "Is Zazi your real name?"

"Isadora is my real name," she says.

He nods. "I remember now."

She says, "Were you born with that on your head?"

"No."

"Remember that time we got tacos?"

"Yes. Do you?"

"Kind of. Mom left you in the middle of the street."

"She was just being careful. But I wouldn't hurt you."

"I know. I went home that night and started cutting off my hair with some scissors to see what picture was on my head. She got mad. Here's the best one." She turns the song up:

> *Staying back in your memory*
> *are the movies of the past*

and Vikar looks at the cassette again. "I like songs about movies," he says.

She says, "I don't care about movies. I like the music."

"Everyone in Hollywood," he says, "likes music better than movies. I hope your mother is coming back soon."

"Why?"

"Because you shouldn't be out here a long time by yourself." He says, "I should go before she returns."

"O.K."

"If I see her on the lot, I'll tell her to come back."

Zazi looks at Vikar. "I want a picture on my head."

"It's from the movies."

"You picked the picture you wanted?"

"Yes."

"I'll get one of Bowie," she says, waving the cassette.

116.

He wanders around the studio in the rain looking for Soledad but doesn't find her. When he goes back out to the gate to check on Zazi, the Mustang is gone.

117.

On the television news is a story that the granddaughter of Charles Foster Kane has been kidnapped. The story says at least one or two of the kidnappers were black, but Vikar is certain some fucked-up white hippies did that business, no matter how hard they tried to pin it on black folks. It's not clear whether they have kidnapped the granddaughter of Charles Foster Kane because they believe *Citizen Kane* is a very good movie or not a very good movie; Vikar wishes he could ask the burglar who broke into his apartment about it. He imagines all of the kidnappers watching *Citizen Kane* on television together in the middle of the night, while the granddaughter lies writhing on the floor, bound and gagged.

118.

When he's finished reading *The Death Ship*, Vikar returns to Book City and buys whatever catches his attention. He reads all the Brontës, *The Book of Lilith* and the *Arabian Nights* which confounds him because it's written by the actor married to Elizabeth Taylor, *The Ogre* by Michel Tournier and *Prose of the Trans-Siberian and of Little Jeanne de France* by Blaise Cendrars, *The Memoirs of Fanny Hill*, a book called *Les Diaboliques* by Barbey d'Aurevilly, *Memoirs of an Opium Eater* and Theodore Sturgeon's *Venus Plus X*, *The Alexandria Quartet* and the Freak Chronicles of one Charles Fort as catalogued in *The Book of the Damned*, with its accounting of a "super" Sargasso Sea in the sky from which reptiles, animals and elements fall to earth. He reads a book by a man named Bataille called *Blue of Noon* that he likes very much except he doesn't understand the politics, this as the radio announces that the President of the United States has resigned.

119.

Nocturnally he begins to tour all the crypts and cemeteries of Los Angeles. Marilyn Monroe is buried in Westwood and Bette Davis is buried in Burbank along with Fritz Lang and Buster Keaton; below Bette's name on her tomb Vikar might expect the inscription to read, *Let's not ask for the moon, we have the stars*. Rather, it says: *She did it the hard way*.

Vikar goes to the graves not to pay his respects. He pays his respects in the movie theater. He goes so that he can, futilely, try to come to grips with a revelation that unsettles him and that he can't articulate. In an old cemetery on Santa Monica Boulevard he finds Douglas Fairbanks, Cecil B. De Mille, Marion Davies, Tyrone Power, Peter Lorre and, just recently interred, Edward G. Robinson. When he reaches Jayne Mansfield's headstone, he sees in the fluttering dark of clouds passing the moon the forms of people moving, and realizes only after a moment what appears to be a man and woman having sex.

120.

Then he realizes there are two men, and the whimpers from the woman sound to Vikar like cries of distress.

Later he'll wonder whether the rage that surges in him is from the act of rape or that it's taking place on Jayne Mansfield's headstone. Within seconds he's yanked one man from off the woman and kicked in the face the other just as he looks up from what he's doing. In the confusion of sex and surprise, neither of the assailants gets his bearings. Vikar kicks the second man again and takes the first by his hair and smashes his face into the headstone.

The man lies still, blood spilling around the *1933 - 1967*. In the dark the woman leaps to her feet, stops for a moment to take one look at the very still man on the headstone and another at Vikar, and bolts.

121.

The one man collects the other and drags him off in the dark. It's hard for Vikar to tell whether the man whose face he smashed into Jayne Mansfield's headstone is conscious or alive. Oh, mother, Vikar says to himself. He rips off his shirt and for the next hour cleans the headstone, mopping up the blood in the moonlight. Vikar tries to think when his last violent episode took place: Was it the morning he first arrived in Los Angeles, that hippie he hit with the food tray? *No, the burglar I hit over the head with the radio. I had violent thoughts as well about the kid behind the front desk at the Roosevelt.* When the headstone is clean, light begins to rise over the eastern hills and Vikar can read what's inscribed: *We live to love you more each day.* Years later he'll learn Jayne Mansfield is not buried here at all but in Pennsylvania where both she and Vikar were born, and then he'll wonder about all the tombs and headstones, and how many hold phantom bodies. The movies are in all times, but the people are in no times.

122.

After he's cleaned the headstone, he begins wandering south, away from the direction he originally came and into which the woman and two men ran. A few minutes later he's stunned to reach the end of the cemetery and find himself at the back of the Paramount lot.

123.

He stashes the bloody shirt in a dumpster in the back of the lot and washes in the men's room. Mid-afternoon he returns to his apartment on his secret street and waits for the police and movie-star chief of detectives who interrogated him on his fourth (fifth?) day in Los Angeles. He watches a movie on TV about a man who is abused as a boy and becomes an arsonist, and then meets a beautiful blond high-school majorette and tells her he's a spy working on a top secret operation. When he commands her to have sex with him in order to prove her loyalty, he believes he has her under his power. But it becomes clear that she has him under her power, involving him in a scheme to murder her mother, after she's already killed several others in an orgasmic rush.

124.

Vikar watches this young blonde in a kind of hypnosis. With her wild-child beauty and demeanor, she's an American Bardot. She made this movie when she lost the role in another movie of a young mother pregnant by the Devil. The studios refused to cast her: Who would believe the Devil ravished this girl when everything about this girl gave every indication of having ravished the Devil? With the death of her father, at the age of three the actress supported her mother and two older sisters by modeling for catalogs; by the age of twelve, she attempted suicide. Was it on a Tuesday, whose name she then took for her own? As Vikar slumps in the couch in front of the TV, he dreams of her on her knees, mad between his legs. As he comes, her mouth curls into that smile of murder, her eyes glow red and he wakes in terror.

125.

When the phone rings, Vikar hasn't seen or heard from Viking Man in nearly a year. "George Stevens man!" booms the voice on the other end. "Kind of a pussy, Stevens, if you don't mind my saying. I'm off to Spain to make a movie."

"I heard."

"I'm psyched, vicar, I must confess. Same part of Spain where Leone's shot a bunch of stuff. A few casting matters to sort out still . . . . I was going to see if I could coax you over to design some sets for me, but Dot tells me you're editing now."

"She's teaching me."

"She says you've got an eye. Big compliment, considering the source." *My eye?* Vikar wonders, touching the tattooed red teardrop beneath his left one. "Maybe we can bring you in on some of the cutting when we get back."

"Thank you."

"Huston's in Morocco shooting his Kipling thing. Maybe I can get you on that too, once they've wrapped."

"I would like that very much," Vikar says.

"Morocco is India in his movie and Spain is Morocco in mine. There's movie-making in a scrotum sac, vicar." There's a long pause. "Take care of Dot, O.K., vicar?" he says.

"All right."

"To the extent she lets anyone take care of her."

"All right."

"You see Margie's Siamese-twin movie?"

"Yes."

"A fucking hit, so that shows what I know."

"Yes."

"Too bad about separating the twins before the story starts. Really wanted to see Margie Ruth joined at the tits."

"Film history will have to survive."

"Ha! God love you, vicar, you're getting wry. O.K., I'm off

to Spain. If I tell you I'll send a postcard, I'm probably lying, so I won't. Hang in there on the editing gig, O.K.?"

"All right."

"Keep an eye on Dot."

126.

All the Los Angeles movies are the same movie, Vikar thinks riding the bus at night into the city of the wrong turn, where there's no love just obsession, which lovers would choose over love even if they had a choice. A hitchhiker gets to L.A. and finds himself at the end of a leash, coiled around the hand of an actress named Ann Savage (. . . *lose my heart on the burning sand / Now I want to be your dog*); blond and bland, not a line of character in his baby face, the actor playing the drifter will spend the end of his life in jail for murdering his wife. A private eye who makes a living pursuing L.A.'s infidelities finds himself at the center of its most forbidden secret, when the woman he's sleeping with is her own father's lover, from whom she's desperately trying to protect the daughter she had by him. Later, the actor playing the private eye will learn his mother is his grandmother and his sister is his mother. God has seeped into Los Angeles after all, and found His instruments there by which to sacrifice the city's children.

In another movie, the most famous and romantic of L.A. private eyes finds himself at the beach, amid the lazy decadence of the seventies. Vikar almost can recognize the beach house where he was seduced by Margie Ruth. When the gangster's girlfriend is smashed in the face with a Coke bottle and people in the theater cry out, Vikar is only surprised that she's not Soledad Palladin; Vikar finally recognizes Soledad among the naked nymphs dancing along the ramparts of Hollywood faux-castles. "It's all right with me," the private eye shrugs, not seeming to care about anything until it becomes clear he's the only one who does care. Three years later Marlowe will move to New York, change his name to Bickle and drive cabs for a living.

127.

Variety, September 24, 1974: "LOS ANGELES—Dorothy Langer, veteran motion-picture editor who worked on the Academy Award-winning *A Place in the Sun* and the Oscar-nominated *Giant* under chief editor William Hornbeck—as well as *The Heiress*, *The Barefoot Contessa*, *Suddenly Last Summer*, *The Diary of Anne Frank*, *The Americanization of Emily* and *The Greatest Story Ever Told*—has been named by Paramount Pictures vice president of cultural affairs effective immediately, it was announced today.

"In a joint statement Gulf + Western CEO Charles G. Bludhorn, Paramount chairman Barry Diller and head of studio production Robert Evans said: 'Dotty Langer is a legend in the business with a deep understanding of both a proud tradition that dates back to Cecil B. De Mille's *The Squaw Man* in 1914—the first Hollywood feature—and the recent winds of change that have produced such modern Paramount classics as *The Godfather*, *The Godfather Part II*, *Chinatown*, *Rosemary's Baby*, *Paper Moon*, *Serpico*, *Lady Sings the Blues*, *Murder on the Orient Express*, and *Love Story*, on which she worked as editor. Paramount Pictures is excited by Ms. Langer's new position and the possibilities it presents for both her and the company, and expects in the coming years to continue a fruitful relationship that already has lasted more than two decades.'"

128.

Vikar stands in Dot's new office. It's less grand than he expected. "She's vice president," he tells the blank-looking receptionist at the front desk, but when he's shown into the office Dotty gently explains, "Vikar, there are about three thousand vice presidents at this studio."

"Three thousand?"

"Maybe not three thousand," she says, "but it's like 'associate producer.' In this town, if you don't have a job or you're not the least bit important, you're an associate producer. At a studio, you're a vice president."

The office is filled with unpacked boxes and Dotty's desk is in disarray, with no sign of the Jack Daniels bottle, although Vikar feels certain he detects bourbon. The office is small and Dotty appears smaller in a big black chair behind a big black desk. "Well," Vikar says, "congratulations."

"God love you," Dotty laughs, "as our viking friend would say, you're probably the only one in Hollywood naïve enough to believe it and sincere enough to mean it. I've been Hornbecked, Vikar. Like what they did to Billy over at Universal, which is one level of purgatory away from retirement. 'Vice president of cultural affairs'? It sounds like I'm having a tryst with Chairman Mao. One morning I'll come into the studio and my furniture will be out on the lawn. The funny thing is I was doing better when the studio was tanking four years ago. Now it's the hottest studio in the business and I'm on the way out." She sees the look on Vikar's face. "Forget it. I hear you're editing the Max Schell picture."

"Another as well, with Rod Steiger as W. C. Fields."

"Jesus," Dotty rolls her eyes.

"There's a very attractive actress is in it." Vikar can't think of her name. "The one from *Lenny.*"

"Our viking friend is in Spain making a big picture," Dotty says.

"He called me."

"It's MGM but maybe we can fix things so you can work on it in post. You probably could learn some things on a big picture like that."

"Viking Man said perhaps a John Huston movie as well."

She says, "You're still vexing them, from what I hear."

"Perhaps I'll always be vexing."

"It's good for the town to get vexed now and then. Don't worry about me, Vikar. It's pretty civilized, really, this vice-president thing. Not that many studios would take the time to ease me out rather than just pull the lever on the trap door underneath, and the writing is on the wall anyway—all the higher-ups are devouring each other, which is what they do when they get successful. Evans is entertaining enough and I'll make the best of it, as long as I don't have to score his coke or deal with the crazy Germans at the top of the food chain."

For several moments, neither of them says anything. Finally Vikar asks, "Are there any movies I should see?"

"What are you in the mood for?"

"Not a comedy," he says.

129.

Because Dotty doesn't hear the "not," she recommends *The Lady Eve* at the Vista. "Positively the same dame!" Vikar remembers from the burglar in his apartment, and is enthralled by Barbara Stanwyck and Henry Fonda's love story of labyrinthine treachery and desire. This is a very good movie, he concludes, disconcerted only by the laughter around him.

He reads a nineteenth-century French novel called *Là-Bas* about a writer living in a bell tower in Paris. The writer becomes obsessed with an historical figure named De Rais, who at the behest of the king of France became Joan of Arc's right-hand man. It's not clear, even to history, whether De Rais betrayed Joan or defended her, but after she was burned at the stake he went on to become the greatest child murderer in history, leading a cult of homicidal priests. Investigating De Rais, the writer receives strange letters from an unknown woman called Hyacinthe. God I hate this book, Vikar thinks to himself as he reads *Là-Bas* in a single night; the next night he reads it again, and the night after that, each time telling himself, God I hate this book, until finally, halfway through the eighth consecutive reading, he whispers to himself, God I love this book.

130.

When Michael has Fredo killed, it isn't just Cain slaying Abel. It's Abraham sacrificing Isaac, because Michael has assumed the role of father to his older brother, who has assumed the role of son. Michael sacrifices the child to the god called Family; he destroys the family in its corruptible human form to preserve the idea of Family that's more divine, and to preserve Michael's love for Family that the older brother has betrayed. God has love only for purity, and everything is washed pure by blood, burned pure by fire, rendered pure by gunshot.

131.

Vikar is in an editing room on the Paramount lot one morning when he gets the phone call. The line has a lot of static and the voice on it sounds as though from the other side of the world, which it is. " . . . making my *Lawrence of Arabia*, vicar," he finally hears. "Barbary pirates, bedouin armies, desert battles, Moroccan castles—well, they're really Moorish castles . . . . "

"You sound far away," Vikar says. There's a delay in the voices back and forth.

"Of course I sound far away," Viking Man says, "I'm in the fucking depths of Spain, not far from Gibraltar. Some grand surfing, though."

"How's the movie?"

"I'm going to be David Lean while I'm waiting to become the next John Ford."

"What about the other David Lean?"

"There you go getting wry on me, vicar."

"They made Dotty vice president."

Sometimes the lag in transatlantic response is longer. "I just talked to her," Viking Man finally says. "Listen, vicar, this call's expensive and I don't know how long the connection will last, so here's the thing. While you're busy getting wry on me, I need you in Spain for a couple of months."

"What?"

"Dot's going to get you out of that W. C. Fields nonsense and I've set it up with the MGM front office, they're making the arrangements. Someone will pick you up—probably day after tomorrow at the soonest—put you on an Iberia jet out of LAX, and someone will be waiting for you on the other end in Madrid."

"I've been reading this book."

"While we're still shooting, we need to sync and assemble as much of a rough as we can if we're going to stay on schedule. We'll do the fine cut back in L.A. Seville is the nearest city but they don't have the facilities so we'll set you up in Madrid and get dailies to you there, fly them in or send them by truck over five hundred kilometers of bad Spanish roads if need be."

"God I love this book."

"We've found a cutting room we can use in the Chueca section of town. We'll put you up in a hotel somewhere around
the Gran Villa."

"I can't come . . . . "

"We're losing this connection, vicar."

" . . . I've read this book five times and need to read it
again . . . . "

There's a particularly long pause and Vikar wonders if the
connection has broken. "What are you talking about, vicar,"
Viking Man's voice finally comes through, "is this book of
yours chained to the Hollywood Sign? You're going to be on
an airplane thirteen fucking hours, you'll be able to read it
another five times."

"I want to stay in Hollywood."

"God love you, vicar, but you're being a pussy. Don't you
understand? *This* is Hollywood."

"What do you mean?"

"This godforsaken stretch of Gibraltar. The cutting room in
Madrid. Paris, Bombay, Tokyo, fucking Norway, wherever—
it's all Hollywood, everywhere is Hollywood, the only place on
the planet that's *not* Hollywood anymore is Hollywood. You
got a passport?"

"No."

"Of course you don't. Well, that's just going to add another day or two. I'll get Stacey or Kate or one of the girls in the
Culver City office to expedite things but of course you'll need
to apply yourself, can't do that for you. They'll also get you a
copy of the script so you can be looking at that. I wish there
was a way to get you shooting boards but that will have to wait
until you get to Spain. Now there's one more thing. You still
there, vicar?"

132.

"Yes," Vikar says.

"The Generalissimo over here," Viking Man says, "is dying and taking his sweet time about it. There are more troops than usual in the streets and things are a bit tense and may get more so. So I'm having the girls in the front office pick you up one of those woolen ski caps nobody wears in L.A., and before you get off that plane and go through customs, I want you to pull that cap down over your head. Do you understand?"

"The General who?"

"Pull that cap down over your head, because one look at you and the officials might get irritable. The Generalissimo may not be a George Stevens man."

133.

Four days later, a limo is parked outside the Paramount Gate with the back door open. Sitting on the black leather backseat is a plane ticket, passport and shooting script, the MGM lion roaring in the upper left hand corner of the envelope. From the radio comes a song—*What are they doing in the Hyacinth House?*—by an old Los Angeles band whose singer died in Paris; perhaps he lived in a bell tower, in pursuit of the world's greatest satanist, the right-hand man of Joan of Arc. Between the limo and the gate, Soledad Palladin sits on the edge of the fountain, arms folded, as though Vikar conjured her.

134.

Four years have passed since she left him on Sunset Boulevard, but she looks at him as if they've seen each other every day since.

Her auburn hair is sun-bleached and she wears a simple black dress, slightly low cut, that seems more like a slip. Perhaps she's more beautiful than when he last saw her, the small cleft in her chin more perfect and irresistible. She nods hello to him more than she says it; across the street, not far from where it was that day in the rain when he last saw Zazi, is the black Mustang. Vikar leans into the limo and says to the driver, "Just a minute."

"This is for you?" Soledad says. "Are you going somewhere?"

"Spain."

She looks at the car. "Right now?"

"Viking Man is making a movie there."

"Oh yes," she smiles, "pirates or something. A boy's adventure."

"They're shooting outside Seville."

"My hometown."

"I'll be in Madrid. I'm cutting a rough from dailies. Do you still see the people at the beach?"

"Everyone is busy now," she says. "I get a small role now and then."

"I saw you in *The Long Goodbye*," Vikar says. He looks across Melrose at the Mustang and the girl in the backseat. "She's gotten big," he says.

"They do that." Soledad says, "I have been wanting to talk to you for a while, but . . . . " She's lost a bit more of her accent. "About that night."

"It's all right."

"What?"

"I vex people."

Her eyes look away and she tilts her head slightly. She takes hold of her hair and wraps it around her fist distractedly. "I wonder if I know what you mean."

"But I would never hurt her."

"Who?"

"Your little girl. Or . . . do anything bad."

She looks back at him. "I wonder if I know what you mean," she says again, except this time she sounds like she really does.

"That night."

"Which night?"

"In the car. When you drove me home from the beach house." She stares at him blankly; he believes she may be most beautiful when she's blank. "When she was in the front and I said you should put her in the back." He adds, "You left me on Sunset."

"Oh," she says. "I had forgotten that. I know you wouldn't hurt her. It had more . . . . " She stops. "It had more to do with . . . other things . . . experiences of my own . . . than with you. I was not speaking of that night. I was speaking of the *other* night."

"The other night?"

"The night," she says, "in the cemetery."

135.

The limo driver says, "Mr. Jerome?"

Stunned, Vikar nods at the driver and turns back to the woman. "Did they hurt you?" he says finally.

She chooses her words carefully. "What matters," she says, "is that you tried to help me. So I have been wanting to thank you . . . . "

Vikar says in a low voice, "Did I kill that man?"

She draws herself up when she says, "I never saw them before and have not seen them since."

"I waited for the police to come to my apartment. I'm not one of the singing family that killed those people." He gazes at the Mustang across the street. "Was Zazi all right?"

"Of course."

"I mean from that night."

"Sometimes I'm certain she's tougher than I. That she's not as beautiful, for which I'm grateful, so the men won't get the same look in their eyes. Perhaps," she shifts from the fountain, "she will not spend her teenage years in and out of institutions like her mother."

"But that night—"

"She was with friends," says Soledad. "With her father." She shrugs. "You don't want to miss your plane," and she turns to cross the street to the Mustang, where Vikar can barely make out Zazi in the back, watching her mother and watching him.

136.

From the liquor cart going up and down the aisle of the airplane, Vikar orders three vodka tonics. Notwithstanding Viking Man's assurance that Vikar would have thirteen hours to read *Là-Bas* five more times, Vikar makes it through only once before pulling the script for Viking Man's movie from the MGM envelope.

He reads the script twice and the third time begins breaking the story into sequences and numbering them as he would identify the parts of an architectural structure. When the sun is behind him, he puts the script away and watches a Spanish movie he doesn't understand; the actress in it navigates between relationships with two men and Vikar keeps seeing Soledad in the part of the woman. At one point he closes his eyes.

In the dark of his lids, the Spanish movie intercuts with the open horizontal rock of his dream and its white ancient writing and the mysterious figure lying on top. Vikar sits up with a start.

When he finally dozes again, it's to the dull roar of the engines and the pitch black of the night above the Atlantic. Upon landing at Barrajas Airport in the late afternoon Vikar remembers only at the last minute, as he steps through the door, to pull the cap from his coat pocket and down over his head.

137.

The customs officials make him take the cap off. In the waiting area beyond the customs control Vikar can see a driver holding a cardboard sign that reads VICAR, with a C. When Vikar takes off the cap, everyone around him—customs officials, police, passengers—stops and a hush falls on the room.

138.

As Vikar is ushered into a smaller room, he looks back over his shoulder at the driver in the distance with the sign. In the room, one of the officials takes Vikar's passport and motions for him to sit at a table. On the wall hangs a portrait of a mild looking man in a uniform, wearing small round spectacles to go with his small trimmed moustache; Vikar realizes this is the General person of whom Viking Man spoke. He doesn't appear fearsome.

Several of the officials lean over Vikar to study his head. "*Anarquista?*" one asks. The official with Vikar's passport vanishes and for a while no one says or does anything. The official finally returns ten minutes later with another who's studying the passport as he walks in the door; he looks at Vikar and says, "Señor Jerome?"

I should have stayed in Hollywood where nothing bad happens except singing families that slaughter people. "Yes."

"Welcome to our country."

"Thank you."

"How long do you plan to be with us, Señor Jerome?" the official asks.

"I'm not sure."

"Is your purpose here business or holiday?"

"Business."

"What is the name of your company?"

I don't have a company, Vikar almost answers, but says, "MGM."

"The hotel," says the official.

"The movies," Vikar says. "I believe there is a hotel as well."

"Las Vegas. Dean Martin."

"*Rio Bravo*," Vikar nods.

The official looks at Vikar, some inexplicable annoyance flashing across his eyes. "I speak English," he says.

"What?"

"Is there someone who can vouch for your business here?"

"A man outside," says Vikar.

"A man?"

"Holding a sign."

The official turns and says something in Spanish to one of the other officials, who leaves the room. The official sits down next to Vikar and looks at his head. He points at Vikar's head and says, "There are not many people in my country who appear like this."

"No."

"In America there are many people who appear like this?"

"No."

The official looks around at the others. "Myself," he confides to Vikar, "I am a great admirer of Miss Natalie Wood."

Vikar just nods.

"I saw her in the film about the two married couples who trade." He shrugs. "This film is not allowed in my country. I saw it while on holiday in Paris. Miss Natalie Wood is very beautiful in this film." A low, desperate groan seems to emanate up from within him. "*Muy, muy, muy.* Do you know this film?"

"Yes."

"She is very beautiful."

"Yes."

"She is very immodest in this film. You hear my English is excellent."

"You should see *Splendor in the Grass.*"

"This *Splendid* film stars Miss Natalie Wood?"

"Yes."

"In this film she is immodest?"

"It's like *The Exorcist*, except better."

"I know of this *Exorcist* film, this is the film about Satanás. Yes?"

"What?"

"*Diablo.* The Devil."

"Yes."

"This film is not allowed in my country."

Vikar nods. "It's not very good."

"*This* film," the official taps Vikar on the head hard, "is not allowed in my country."

Vikar says, as politely as possible, "It's not Natalie Wood."

The official rises slightly from the chair, looks at Vikar's head. He studies the woman's face.

"It's Elizabeth Taylor," says Vikar.

"Elizabeth Taylor?"

"And Montgomery Clift. *A Place in the Sun.*"

"*Qué?*"

"The name of this movie," Vikar taps his own head in turn, speaking slowly, "is *A Place . . . in . . . the . . . Sun.*"

"This," the official says, tapping Vikar's head back even harder, "is . . . " *tap* " . . . not . . . " *tap* " . . . the. . . " *tap* " . . .

film with Miss Natalie Wood about the young degenerate American hoodlums who are probably homosexuals?"

"No."

"Do you know this film that I mean?"

"*Rebel Without a Cause.*"

"This is the one I mean," the official nods, "it is not allowed in my country." The two men say nothing more but sit at the table looking at each other. Five minutes pass, then ten.

139.

The door opens and the other official returns, and says something in Spanish.

The official sitting with Vikar continues to stare at him as if barely registering whatever has been said. Then he stands. He hands Vikar his passport. "This film you are working, is Miss Natalie Wood in this film?"

"I don't believe so," Vikar says.

"Perhaps your film will be allowed in my country."

"I'm certain it will be a very good movie," Vikar says.

140.

When the phone rings in his hotel room, Vikar assumes it's Viking Man. But amid the static of the phone call he hears a female voice saying his name; for a moment he imagines it's Soledad and only after the phone has gone dead does he realize it was Dotty. He waits for the phone to ring again but it doesn't, and finally he sleeps.

141.

When he wakes in the morning, someone seems to have been knocking at his door for hours.

The same driver who met Vikar at the airport and drove him to the hotel now drives him through a depressed part of Madrid to an ugly industrial building twenty minutes away. In the editing room Vikar finds bread, butter and jam but no knife to spread them, coffee and bottled water, and a stack of film cans that have just arrived from a lab. There are no instructions from Viking Man or anyone else.

For a while Vikar sits staring at the cans. He eats the bread with the butter and jam that he spreads by using the other end of the china pencil with which he'll mark the print. He doesn't drink the coffee.

142.

He sits a while longer staring at the cans. He believes his life itself is in a kind of jet lag. After half an hour he gets up and begins stripping away posters, photos and memos from the room's largest wall until it's bare.

He takes the film can on top and separates the lids. He threads the film through the drive mechanism of the viewer. For the moment he doesn't concern himself with what kind of splices to make, with fades or dissolves or wipes, let alone with lighting or color. He's putting miles of film into order, which means locating the sequences that he's marked in the script, and the camera set-ups within each sequence.

143.

Over the weeks to come, first he'll match the exposed film with the soundtrack, then select a representative still from each set-up, sometimes more than one.

If there is, for instance, a sequence in which the Berber chieftain lops off the head of a thief, Vikar will choose a single still of perhaps a flying head, or a head rolling on the ground. He'll print an enlargement of the still and number it and tack it onto the bare wall that he's stripped. He'll group set-ups chronologically into sequences, then number and group sequences as they're represented by the set-up stills, until finally he's determined the sequence for everything that's been shot. He'll catalog images and sounds by a synchronization code, then begin splicing together footage. Sometimes he'll make a decision for one take over the others when the choice seems clear, particularly from a technical standpoint.

As Vikar does this, more rushes come each day or sometimes arrive every two or three days, or occasionally two or three times in one day. He works nine hours a day. Around one o'clock his driver brings lunch, and sometimes he eats dinner around ten o'clock in the Spanish fashion. Not once in the weeks to come will he receive a phone call from Viking Man.

144.

At night, after his work, he falls asleep in the back of the car, and the driver shakes him awake when they reach Vikar's hotel. Vikar doesn't go out into the city at all; he doesn't care about the city. Madrid is a ghost town, fixed in the suspension of the Generalissimo's pending death. Black wrought iron wreathes the city's doors and balconies and fountains and windows. As the weeks pass, on the Fuencarral below his hotel window Vikar notices first the appearance of one streetwalker, then another, then another.

145.

After he's been in Madrid three weeks, one night on the way back to his hotel Vikar wakes not to the driver's touch but rather the jostling of the car, and realizes he's blindfolded.

He also realizes his hands are bound. "What's happening?" he says; he can feel someone on each side of him in the backseat. "What's happening?" he says again, and someone answers, "Please do not talk. We will be there soon."

"Where?"

"Please do not talk."

146.

Soon he feels the car come to a stop. All the doors open and someone pulls Vikar out of the backseat. Led blindfolded for several minutes, at one point Vikar trips and two men catch him and pull him to his feet.

They stop and there's the metal creak of an opening door. "There is a step here," someone says. Vikar lifts his feet to step inside the door, which he hears pulled closed behind him.

147.

Vikar assumes he's been arrested by the same officials who interrogated him in customs when he entered the country. When the blindfold is taken off, he expects to see the fan of Miss Natalie Wood waiting for him.

Instead he's in some sort of warehouse. On the far side is

what appears to be a makeshift soundstage with a bed, and in one corner a particularly old moviola. Lined against the wall are a dozen guns and rifles and rounds of ammunition.

There's also a small screen and projector with a low table nearby and someone sitting on a stool watching a movie. Vikar looks around him; one of the men, his driver, holds several film canisters. The other men wear rifles on their shoulder or guns in their belts. The figure on the stool doesn't turn to look at Vikar but continues watching the movie.

148.

When the man on the stool turns from the movie to Vikar, he doesn't look like a policeman or customs official.

He's slight in stature, dark, in his late twenties. He wears dark pants and combat boots and a kind of workshirt; a scarf is tied around his neck. On the table next to the stool where the man sits, next to a bottle of wine and several glasses, Vikar sees a military issue .45.

The man on the stool notes Vikar's bound hands. "Untie his hands," he says to the other men. He says to Vikar, "I apologize for the ropes. Please," and indicates another nearby stool for Vikar to sit. He turns his attention back to the movie, and together the two men watch.

149.

The movie is about a young bride who travels to Thailand to be with her French diplomat husband. Among the embassy's aristocratic females, the bride has a number of sexual relationships, then is sent by her husband to be trained by an older man in the art of sexual submission.

Vikar believes that the young woman is very attractive but perhaps the movie is not so good. "This film is not allowed in my country," the man on the stool says to Vikar. "You know of this actress?" Over the man's shoulder, Vikar watches the driver of his car set the film cans on the editing table.

"No."

"Miss Sylvia Kristel," the man says, as though this explains everything.

"Is she French?"

"The film is French. She is . . . " he thinks, " . . . Dutch, I believe."

150.

They watch awhile longer, the man riveted by the Dutch actress. Then he reaches over and turns off the projector. He says, "You are Señor . . . Vicar? How do you say it?"

"Vikar."

"Like a church name."

"With a k."

This isn't altogether clear to the other man but he says, "I am Cooper Léon. Are you hungry?"

"No, thank you." There are seven or eight men besides Cooper Léon. One is an older man who sits on the soundstage bed smiling at Vikar, and who appears to Vikar to be wearing some sort of military costume and make-up, although from the distance Vikar can't be sure.

"Have a little wine," says Cooper Léon, who takes the bottle from next to the pistol on the table and pours a glass and hands it to Vikar. "Of course Cooper Léon," says the man, "may not be my real name. Or it might. It might be that my parents really did name me after Gary Cooper who fought for the Republic in *For Whom the Bell Tolls*. If that is so, then it places you in a potentially untenable position, since I have told to you my real name."

"But it might not be your real name," says Vikar.

"Exactly. It is as with the chamber of a gun that may or may not have a bullet in it. But the larger point is that if you cooperate, you will be all right in either case and it will not matter if it is my real name." Cooper Léon says, "Do you know who we are?"

"No."

"We are the Soldiers of Viridiana."

"I don't know what that is."

"We are the resistance to the fascist assassin the Generalissimo."

"The man who's dying?"

"Ah." Cooper Léon is pleased. "*Gracias*. We arrive at the heart of the conversation without further preliminaries."

"You're welcome."

"Dying is not dead, this is the mournful truth of our situation. The assassin dies and dies and dies and dies, it goes on and on and on and on, which is to say he lives and lives and lives and lives. It is a tedious thing."

Vikar says, "He should die more quickly."

"He should die NOW!" Cooper Léon roars in Vikar's face, then pulls back, hands raised. "You see?" he waves to the men around him, then places his hand on his chest. "It unsettles us. It unsettles all of Spain." He pours himself more wine and stares at the blank movie screen, lost in thought.

151.

Cooper Léon says, "What is cinema, Señor Vicar?"

"What?"

"What is cinema? Cinema," he answers himself, "is

metaphor." He looks at his men around him to gauge the awe with which this insight has been received. "Cinema is metaphor, and this is one of the things that cinema has in common with politics, which often is metaphor as well. The assassin the Generalissimo, it is no longer a question of his power. He is dying, and in his dying he has no true practical power anymore. Slow but sure the country rustles itself to freedom and justice. On the Fuencarral by your hotel, for instance, you have recently noticed more women of the night?"

"Yes."

"This is what I mean."

Vikar considers the political implications of the women he has seen on the Fuencarral.

"But in his unseemly insistence on continuing to live, the assassin the Generalissimo holds another kind of power over the minds of the countrymen he has oppressed for more than thirty-five years. Do you understand what I am saying?"

"No."

152.

Cooper Léon waves it away. "It is of no matter," he says. "We are going to make a film about the death of the assassin the Generalissimo."

"The one who hasn't died."

"That is why we make the film. Cinema is metaphor, and when politics is metaphor as well, then cinema is guerrilla action. So that although the assassin may live another thirty-five years, he will die in the imaginations of the people, which is what matters. I am certain you understand." Vikar doesn't understand. Cooper Léon indicates the old man sitting on the bed on the soundstage. "My papa here, he is playing the assassin the Generalissimo. You will direct the scene."

"I'm not a director."

"You will direct the scene, and then you will put the film together with what we have filmed, and with documentary footage we have gathered of the assassin the Generalissimo over the last thirty-five years, and with what you have cut from the film that you have been working on in Madrid."

Vikar looks at the soundstage and the little old man, and looks at the cans of film that his driver has placed on the far editing table. "Those," he says to the canisters, "are what I've cut from Viking Man's movie?"

"Who is this viking?"

"That is footage from the movie I've been cutting?"

"Some is other footage, as I said. As well," he adds, patting the projector, "we might put in some of this film."

Vikar looks at the projector. "The French movie starring the naked Dutch actress?"

Cooper Léon frowns. "I have to consider this. I have to consider whether it is proper to sacrifice this film for this purpose. Perhaps some parts of this film that are not as," he's at a loss for the precise word, "stirring. If you cut something from this film," patting the projector again, "you can put back together what is left?"

"I can splice it," says Vikar.

"That is it," Cooper Léon points at Vikar triumphantly, "splice!"

"You want to make a movie of your father," says Vikar, looking at the little old man on the set, "and Viking Man's movie and old documentaries and the movie with the naked Dutch actress?"

"You keep saying this viking."

Vikar says, "I don't believe I can make this movie you want."

Cooper Léon's face goes cold. "This has been a civil conversation, has it not?"

"I'm very busy with the other movie."

"It has been a pleasant conversation, no?"

"All right."

"Let us not be uncivil. Let us not be unpleasant. You will do this."

Vikar looks at the .45 on the table and at the stage behind Cooper Léon.

"Pablo," Cooper Léon calls. One of the other men raises a handheld camera.

"Viking Man's movie," Vikar nods at the cans of film on the editing table, "is about long ago. It's about the desert and people who ride horses and wear robes and have swords. I don't believe," he says, "your movie is going to make sense."

Cooper Léon smiles, having anticipated this objection. "Señor," he says, "do you know of Buñuel?"

"Yes."

"He is known in your country?"

"People who know about movies know about him."

"He is considered a good director?"

"Yes."

"Your great American novelist Henry Miller said, 'They call Buñuel many things but they do not call him a lunatic.' Señor Vicar, have you seen a film by Buñuel that makes sense?"

"No. I believe the movie of Catherine Deneuve getting splattered with mud is a very good movie."

"That is my favorite as well," Cooper Léon nods. "The mud splattering especially."

153.

Vikar says, "Do you know Buñuel yourself?"

"This is what I have just said."

"I mean, do you *know* Buñuel?"

"You mean Buñuel the man?"

"Yes."

"Buñuel has not been in Spain a long time."

"Do you know his daughter?"

"I know of no daughter. I know he has sons."

"No daughter?"

"If Buñuel had a daughter, would he not acknowledge it?"

"You would be surprised," says Vikar, "what fathers do to their children."

154.

The car returns Vikar to his hotel where he sleeps three hours, then rises to find the car waiting to take him to the cutting room where he edits Viking Man's movie. Every night the car picks up Vikar from the cutting room; three or four other men are always in the car, where Vikar is blindfolded but his hands are no longer bound. By night Vikar "directs" the death of the Generalissimo, starring Cooper Léon's papa. By day he cuts Viking Man's Barbary pirate movie.

155.

As the Generalissimo's death is filmed, one of the Soldiers of Viridiana cooks what the men call the "Basque Breakfast"— although it's the middle of the night—a hash of fried eggs, potatoes, onions and chopped tomatoes. It becomes the one thing Vikar looks forward to, eating it out of the skillet with the other men and drinking it down with Spanish red wine.

Pablo with the handheld camera shoots the Generalissimo's death scene from every angle. For the "lights" on the makeshift soundstage, three stainless-steel standing floor lamps that twist into shapes appear to have been liberated from a gynecologist's office. Cooper Léon's papa is lit and shot in every position that might conceivably suggest a dictator on the verge of death. Vikar shoots and shoots night after night because, first of all, he has heard that when a director has no idea what he's doing, he should shoot as much film as possible, and because, second, he's trying to prolong the filming so that he might finish Viking Man's movie first and slip out of the country.

"Perhaps you should moan," Vikar suggests to Cooper Léon's papa during filming. For a "soundstage," the set is remarkably absent of any kind of sound equipment—perhaps, Vikar believes, because it's the style of European filmmaking to dub in the sound later. Nonetheless Vikar also believes Cooper Léon's papa should moan even if no one can hear it; the camera will hear it. These directions are translated to Cooper Léon's papa and he moans. I don't believe it's a very good moan, Vikar thinks. But perhaps this is the way they moan in Spain when they're dying. "Perhaps," Vikar says to the translator, reconsidering, "he should not moan," and Cooper Léon's papa stops moaning.

156.

Two weeks pass. Cutting Viking Man's movie by day and the movie for the Soldiers of Viridiana by night, Vikar feels not only his eyes going but whatever distinctions onto which he's been able to hold. In Cooper Léon's movie, Vikar intercuts footage of Cooper Léon's papa in bed with the old documentary footage of the Generalissimo and left-over shards of Viking Man's movie, to show the Generalissimo flooded by memories and strange dreams as he dies. Bits of the sequence in Viking Man's movie where the Berber chieftain chops off the thief's head become a dream in which the Generalissimo as a child has his own head chopped off by his father, dressed in the black robes of death.

Vikar believes perhaps the movie doesn't look so much like Buñuel. He's also not certain how Viking Man would feel about some of his movie making its way into a movie by the Soldiers of Viridiana. Cooper Léon insists that a bit of the French movie with the naked Dutch actress should be included, preferably some stray moment from the film's "most superb scene" where the young bride is raped in an opium den. At the same time, Cooper Léon doesn't want his print of the French movie too violated; Vikar decides to surgically remove a single frame from the opium den scene and drop it into the Generalissimo movie. He feels a bit like God doing this, sending a clandestine message to anyone who sees the movie. "But no one will see only a single frame," Cooper Léon protests.

"They will not see it but they will," says Vikar.

Cooper Léon's eyes narrow. "They will not see it but they will," he repeats slowly, then again, "*they will not see it but they will!* It is like a secret weapon, then, that explodes in the imagination of the viewer!"

"Yes."

Cooper Léon looks at Vikar and his eyes glisten. "You are a man of vision," he declares quietly.

"Uh."

"Spain is fortunate you were sent in this trying hour."

157.

Editing the death of the Generalissimo, Vikar notices that in scenes shot from one side Cooper Léon's papa is not ominous in the least, but that in scenes shot from the other side, a menace presents itself that was unseen either on the stage or in the camera's lens. It's as though one profile of the old man is possessed in a way that only film captures. He uses all the footage from the menacing profile and rejects the rest.

158.

One night, after sleepless nights and days of Vikar working on both movies, the car that always waits for him isn't there.

Vikar gets a taxi back to his hotel. The next morning at the hotel, the car still isn't there, nor that night, nor the next morning and night. It never appears again. The driver never returns, and no one brings Vikar lunch.

Sitting at the window of his hotel room one night, Vikar notes out of the corner of his eye the mirror over the bathroom sink, and in it his reflection.

159.

Looking at his reflection in the mirror, Vikar thinks about the scenes of Cooper Léon's papa and how by cutting to someone's right or left profile in the editing, he can expose something. He can expose the side of the person that's true and the side that's false. He can expose the side that's good and the side that's evil.

160.

He can—he's still thinking to himself a week later, on the plane home—expose the side that punishes and the side that receives, the side that dominates and the side that submits. It's different with each person and each profile: what's represented by one actor's right might be represented by another's left. George Stevens understood this in *A Place in the Sun*; Vikar remembers what Dotty said about the close-ups of Taylor and Clift on the terrace, how Stevens had no regard for continuity in cutting from one profile to the other. As Vikar begins to decipher which profile is which—although he can't articulate it to himself let alone anyone else—a new visual vocabulary of meaning becomes available to him.

161.

Variety, January 5, 1976: "LOS ANGELES—Long-time motion-picture veteran Dorothy Langer is leaving the studio after more than 25 years as editor and vice president, effective immediately, it was announced today by Paramount Pictures. Neither Ms. Langer nor a spokesman for the studio could be reached for comment."

162.

Back in Los Angeles, Vikar goes by Dotty's office on the chance she's still there. He tries phoning her once, to no answer.

Over the coming weeks and months, he walks out to the Paramount Gate looking for Soledad against the fountain, arms folded. He searches everywhere and asks anyone who might know her; he calls information over and over for her number, but there never is one.

163.

Kubrick's *Barry Lyndon*. Kurosawa's *The Bad Sleep Well*. Penn's *Night Moves*. Warhol's *Heat*. Huston's *The Man Who Would Be King*. Borowczyk's *Immoral Tales*. Meyer's *Up!* Sarre's *The Death of Marat*. Roeg's *The Man Who Fell to Earth*. In *The Story of Adele H*, the daughter of a famous nineteenth-century author falls in love with a soldier. She follows the soldier from France to Nova Scotia and haunts the streets of Halifax looking for him; everything she believes or has believed has collapsed into his form. She is Joan of Arc but without a god; she becomes so pure in her crusade that, by the end of the movie, the soldier himself means nothing to her and is unrecognizable to her. She's beyond love, beyond the pettiness of her own heart; she's beyond God. By the end of the movie, she's gone somewhere God can't reach her.

164.

Later he'll tell himself it's for Dotty, but he doesn't really believe that. Deep in the bowels of the Paramount archives one afternoon he sees it, there on a shelf like this week's disposable magazine: *place in the sun / stevens* scrawled on the edge of the canister; and he stands looking at it a long time as if deciding whether to steal it rather than how. But really he's deciding how.

If they hadn't fired Dotty, I wouldn't, but he knows he would and feels no guilt. He also knows he cherishes this movie more than its owners ever could. Finally he simply carries the cans out of the building under his arm in broad daylight, making no attempt to hide them; when no one stops or questions him, the theft is only validated. Back in his apartment on Pauline Boulevard, he makes a shrine for it.

165.

Dietrich and Von Sternberg's *The Devil is a Woman* is next. As the pirated movie collection grows, the shrine grows; soon it's filled a wall. *I'm going to need more walls.*

166.

He goes to the Fox Venice one night to see an Antonioni double bill. In the first film, a group of vacationers visits an island where one of them vanishes; the woman is never found, and by the end of the movie she is all but forgotten. In the second film, the private eye from *Chinatown* has become a foreign correspondent who changes places with a dead man, leaving in his wake a successful career and an estranged wife. So really the second half of the double bill solves the mystery of the first, and of the vanished woman on the island, who clearly also has exchanged places with someone. Vikar knows she has become Soledad Palladin, who was originally supposed to play the part. By the end of the double bill the foreign correspondent has assumed not only the dead man's itinerary but his destiny, and a growing hush falls over not just these movies but all movies—the hush of looming cataclysm, the slow pan of the camera across an empty town square outside a hotel room, where a body lies.

167.

Vikar returns to Jayne Mansfield's headstone at Hollywood Memorial one night and lies on the headstone waiting for her. But she doesn't come.

168.

After three projects as an assistant editor, Vikar hasn't worked for eight months when he gets a phone call.

"Mr. Jerome?" The voice on the other line is pleasant and self-assured. "Mitch Rondell with United Artists in New York. How are you?"

"I'm all right."

"I'm wondering if we can fly you back here to discuss a project. It would be on our dime, of course."

"When?" says Vikar.

"I don't mean to be pushy, but as soon as possible. This afternoon or, if that's not feasible, tomorrow."

"Can you tell me what it is?"

"I would rather talk about it in person. It's pressing and a little delicate."

"It doesn't take thirteen hours, does it?"

"To New York?"

"The last plane I flew took thirteen hours."

"You must have gone farther than New York."

"Spain."

"That's farther than New York. Have you ever been to New York?"

"No. I've been to Philadelphia."

"Well, that's close to New York. It didn't take you thirteen hours to fly to Philadelphia, did it?"

"I took a bus from Philadelphia. That took longer than thirteen hours."

"I would think so. Can I have my assistant call you back in twenty minutes or so to make the arrangements?"

"Someone will need to drive me to the airport."

"Of course. Someone will be waiting for you at JFK as well, and bring you to a hotel here in the city, probably the Sherry-Netherland, and we'll take things from there. Everything will be handled on our end."

"Thank you."

"See you in the next day or two, Mr. Jerome."

"You may call me Vikar. With a k."

"You can call me Mitch with an M," although Vikar can't imagine how else he would spell it.

169.

The sign the driver holds the next evening when Vikar arrives at JFK doesn't say "Vikar" by any spelling, but MR. JEROME. The car takes Vikar to his hotel; he has a small suite overlooking the park.

The next morning Vikar is driven to the company offices at Forty-Ninth and Seventh. It's the worst neighborhood he's ever seen; a porn theater is across the street. He's wandering the building's twelfth floor, lost, when someone says, "Vikar Jerome?"

"Yes," Vikar says.

"Your head precedes you," the man laughs. He looks like one of the actors in *Carnal Knowledge*, who also was half of a singing duo Vikar once saw on television, with the same blond brillo hair except thinning. "I'm Mitch."

"Hello." Vikar shakes his hand.

"How was your flight?"

"All right, thank you."

"Not thirteen hours."

"No." Vikar says, "I know New York is closer than Spain."

"How is the hotel?"

"It's nice. Thank you."

"Have you had lunch?"

"No."

"Let's go have lunch."

170.

The two walk along Forty-Ninth to a restaurant called Vesuvio's, where Rondell has a salad and Vikar orders a pizza.

"Let me get right to why I called you," says Rondell, his voice dropping. He looks around. "For some time we've been in production on a picture called *Your Pale Blue Eyes*. Have you heard of it?"

"Yes," Vikar says.

"I'm afraid," Rondell sighs, "many people have heard of it, and have heard all the wrong things." He glances around him again. "The company is going through an interesting period, Vikar. On the one hand, we've won the last two consecutive Oscars for best picture. I would love to say it's part of a grand plan but of course you know better. *Cuckoo's Nest* was kicking around ten years—and a B-picture about a boxer shot in four weeks for a million bucks, starring and written by somebody whose biggest credit was *The Lords of Flatbush*? On the other hand, the moneymen in San Francisco are making changes, everything is moving west, and soon there probably won't be any New York office—which, I grant you, if you saw the neighborhood as you were driving in, maybe isn't such a terrible thing. There's serious talk that the guy who's been running the company thirty years is on his way out to start another company. None of which any reasonable movie fan cares about, I know, but that's the back story. How's that pizza?"

"It's very good pizza."

"Now we have this picture. A very New York picture, which made it seem right for us, budgeted at five million. Well, it's going to cost ten if we're lucky, likelier twelve-plus. Ridiculous that this picture should cost that, and if we could turn back the clock and pull the plug on the whole thing, we would, but we can't. Two days ago, the day I called you, the director quit. Do you know who I'm talking about? Don't say his name if you do, not here, anyway."

"He made the movie about the Devil."

"Right."

"*Splendor in the Grass* is better."

Rondell appears slightly befuddled but says, "That's probably true."

"It's all right," Vikar assures him. "Sometimes I vex people."

"Thank you. I'm glad you told me."

"You're welcome."

"In a lot of ways, we're not sorry to see him go. Certainly none of the crew is sorry to see him go. The original D.P. couldn't work with him and quit, and none of the major talent we wanted will work with him either. Now he's walked off and we've had to bring up the second-unit director to finish the picture—it's just a situation that we have to make work for us. They're trying to wrap on a soundstage in Queens as we speak."

"Is that close?"

"Forty minutes by car."

"Closer than Spain, then." Vikar says, "I'm being wry."

"Closer than Spain," Rondell laughs. "None of this I've told you has gotten out so far in the press, but of course such discretion won't last long. It probably won't last another day. The phone calls from *Variety* and the *Hollywood Reporter* and the *L.A. Times* will start pouring in," he looks at his watch, "about five minutes ago."

"Five minutes ago?" Vikar asks, confused.

"It's an expression. We'll have DGA arbitration and, until the Guild sorts it out, this picture is officially directed by nobody. This is why we needed to see you quickly. We're unofficially scheduled to screen at Cannes in seven months, and while the rational thing might be to pull out, if we do that then between the official undirector and the unofficial withdrawal of the unofficial Cannes selection, what we wind up with is a very official disaster. How is Dotty Langer, by the way?"

It takes Vikar a moment to answer. "I haven't talked to her in a while."

"She worked on that picture, right?"

"What?"

"*That* picture," Rondell says, his eyes cast slightly upward.

"Oh." Vikar touches his head. "I forget it's up there."

"I imagine people remind you."

"Yes."

"The truth is that if we can get away with it, we would rather go with someone a bit under the radar than some powerhouse editor who will attract attention—I mean," he laughs a bit, "a different kind of attention than you attract. Please don't be offended if I say this may prove to be out of your depth, assuming you take it on. But whether you realize it, and I know you haven't been in the business long, you're developing something of a reputation for coming into troubled projects and sorting things out."

"I've only done it two or three times."

"We understand that. We also understand that this project requires more than just sorting out. This will be the biggest thing you've done—it's not some madman in the south of Spain who thinks he's making *Lawrence of Arabia*—and I hope I don't offend you again if I say that in the long run we may wind up bringing in that powerhouse editor after all, who may wind up doing no better than you. This is not a reflection of any lack of confidence in you. It's a lack of confidence in the circumstances."

"I'm not offended."

"Most of the time we feel like we don't know what this picture is. We don't know if it's a thriller or an art film or—"

"Perhaps it's a thrilling art film. I'm being wry again."

"We'll settle for a thrilling art film at this point," says Rondell. "We'll settle for salvaging the situation, forget any sort of actual *success*."

"Is there a rough yet?"

"Someone's assembling one now."

"I hope not too much footage is being cut. I would like to see it."

"I appreciate that. Do you appreciate, in turn, that time is of the essence?"

"Yes." Vikar says, "You need the movie in the can if the movie is going to be in the Cannes." He laughs.

"Six months from now we need something as close to an answer print as possible. An actual booking print would be a dream."

"All right."

"What about terms?"

"Terms?"

"We'll more than match whatever you're making now for whatever you're working on."

"I'm not working on anything. I'm probably not supposed to say that, am I?"

"I'll pretend you're being wry again. Let us know what you made on your last job and we'll increase it twenty-five percent, if that's acceptable. How's the room at the Sherry?"

"It's nice."

"We keep it for situations like this. Maybe not lavish, but a month from now you won't feel like the walls are closing in on you, either. Can you be comfortable there for a while?"

"Yes. There's something else."

171.

Rondell says, "What's that?"

"Old movies."

"Old movies?"

"I collect old movies." Vikar believes it sounds better to say he collects them than that he steals them. "Prints of old movies. Can I get prints of old movies you've made?"

"Are there any you have in mind?"

"I wouldn't sell them or anything. I would keep them for myself."

"It would depend on what you have in mind. You know, *Broken Blossoms*, probably not."

"Not that old. The private-eye one at the beach," he says, "*The Long Goodbye*. Is that yours?"

"Yes, that's ours. I might be able to get you that."

"*Kiss Me Deadly. Sweet Smell of Success.* Those are yours?"

"Yes."

"Especially *The Long Goodbye*."

"I'll see what I can do."

172.

He's in New York through the end of the fall, into winter. The winter reminds him of Pennsylvania, bitter mornings rising in his room back at Mather Divinity. As when he was in Madrid, for a while he doesn't go out into the city, beyond shuttling between the hotel at Fifty-Ninth and Fifth and the editing room at Forty-Ninth and Seventh, where he works nine, eleven, sometimes fourteen hours a day.

173.

Then one Sunday, the cold breaks and he leaves his suite and walks out into the city. He believes he's going to cross the street over to the park; instead he turns south, down Fifth past the Empire State Building all the way to Union Square, cutting down Broadway to the Bowery. The afternoon passes and he wanders along St. Marks Place; there aren't any hippie buckaroos or even many space-age drag queens. People wear motorcycle jackets and jeans with holes in the knees and T-shirts with pictures of Captain America, and Mickey Mouse doing something strange to Minnie, and the words I KILL MOONIES.

What are Moonies? Some wear rings in unusual parts of their bodies, and their wrists are wrapped from suicides attempted or postured or postponed.

At one point, Vikar and a girl on the street with cropped, dyed-black hair stop and stare at each other, she at Elizabeth Taylor and Montgomery Clift, he at the words on her chest. GABBA GABBA HEY, says her shirt. "Hey, man," she calls to someone across the street, "check this out." It's difficult to know who finds the other more mystifying. As these people are nothing like he's seen, he is nothing like they've seen; and then, as dark falls, he hears something for which—he realizes in retrospect—he's been listening for years.

174.

It's not just a music, rather it's the Sound, the real Music everyone has tried to tell him over the years that all the other music was when it wasn't.

Vikar is standing on the Bowery outside what seems to be a tunnel cut into a bunker. The sidewalk is crowded with more kids like he saw on St. Marks Place, as well as old people sleeping under newspapers and drunks stumbling through the crowd asking for money. A dirty barefooted woman shivers under a yellow awning in nothing but the paper-thin gown that patients wear in hospitals.

The address on the awning is 315. There are nonsensical letters on the awning that spell nothing. A mystifying handwritten cardboard sign on the black glass doors says

HEARTBREAKERS
MAXXI MARASCHINO
SIC FUCKS
SHIRTS

and while nothing about this is comprehensible to him, the

154 -- STEVE ERICKSON

illicitly narcotic Sound is irresistible and he goes inside, the doorman eying him with wonder.

175.

Inside, the club isn't much bigger than Vikar's hotel suite. There are two stages, the main one in front, a smaller and lower one off to the side. There's a pool table and a couple of pinball machines. The walls are peeling and needles litter the shadows and wafting clouds of urine collide with clouds of beer. The Sound, made by the band on the main stage, is overwhelming; people at the front fling themselves wildly into each other. Something wells up in Vikar. There's a break, then a singer who reminds him of Brigitte Bardot or Tuesday Weld.

176.

It was never the Music at all, it was always the Sound; and though there's no way for him to understand this, perhaps the Sound moves him now because, a little more than twenty years after its birth, the Sound has become about itself, the Sound is about its own truth and corruption in the same way that, a little more than twenty years after the Movies found their sound, there was a wave of movies about the Movies: *Sunset Boulevard*, *Singin' in the Rain*, *The Big Knife*, *The Bad and the Beautiful*. When the Sound has circled to swallow its tail, it becomes a world of its own, god or no god, or in which Vikar is god—or in any event a god that kills fathers rather than sons.

177.

Vikar returns to the club the next night and the next, and the next five after that. There's never a moment when he says *God I hate this music* before he admits *God I love this Sound.* By his third night, when he steps over the woman in the hospital gown sleeping in the doorway and walks into the club, everyone turns to look and in the din he catches stray fragments of buzz, "He's here . . ." and people part before him. When the audience begins its tribal smash-ups, the thing in him wells up and he lurches into the crowd, slamming into everything and everyone, toppling over the edge of the stage. He feels people's hands on Liz and Monty. Later behind the club, a feline Asian named Tanya and her "slave" Damitra take turns putting him in their mouths, and as he leans back against the wall he can feel the vibration, like the vibration he felt when he went to the silent-movie theater one night on Fairfax, and Chauncey played the organ to the ride of the Klan in *The Birth of a Nation.* Returning to the editing room in the mornings he glows with a bruised blue, and the secretaries and assistants regard him even more strangely than usual.

178.

For a while he realizes he's come to care more about the Sound than the Movies, and in his infidelity he's ashamed, memories washing over him of his first days in Los Angeles when no one seemed to love the movies. I would never betray you, he promises the bathroom mirror, caressing his head. I might cheat on you for Kim or Natalie or Tuesday, but I would never betray you for any sound or music.

179.

One early morning in the dark after returning to the hotel, Vikar sits looking out the window at the park. It's turned cold again. Christmas decorations go up all over the city. The heat of his night at the club, however, makes him unlatch the window and push it open. The park reflects off the glass of the window in the light from his suite. He keeps pushing the window in and out, the image of the park shifting with its reflection in the glass.

180.

I would never betray you, one lover might say to another in a scene, but by choosing one profile over the other, Vikar can lay bare either credibility or mendacity in the character, irrespective of the actor's intention or the writer's or director's.

As people have right profiles and lefts, so places and moments have them. Vikar looks back and forth from the park below to its image in the window, listening to the image's stereo. In a movie, every shot is a profile of *something*. By cutting from rights to lefts or vice versa, or from rights to other rights or from lefts to other lefts, Vikar reinforces or sabotages the audience's perceptions, not to mention the film's. He sets free from within the false film the true film.

He's been working on *Your Pale Blue Eyes* for two months when, going over the previous day's rushes, he hits the stop button and looks at the face in the frame before him.

181.

He picks up the phone and puts a call through to Mitch Rondell.

"I hear you're a busy man these nights, Vikar," Rondell says. The tone of concern is unmistakable. "At some point soon, it would be helpful if we took a look at what you're doing."

"It's better if you trust me," Vikar says.

"I'll be honest—that makes us nervous. Why is it better?"

"Because otherwise it would be hard for someone to understand or for me to explain." There's silence on the other end of the phone. "Let me finish a little more." Vikar adds, "Hiring another editor now would be bad."

"We'll be the judge of that," Rondell says. "I didn't say anything about hiring another editor."

Vikar doesn't answer.

"Tell me honestly how you feel it's going."

"I don't know yet. That doesn't mean," Vikar says, "it's not going well."

"What does it mean?"

"It means I have to finish to know. It's a matter of faith."

"The faith feels a bit blind."

"In one eye, perhaps."

"This is all very poetic, Vikar, but both eyes would like to see what you're doing. Take until the end of next week and then you need to show us something."

"All right."

"I'm also sending something over to your suite this afternoon. Depending on what I see next week, there will be more where that comes from." Is it illicit narcotics? Vikar wonders. "You'll find it when you get back to the hotel. You are going back to the hotel these nights, aren't you?"

"Sooner or later."

"They're your nights, as long as it's not hurting the picture."

"All right."

"We understand and accept that a certain amount of mystery is part of your personality, Vikar. You do understand that sometimes it unsettles people?"

"Yes."

"Do you ever get unsettled?"

"I don't believe so."

"I guess that's good."

"I get other things." Looking at the face in the viewer before him, Vikar says, "But I called about something else."

182.

When Vikar returns to his suite that evening, a large stack of film canisters waits for him on the table in the front room. *The Long Goodbye, Kiss Me Deadly, Sweet Smell of Success, Body and Soul, Monsieur Verdoux, To Be or Not to Be, A Hard Day's Night, One Million B.C.* (the final movie D. W. Griffith produced, and part of which he may have directed). When I get back to Hollywood, Vikar thinks, I'm going to need a bigger place.

183.

He doesn't go to the club that night, and the next day he leaves the cutting room early and returns to the suite. He waits for a phone call, or a knock on the door.

184.

She holds her hair, wrapping her hand in it. She wears a black dress like the last time he saw her. "Hello," he says.

"You are editing my film." She smiles. "*My* film."

"Come in."

"I can't. But perhaps we can go out Friday night."

"Do you want to give me your phone number?"

"I will just come over, O.K.?"

"Yes."

"We can go out and have a drink or go dancing or go to a club."

Vikar says, "I know a very good club."

185.

Until the last second, some part of him believes she'll disappear again. When he answers the door Friday night, she wears a shorter, sexier dress and her lips glisten; she's slightly flushed, and across her eyes is a mysterious veil, as though the eyes and lips are each of a different face. "I have to make one stop," she says breezily in the taxi on its way down Fifth Avenue.

186.

The streetlights ripple across her face. A full moon hangs over Grand Central Station. "Is it waxing or waning?" she says. "I've been on the set so many nights I don't know."

"Which is which?" he says. "Which is becoming and which is begoing?"

"Waxing is becoming."

"It's waxing." He says, "I didn't know you were in this movie until I saw your face in the viewer."

"I didn't know you were on it," she says, "until they told me."

"What did they tell you?"

"They told me you were cutting the movie." She half laughs, "I play the model's friend."

"I know."

"It's not a big part. I tried out for the part of the model."

"I saw you in *The Long Goodbye*."

"Yes, you told me."

"I did?"

"That afternoon at Paramount. There was a limousine for you and you were going to Spain." She says, "I was supposed to play the gangster's girlfriend."

"The scene with the Coke bottle."

"At the last minute, the director decided no one would smash my face with a Coke bottle. They needed a more . . . disposable actress with a more disposable face. I lost the lead in *L'Avventura* for the same reason."

"The woman who disappears on the island."

"She was the second lead," Soledad corrects herself, "she was a disposable character too. As with Altman, Antonioni said, 'No one would lose *you* on an island.' Driver, turn left here please."

187.

The taxi turns on Thirty-Fourth Street. "Another block and a half," Soledad says to the driver.

The taxi crosses Park Avenue.

"Pull over here please." The taxi pulls in front of a parking structure. "I will be right back," she says to Vikar, opening the door.

"Where are you going?" Vikar says.

"I will be right back."

"I'll go with you."

"Stay and hold the taxi. I will be back."

188.

Inside the club, Soledad says, "What is this?"

"Why did we stop at that parking structure?" asks Vikar.

She gazes around her. "I thought we were going to a club."

"I believe this is a very good club."

"I thought we were going to a disco, I thought we were going dancing." She's stricken by the spectacle; for a moment, her accent flares. "Everyone is looking at me," in her short sexy dress, there among the ripped jeans and leather.

"They're looking at me," Vikar says. They're both right.

"I don't like this club."

"I believe it's a very good—"

"I hate this music. It's not even music."

"No," Vikar agrees, "it's the Sound."

"It's . . . " she thinks, "*bárbaro*. Barbaric."

"Yes," he says, "that's it, barbaric," and throws himself into the roiling pit of the audience.

189.

Outside, he tries to hail a cab while she waits under the awning. Standing in the empty street he turns to see Soledad gazing down at the sidewalk and the dirty barefooted woman in the hospital gown who always sleeps in the club doorway.

To Vikar's astonishment, Soledad pulls off over her head her flimsy black dress, laying it over the woman as though it could keep her warm, and stands on the freezing New York sidewalk in nothing but her panties, high heels and a glimmer of recognition rooted seven years before and three thousand miles away, on Pacific Coast Highway.

Vikar looks around to see if anyone is watching. Some people stop to stare at the nearly naked woman but others just pass by; finally flagging the attention of a distant taxi, Vikar dashes to Soledad and removes his coat, draping it around her shoulders.

190.

"As we get older," Soledad says in the cab back to the hotel, shivering in Vikar's coat, "does the wall between youth and madness become higher? Or do we just learn how to . . . better stay on our side of the wall?"

"I don't know," Vikar answers.

"That club," she says softly. "There was no wall."

"No."

"The bathroom was a cesspool."

After a while Vikar says, "How is Zazi?" Soledad turns to him in the backseat; her breasts fall out of his open coat and press against his sweat-soaked shirt. "I wonder if I know what you mean, Mister Film Editor," she says, and this time he knows she doesn't wonder at all. "I wonder why you ask about that. She's in L.A. With friends. With her father." She whispers, "You want to get *bárbaro*, Mister Film Editor?" inches from his mouth, the passing lights from the street outside rolling across her face. She pulls his belt out of the loops of his pants and unbuttons the front and takes him in her hand.

191.

Back at his suite in the hotel, she says, "What's this?" She holds it up before her eyes. In her other hand she still has his belt, carried defiantly through the hotel lobby.

"Something I made," he says, "a long time ago."

She examines it. "A toy house?"

"It's not a toy, it's not a house." Vikar takes two small bottles of vodka and red wine from the mini-bar. Is this the moment for such autobiography? Is there any moment for such autobiography? "It's a model of a church."

She turns the model in her hand. "You take it with you wherever you go?"

"I was an architecture student."

"I remember." She points at one wall. "It's bent."

"From the earthquake. The big one, seven years ago."

She studies the small steeple with its crowned lion holding a gold axe. "There is," her eyes narrow at the other tiny walls, "no way out."

"That's what I believed. The review committee," he says, "saw it as no way in."

She smiles at him and hurls the model into the wall, like a champagne glass into the fireplace.

192.

He stares at the shards of the smashed model on the floor. She reaches over to the wall and flips off the light; in the dark, his coat slides off her bare body and she wraps his belt around his neck, running it through the buckle and tightening it. "When we fuck, Mister Barbaric Church Builder," she says, giving the belt a yank, "do we make death an ecstatic experience rather than a lonely one?" What? thinks Vikar. She takes him out of his pants again and gets on her knees and puts him in her mouth; he stares through the window at the lights on the park outside. After a while she pulls herself back to her feet by the belt around his neck and says, "Put it inside me." He sways where he stands and she pulls him into the other room as if she's been in this suite a hundred nights. In the dark, she stretches herself out on the bed. "Put it inside me."

193.

He sways where he stands, caught in the lights off the park. "I can't."

"Why not?" she says.

"I don't know."

"You're hard."

"That's not why."

For a moment nothing happens and then she says, "O.K." In the dark she pulls him by the belt onto the bed where she curls between his legs, breasts pressed against his thighs, and takes him in her mouth again.

194.

Afterward she says, "It's O.K. We can do it however you like," and he drifts to sleep.

195.

He wakes a couple of hours later. It's still the middle of the night; she's sitting at the edge of the bed in the dark, with her back to him. "What?" he says. He can't hear her when she answers. "What is it?" he says.

He hears her say, "You should not have used what I told you in that way."

"Used what?"

"It was cruel."

196.

Vikar says, "I don't understand."

"Your little church. I know it's not a church."

No, he admits to himself, it's a movie theater: Did she see the tiny blank screen when she threw it at the wall?

"It's a private thing," she says, "that belongs to me."

"What do you mean?"

"You know."

"No." He sits up in bed.

"The institution."

"What institution?"

"I told you. When I was a teenager, in Oslo."

"Oslo?" he says.

"In the institution there."

He remembers about the institutions. "I remember now about the institutions, but not Oslo."

"You made a toy of it."

"My model looks like an institution in Oslo?" Perhaps someone did tell him about Oslo, he thinks, but it wasn't her.

In the dark she turns to him. "You're making it worse."

"I made it before I knew you. I've never been to Oslo. It's far, isn't it? Farther than Spain?"

"Why won't you admit it's cruel?"

"I promise it was a church," he lies.

He feels her staring at him. "A lion wearing a crown? Holding a gold axe?"

"I don't know where that came from."

"A crowned lion holding a gold axe," she says, "is the symbol of Norway."

197.

He wakes again at five-thirty in the morning. It takes him a moment to realize she's up and moving around in the dark. "I have to go to work," she says. Is she rummaging through his clothes? "I'm taking a pair of your jeans," she says. In the dark he can see her holding one of his white shirts. "I'll use your belt. May I take your belt?"

"Yes."

She cinches around her waist the belt she tightened around his neck the night before. She says, "Your work, how is it?"

"All right."

"Go back to sleep, but not too late. You don't want to miss work."

"I won't."

"It's a good job. You don't want to lose it."

198.

Every night she lies between his legs like his dream; and then one night he turns

199.

to the suite's empty doorway, and the cylinders in his head click into

200.

place, and he sits up from the bed. She stops and says, "What is it?"

"Where's Zazi?"

"What?"

"Where's Zazi?"

"I told you. She's in L.A. With friends."

"You said with friends. Then you said with her father. Then you said with friends."

"What does it matter?"

201.

"'What does it matter?'" he repeats. He gets up from bed in the dark and begins putting on his clothes.

"Where are you going?" she asks. He doesn't answer. He finishes dressing, slipping on a coat.

202.

By the time he's down to the hotel lobby, she's caught up with him, pulling on her own clothes. "Stop," she says, grabbing him by the arm, but he doesn't stop. Out at the street in the cold night, the doorman hails a cab.

He says, opening the cab door, "You can come or not." A panic is in her eyes. He gets in the cab and she darts in after him before the cab pulls away.

203.

It's one-thirty in the morning. At the parking structure on Thirty-Fourth Street, he gives some money to the driver and gets out, leaving the door open behind him. "What are you doing?" she keeps saying. He walks into the structure and wanders among the aisles of cars on the first level, then walks up the concrete stairs to the second level, then the third.

204.

In the midst of the parked cars on the third level, he turns to her and says, "Where is it?"

"What?"

"The car." He begins searching again.

"I moved it," she says, "it's parked in another structure now."

"Where?"

She shivers in the parking lot. Her mind races almost audibly. "Back uptown," she says. Then, "Out in Queens."

"Is it uptown or out in Queens?"

"I . . . ."

"Is she with friends or with her father?"

205.

When she doesn't answer, he turns and sees a black Mustang at the end of the lot. Three thousand miles from Los Angeles, he didn't believe it would really be the black Mustang.

206.

He walks toward the car. Again she grabs him by the arm to pull him back, again he pulls his arm away. She stops in her footsteps and begins screaming. "All right then! All right!" He reaches the Mustang and peers through the window into the backseat and sees a form huddled under some blankets. The form sits up and looks back at him.

207.

He rattles the handle of the car door. The young girl inside the car reaches over and unlocks it.

208.

Vikar sticks his head in the car. It's strewn with the cellophane wrap of eaten junk food, MacDonald's bags, styrofoam cups. Zazi must see something in his face because she retreats, pulling the blankets up around her.

209.

When Vikar turns to Soledad and steps toward her, in this moment she sees in his eyes the person she was afraid of when they first met.

He slams the back window of the car with his fist and glass implodes. Both Soledad and Zazi scream.

His bloody hand hangs at his side. The girl begins crying. "Oh mother," Vikar says, then reaches to Zazi with his other hand as she draws away from him amid the glass.

210.

Soledad sobs, "You're frightening her."

"I'm frightening her?" Vikar says. The wrath that seemed momentarily satisfied when he smashed the window returns.

"No," Zazi calls to Vikar when he takes another step toward her mother.

"Now do you want to see *bárbaro?*" Vikar says to Soledad, raising his bloody fist.

"Don't," says the girl.

"All these nights your daughter is sleeping in the car?" says Vikar. "Do you believe you're the Whore of God, to sacrifice your child on the altar of pleasure?"

"*Mi dios,*" Soledad cries.

"He's not *my* god," he says. "Look." He turns his head. "This is the profile of the one who wants you," and turns his head back, "this is the profile of the one who would kill you, for sacrificing your nine-year-old child."

"*Diablo.*"

Zazi says to him, "Don't. I'm O.K." She adds, "Actually, I'm eleven now."

211.

In the corners of the parking lot's concrete bunker, homeless people look up from the rags where they sleep. Crying, Soledad rushes Vikar and pounds his chest. "Don't you think I'm trying?" she blurts. "Don't you think? Driving all the way from L.A. for this shitty little part in this shitty little movie?"

"By spending your nights with me?" he says. "You try to take care of her by sp—?"

"Yes!" Her pounding exhausts itself. "It's *exactly* what I'm trying to do!"

Vikar begins walking away. He gets halfway across the parking lot and turns; his hand leaves a trail of blood. "Come on," he says.

Soledad still cries.

"Come on." He motions to Zazi.

"Where?" Soledad finally says. "I can't sleep with you when she's with us. It's not right."

"Come on."

212.

Back at the suite, mother and daughter sleep in the bedroom and Vikar finally falls asleep on the couch. Both are gone when he wakes. He doesn't go to work but lies on the couch looking at the remains of his model church on the floor.

213.

On the fourth day, someone slips something under the door. He still lies on the couch. Another hour passes before he rises from the couch and walks to the door; it's that day's *Variety*. A small notice in the bottom left-hand corner of the second-to-last page is circled in purple, announcing that United Artists has brought onto its "troubled" production of *Your Pale Blue Eyes* a "respected Academy Award-nominated" editor to take over the project in its "final stage." *I wonder if this is how Dotty found out.* An hour and a half later Vikar gets a call from the Sherry-Netherland front desk, informing him his balance is paid through the next day.

214.

Vikar takes a cab to the parking lot on Thirty-Fourth Street. Soledad's Mustang is gone from where it was parked; the space still glimmers with broken glass. He walks up and down the aisles and up and down the structure from one level to the next, but the car is gone.

215.

He arranges with the hotel to stay in New York another forty-eight hours. In his inertia he manages to ship to Los Angeles the stack of movies: *I'm not giving them back.* The night before he is to catch his plane, he shakes himself from his torpor for one more trip down to the Bowery.

216.

He finds himself watching the band without seeing it, listening to them without hearing, until someone pulls at his elbow. There in the dark he almost can't register her; she's shorter than everyone else. He says, "What are you doing here?"

"Mom told me about it," she says. "The more she talked about how disgusting it was, the cooler it sounded."

217.

He says, "How did you get in here? You're nine."

"I'm eleven," Zazi says, "almost twelve."

"You're not supposed to be here."

"I'm not drinking or anything." She says, "Everyone seems to know who you are."

"Where's your mother?"

"You missed this great band. They're from England and the lead singer's this little fat chick with braces and I can't tell if she's black or white or what, and get this, the sax player is a chick too."

"Where's your mother?"

"There are ten million fucks in the naked city, and she's

with one of them. Or maybe," Zazi shrugs, "three or four." She sees the look on Vikar's face. "Sorry," she says.

"You're nine," he says, "you shouldn't say things like that." He gives her fifty dollars and the key to his suite. "Do you need a place to sleep? Do you remember where my hotel is?"

She looks at the money and key for a moment. "Thanks," she finally says. "Aren't you staying?"

"No."

218.

Back at the hotel he gets another key from the front desk, goes up to his suite and packs and leaves a folded blanket on the couch in the sitting room. He goes to bed and sometime in the night hears the door open and close. In the morning the couch is empty, the blanket draped over the end.

219.

When Vikar reaches the TWA ticket counter at JFK, Mitch Rondell is waiting with an assistant. "Can I talk to you?" he says to Vikar. *He wants his movies back.* Vikar imagines an armed struggle there in the terminal. "Don't check him in yet," Rondell says to the woman behind the counter.

220.

Vikar says, "I've already shipped them."

"What?"

"I've already shipped the movies back to Los Angeles."

"What movies?"

"The ones you gave me. *The Long Goodbye*."

"The movies are yours, Vikar. I want to talk to you about what happened."

"It's all right. I saw the *Variety* article."

"I need to talk to you."

"Why?"

"Can we go into the lounge and talk?"

"I'll miss my flight."

"We'll put you on another flight, if it comes to that. In first class. I need to talk to you." Rondell puts his hand on Vikar's shoulder and the assistant picks up Vikar's bag.

221.

In the lounge Vikar and Rondell sit at one table and the assistant with Vikar's bag sits at another on the other side of the room. "We would like you to come back," Rondell says.

"What happened to the respected Academy Award-nominated editor?" Vikar asks. From anyone else, it would sound sarcastic.

Rondell leans across the table, speaking with more intensity than Vikar has heard from him. "No one understands you or what you're doing," he says. "No one understands what this picture is as you've cut it. I don't understand it. It's not an art film and it's not a thriller and maybe it's a thrilling art film but I'm not getting it."

"It would be better if it were finished."

"Maybe it would and maybe it wouldn't. I'm accepting that I may never get it. That's O.K., I don't have to get it, not at this point. We brought in a very smart editor, very hip, he did the sound edit on Coppola's last two pictures and just cut Zinnemann's last picture, two Oscar nominations in the last four years. He looked at what you've done and we talked about it."

"Is it faster in first class?"

"What?"

"Is it faster in first class, back to Hollywood?"

"It's the same, Vikar. Listen, this guy didn't understand what you're doing either. But he was more or less convinced you're doing *something*. He said the first ten minutes he thought you were completely incompetent but by the time he got to the end he knew that wasn't it. He said he has no idea whether the picture is working or any good but that every decision you're making is original at best and counterintuitive at the least."

"I don't know what that means."

"Me neither. But the way he explained it is that most editors, if they're cutting from a shot where the action is going on at the right of the frame, then they cut to another shot where the action is at the right so the audience can follow it, unless the picture wants to unsettle the audience at that moment, then they do it the other way around. I gather you're doing everything upside down, not to mention you've taken the central murder plot about the artist and the nightclub and framed it with the sub-plot about the supermodel rather than vice-versa, which is also backward from what anyone else would do."

"Scenes have profiles like people and things. All stories are in the time and all time is in the stories."

Rondell blinks. "If you say so, Vikar. So I asked this guy, 'What are you telling me, he's some kind of genius?' and the guy says of course not, there are no geniuses other than Bach and Rita Hayworth, but I *am* telling you, the guy says, that he's editing in a way I haven't seen before and now there's an internal logic to this picture that you would be better to follow through on rather than try to fix, if that's the word. The die is cast and we should go with it. Make it work for us. Is what he said. Otherwise we're messing with the aesthetic continuity of the thing. Is what he said."

Vikar says, "Continuity is one of the myths of film. In film, time is round like a reel. Fuck continuity. In every false movie is the true movie that must be set free."

Rondell sighs heavily.

222.

"That, vicar," Viking Man will explain a few months later, "is the sound of a studio executive, God love him, staring into the Nietzschean abyss of his own ignorance, venality and spinelessness," but Viking Man isn't here to say it now.

"No," says Vikar.

"Pardon me?" says Rondell.

"I don't want to anymore."

"We have an agreement."

"You fired me."

"Does this have anything to do with Ms. Palladin?" Rondell rubs his brow with both hands. "Vikar, the company is going through a great deal at the moment. All the top people have left to go form another company, including the man who's headed ours more than a quarter century. They'll take talent with them, Woody Allen, others. We need to salvage whatever of this picture can be salvaged. Cannes is in seven and a half weeks. All the principal shooting is done, we're down to a few final establishing shots, pick-up stuff. We don't need to absolutely lock the picture but we do need something more than a fine cut. It may still be we can make Cannes work for us. I don't want to withdraw the picture. We can't withdraw the picture. Very bad if we withdraw the picture. What do you want? We'll raise your pay and I'll take you down to the archive at midnight myself, as many pictures as you can carry out. Do you want to make a picture of your own?"

"There's a book. It's in French. I've read it many times."

"We can make a lot of things happen if you pull this out for us."

223.

Vikar says, "About Soledad."

"You want her off the picture."

"Why would I want that?"

"What, then?"

"Off the picture?"

"Vikar, listen. You said to find her so we found her. You saw her. If that's what it took to make you happy, then that's what we were ready to do. If you were a normal person we would have done things the normal way and supplied you with the usual kilo of coke." He adds, "She had her own interest at stake, too."

"It's her daughter."

"Her daughter?"

"She's sleeping in cars and going to clubs she shouldn't go to and she's nine." He says, "Actually, she's twelve."

"A little young for you, wouldn't you say, Vikar?"

"What?" Something barely comprehending compels him to say, "Her mother doesn't take care of her," with an undertone of violence that makes Rondell draw back.

"Sorry," Rondell laughs uneasily, "bad joke."

"Find her and make sure she's all right. Get her a room in a hotel."

"And her mother?"

"If she's with her mother," Vikar says.

"I'll do what I can. It's all I can promise."

"Do what you can."

224.

He returns to the Bowery at night looking for Zazi, but she isn't there and no one has seen her. "We can't find her," Rondell says when Vikar phones four days later from the cutting room, "on my word we've tried. Production wrapped a week ago, they're probably driving back to L.A. Short of the Highway Patrol putting out an APB, I don't know what else to do." On Vikar's last night in New York, confronted with a choice between the Sound and the Movies, he finds he loves the Movies after all, raiding the archives one last time.

225.

Variety, May 8, 1978: "NEW YORK—A subject of intense gossip, rumor and speculation over the past year, United Artists' production of *Your Pale Blues Eyes* will premiere in competition at the 31st annual Cannes film festival beginning next week, it was announced today.

"Rife with difficulties during production, the motion picture is now at the center of a heated dispute leaving it without an officially credited director, pending arbitration before the DGA. Editing of the picture reportedly has changed hands several times in the last eight months.

"Other U.S. pictures in competition at Cannes this year include *An Unmarried Woman, Coming Home, Midnight Express, Pretty Baby* and *Who'll Stop the Rain*. The jury that bestows the Palme d'Or and other prizes is headed by an American, director Alan J. Pakula (*All the President's Men, The Parallax View*), for the third time in the festival's history, following screen legend Olivia de Havilland in 1965 and, two years ago, playwright Tennessee Williams."

226.

The large boxes packed with movies are waiting when Vikar returns to Los Angeles, after being gone nearly six months. He unpacks his library that now crowds his apartment, and falls asleep to visions of smashing Soledad in the face with a Coke bottle.

227.

Vikar doesn't know it, but everything now has been reset to zero.

226.

The first movie he sees back in Los Angeles is a French gangster film where a beautiful samurai hit man floats through Paris without expression, in white fedora and gloves. Vikar is most taken with a scene involving a huge ring of keys that the hit man uses to steal cars. In the driver's seat of a car that isn't his, the hit man in white coolly lays out on the passenger seat beside him a ring of what must be a hundred keys; one by one he takes each key from the ring and tries it in the car's ignition until finally the correct key starts the car. As each key fails, the hit man lays it with precision on the passenger seat next to the previous key. In the movie, the fourth attempt starts the car—but what if he had begun at the ring's other end? The car wouldn't have started with the fourth key but the ninety-sixth. Under what growing spell and for how long would the audience be held as each key failed? The entire scene is shot from the vantage point of the passenger's seat, which is to say the hit man's right profile, the profile that reveals his calm, resolve, grace.

225.

For a week and a half Vikar hires a car to drive him around the city, looking for a black Mustang. He phones the beach house where he hasn't been for years now, Viking Man whom he hasn't spoken to since before Madrid, anyone who might know where the daughter and mother are. He calls methodically as though laying out on the passenger seat the keys of a car to be stolen.

224.

Over the course of the following week the phone doesn't ring at all, then one morning he receives three calls, the first two from the *Los Angeles Times* and *Variety* asking for Vikar's reaction to the response at Cannes to *Your Pale Blue Eyes*. "The true movie has been set free from within the false movie," he says, to silence on the other end of the line. The third call is from Mitch Rondell.

223.

Vikar says, "You found them."

"What?" says Rondell.

"You found Zazi and her mother."

Rondell sounds slightly flustered. "I'm at JFK, about to get on a plane for France. Vikar, we need you to come over."

"To New York?"

"Europe. There's an Air France flight this evening. We've booked you a first-class seat."

"Newspapers are calling."

"About the picture?"

"Yes."

"So you've heard."

"Heard what?"

"It screened in competition at Cannes a week ago. Apparently it was riotous. You didn't hear?"

"No."

"Not *Rite of Spring* tear-up-the-theater riotous, but the sort of commotion one picture in the festival always whips up every year. I gather it was hard to tell whether the applause or boos were louder."

"Boos?"

"Air France will fly you into Nice and someone will meet you and drive you to Cannes, which is the next town over."

"People booed?"

"Vikar, it's the picture everyone's talking about."

"They booed." Vikar is fascinated.

"We've booked you a small suite at the Carlton, which at this point was difficult. Truth is we had to move someone else out."

Vikar says, "Is it farther than Spain?"

"You may have to change planes in Paris . . . . "

"Perhaps I'll come in a couple of weeks. I just got back to Los Angeles."

"Vikar, there won't be a festival in a couple of weeks." Now the tension in Rondell's voice is unmistakable. "The closing ceremony is tomorrow night. The driver will take you straight to the Palais."

"The director of the movie should be there."

"There *is* no director of this movie. Literally, at this point there is no 'Directed by' in the credits. Until the DGA decides otherwise, this picture directed itself."

"I don't want to."

"What?"

"I don't want to come."

222.

Vikar can hear the panic rise in Rondell's voice.

"Listen to me," comes the voice on the other end of the line, "three hours ago we got a call in our offices here—I can't say who—to get you to Cannes. Do you understand? This person wouldn't say more, he wasn't even supposed to say that much, but . . . . The head of the festival jury is an American director who just did a Jane Fonda-Jimmy Caan picture for us . . . modern Western thing he's nervous about . . . do you understand what I'm getting at?"

"No."

"I mean this guy wouldn't be jerking us around five thousand miles away if there wasn't something afoot. Listen. What about that French novel you want to film?"

"God, I love that book."

"That can become a very real possibility, but you have to get to Cannes."

"You don't believe Zazi and her mother are there, do you?"

"I've got to catch my plane, Vikar. We're sending a car to pick you up in . . . what time is it in L.A.?" There's the sound of the phone on the other end changing hands as Rondell checks his watch. "Eleven-thirty in L.A., right? A car is going to pick you up in five hours. Please tell me you have a passport. You must, because you went to Spain for that madman."

Vikar says, "I live on a secret street."

"What?"

"It might be hard to find me."

"Someone will call you in the next thirty minutes and sort everything out. The driver in Nice will have formal wear for you . . . you'll have to change in the limo." A moment's pause. "We'll get a hat for you." Another moment's pause. "No, you know what? No hat. Better no hat. We'll make it work for us. See you tomorrow night on the Red Steps."

221.

In the limo traveling southwest from Nice, looking at the coast Vikar can almost believe he hasn't left Los Angeles at all, that the plane flew around in the air twelve hours and returned where it took off. "Is that the Atlantic Ocean?" he asks the driver, who glances at Vikar in the rear-view mirror. "Monsieur, it's the Mediterranean," the driver says. In a large plastic bag in the seat next to him, Vikar unwraps the black pants, jacket and tie, white shirt, socks and shoes. In a smaller plastic bag are strange black beads that he lays precisely on the seat side by side, like a series of keys that have failed to start a car.

220.

The limo drives twenty-five kilometers to the outskirts of Cannes, along the rue des Belges before cutting down to the Croisette. In the distance Vikar sees a large round building bathed in a light. Reaching a point where other traffic is being turned back, the limo is waved through and then suddenly it's in the midst of a throng caught between the sea, where the white beach tents are visible in the night, billowing like parachutes as though everyone has dropped from the sky, and red-carpeted steps on the other side, nearly as wide as they are long, leading up to the Palais. The limo stops and Vikar doesn't move; someone outside opens his door. "Am I supposed to get out here?" he says to the driver. He's slightly astonished to find that the shirt has no buttons. He lays the tie on the seat next to him with the black beads.

219.

He gets out of the limo. From out of the throng, Mitch Rondell appears. *He has a shirt that buttons. I should have gotten one of those.* All around is an explosion of bulbs flashing from cameras that Vikar can't see. Rondell stares aghast at Vikar's completely open shirt. "There are no buttons," Vikar explains. Rondell frantically sticks his hand in the pockets of Vikar's coat searching, then peers into the limo at the black buttons sitting on the seat. He begins to reach in and scoop them up, and another round of flash bulbs goes off around them. "You know what?" he says to Vikar, withdrawing from the limo, "better without the buttons. We'll make it work for us," and then one of the ceremonial escorts leads Rondell and Vikar up the long red steps, camera flashes barraging the man with the unbuttoned shirt and the tattoo of Elizabeth Taylor and Montgomery Clift on his head.

218.

In the yawning theater where the festival's closing ceremony takes place are more people than Vikar has ever seen. They fill the mezzanine and a grand balcony above him; he didn't know a building could hold this many people. He stands in the middle looking around, everyone looking back. Everyone looks at him but not the way people used to when they would throw themselves off hillsides and not the way they did in the Bowery when he came into the club. A golden glow settles on the theater, and up onstage in a box to the right are nine people that Rondell explains to Vikar are the festival jury. They include a famous Swedish actress whom Vikar recognizes from several Ingmar Bergman movies he can't think of because all Ingmar Bergman's movies are the same to him, and one of the producers of the James Bond movies. Mitch Rondell seems fairly beside himself. "My God," Rondell says, partly to Vikar, mostly to no one, "do you suppose we might actually win the fucking Palme d'Or?"

217.

The fucking Palme d'Or is presented to a three-hour Italian epic about a peasant boy on a long walk home from school who breaks his shoes. Italians, Vikar believes, like to make movies about things that break or get lost, like shoes and bicycles. Two so-called Grand Prizes are presented to a British movie by a Polish director about a man who's learned from Aborigines a shout that kills people, which people in the movie insist on hearing anyway, and a French movie by an Italian director with Marcello Mastroianni and Gerard Depardieu about a man who finds the body of King Kong washed up on the beach; the title translates as *Bye Bye, Monkey*. "That sounds like a very good movie," says Vikar.

It's also announced that this year the jury has created a special award, the Prix Sergei, presented "to the film *Your Pale Blue Eyes* and editor Isaac Jerome for an original and provocative contribution to the art of montage and the creation of a revelatory new cinematic rhetoric."

"That's not my name," Vikar says.

"What?" Rondell says, the applause around them swelling. Neither notices the sprinkling of boos.

"That's not my name."

"Vikar," Rondell whispers urgently, "please go up there now."

"Who put that name on the movie?" In the midst of the ceremony audience, Vikar is an eye-twitch away from ripping Rondell's head off his shoulders, while Rondell appears on the verge of leaping out of his body. "I'm sorry, it was a mistake," he begs, "a terrible, terrible mistake. We'll change it, we'll do anything you want, we'll make it right. Just please please please go up there."

216.

Vikar reaches the stage several seconds after the mystified applause has died. Applause rises again in what sounds to Vikar like a swarm of bees—a collective murmur at the sight of the man with the unbuttoned shirt and tattooed head. The boos apparently have been stunned into silence. The jury president leans slightly away from Vikar as he hands him the award scroll, rolled and tied in the center with a red ribbon, and shakes his hand. A third wave of applause rises and Vikar steps to the microphone. "That's not my name," he says and walks off, strangling the award in his fist.

215.

Dashing through the salons of the Palais, Vikar finally staggers out into the Mediterranean air. Small food and drink stands begin to close, as well as an outdoor café only a few meters away. Since he has no idea where he is or where to go, he takes it as something of a sign that there before him, just around the bend of the Croisette, are the nouveaux cupolas of the massive Carlton. Its vertical banners hang from the hotel's rafters, mildly ruffled by the breeze off the harbor.

214.

Thoroughly conflicted by Vikar's tattooed head, his state of undress and the throttled red-ribboned scroll in Vikar's hand, the concierge at the front desk apologizes that the suite isn't ready. "We weren't expecting you for at least another hour or two, monsieur," he says, "are the ceremonies over?" He invites Vikar to wait in the Petit Bar, where someone will come retrieve him.

213.

The bar is mostly empty. Everyone else is at the Palais except two men at a far table talking and an attractive blonde in her early fifties at another table, wearing a wide-brimmed fedora and sunglasses even though it's night and the lounge is dark. At another table is a younger woman, around thirty, with dark curls, wearing a long white coat; she drinks a glass of red wine and seems to be waiting for someone. She surveys Vikar for a full minute with a cool and overt curiosity. Vikar orders a vodka tonic.

212.

Now one of the two men talking at the far table looks at Vikar. He gets up from the table and comes over; he's sharply though informally dressed in a light cotton summer jacket, and Vikar realizes he's familiar. "Monsieur Vicar," the man says, Vikar still trying to place him. "It is I, Cooper Léon."

"Yes," Vikar says, uncertainly.

Cooper Léon puts out his hand. "How are you?"

Shaking the other man's hand, Vikar says, "All right."

Cooper Léon looks at the crumpled scroll on Vikar's cocktail table. "You have received one of the prizes at the ceremony tonight?"

"They said my name wrong."

"May I sit with you?"

"All right."

Cooper Léon sits down. "Felicitations. I am not surprised in the least. I knew three years ago in Madrid that you are a man of vision."

211.

Now Vikar remembers. "The movie about the General."

"Yes."

"For the soldiers of . . . . "

"The Soldiers of Viridiana."

"Are they here?"

"Who?"

"The soldiers."

"In Cannes?" Cooper Léon says, surprised. "I am no longer leading the revolution in Spain. The assassin the Generalissimo died, and now many good films are allowed in my country. Thanks to you."

"I don't believe the movie I made for you was a very good one."

"That, Monsieur Vicar," Cooper Léon points to the award, "says differently." Vikar notices that Cooper Léon's Spanish accent has turned to French. "I no longer am living in Madrid. I live in Paris now."

"Are the soldiers there now?"

"Monsieur, there are no more soldiers. Please forget the soldiers. Now I am a publicist for Gaumont. We are here at the festival representing the new film by Claude Chabrol with

Isabelle Huppert. I believe she won a prize this evening as well."

"I don't know."

"We also are sponsoring a retrospective, as . . . " he pauses, " . . . as an unofficial tangent, you might say, to the official festival, a retrospective of one of your great American auteurs. Well, actually he is British, but he made all of his films in America. Irving Rapper."

"Irving Rapper?"

"You know of Monsieur Irving Rapper?" Cooper Léon asks.

"*Now, Voyager.*"

Relief floods Cooper Léon's face. "Of course I was certain a scholar of film such as yourself would know of Irving Rapper. Cinema's great poet of *la femme dérangée*. As you say, *Now, Voyager. Deception. The Glass Menagerie. Marjorie Morningstar.* Would you care for another?" He points at Vikar's vodka tonic.

"I'm waiting for my room to be ready."

"Of course. Allow me please to buy for you another drink while you wait. It would be my honor." Cooper Léon calls out something to the bartender and turns back to Vikar. His brow furrows. "Monsieur Vicar, I feel it is fateful that I should see you here this evening. I wonder if I might make a confession to you that I never have told to anyone else."

"All right."

"It seems proper that you are the person to whom I should confess this."

"All right."

210.

Cooper Léon says, "Monsieur Vicar, perhaps you are wondering how it is I no longer am leading the revolutionary struggle for justice and rather have become a publicist for Gaumont."

"Uh," says Vikar.

"It is a difficult thing to comprehend, even for me sometimes. It is a result of a moment of truth I had, as it happens, not long after we met and worked together on our film about the death of the assassin the Generalissimo." He pauses as if waiting for Vikar to respond.

"Oh."

Cooper Léon shrugs. "Not long after we worked together on our film, I had a dream. Do you know who came to me in this dream?"

"God?"

"Luis Buñuel."

"Oh."

"Luis Buñuel, who once stayed in this hotel, this same hotel where he slept on the floor of his suite rather than the bed, as a revolutionary act. This dream was so real that I might almost have thought it was not a dream at all but the ghost of Buñuel, visiting me in the night, if Buñuel were not still alive. So it could not be his ghost."

"No."

"In this dream, Buñuel gave me a choice. Do you know what this choice was?"

"No."

"Buñuel said to me, 'Cooper Léon, you may have one of two things.' Monsieur," Cooper Léon's voice breaks, "this is a difficult thing to confess."

"You don't have to."

"Buñuel said, 'Cooper Léon, you either may see the fruits of your revolutionary struggle and have justice and freedom for all people in the world, or you may fuck Miss Sylvia Kristel.' Of course you remember Miss Sylvia Kristel, Monsieur Vicar?"

"Yes."

"From the French masterpiece *Emmanuelle?*"

"Yes."

"And *Emmanuelle 2?*"

"I guess."

"And *Emmanuelle '77?*"

"Uh."

"And *Goodbye, Emmanuelle?*"

"I don't know about those last ones."

"So then. 'Now I know what you are thinking,' Buñuel went on in my dream. 'You are thinking that you will fuck Miss Sylvia Kristel and it will be over in the usual forty-five seconds and that is hardly worth it. No,' Buñuel said in my dream, 'if you choose to fuck Miss Sylvia Kristel, I will give you an erection not as in real life but a cinematic erection, as men have in films. It will last as long as you want, it will last hours, days if you want. But,' and Buñuel was emphatic about this, Monsieur Vicar, 'but once you have reached climax and the fucking is over, then . . . no more.' And as soon as Buñuel said this, I woke." Cooper Léon sighs heavily. "I woke, monsieur, to the truth that I would trade the freedom and justice of all the world's oppressed masses for one chance to fuck Miss Sylvia Kristel. And of course the tragedy, monsieur, is that I woke to this truth that I have to live with forever *without ever having actually fucked Miss Sylvia Kristel.* So it is as though I made the choice in my soul without ever having received the benefit of that choice. Do you understand?"

"I believe so."

"I believed that you would," Cooper Léon nodded. "I believed that you of all people would understand that this is the exquisite cruelty of cinema, confronting men with truths about themselves that they must live with without ever actually getting to fuck Miss Sylvia Kristel."

"I've cheated on Elizabeth Taylor," Vikar says, patting his own head.

"Yes, monsieur," the other man says dismissively. "But Elizabeth Taylor has cheated on you far more often."

209.

"*Mon dieu*," Cooper Léon says, looking across the room.

"What?" says Vikar.

"Do you know who that is?" He's looking at the two women on the other side of the room, the older blonde in the wide-brimmed fedora and sunglasses, and the younger one with dark curls in the long white coat. Vikar isn't certain which one he means.

"Which one do you mean?"

"That one."

Vikar believes Cooper Léon means the older blonde but he still isn't certain.

"That, Monsieur Vicar, is Christine Jorgensen."

A worrisome recollection flickers across Vikar's mind.

"She is here for the Irving Rapper retrospective. Monsieur Rapper filmed the story of her life eight or nine years ago. You know of Christine Jorgensen, of course."

Vikar doesn't say anything. He looks back and forth from the older blonde to the younger woman in the white coat.

"You know of the story of her life. She was a man. She was an American soldier who—"

"I know the story."

"—had herself, how would you say, altered surgically—"

"I know the story." It has to be the older blonde.

"Allow me to introduce you."

"No, thank you."

"It is no trouble."

"I believe my room is ready now." Vikar stands up from the cocktail table.

"Are you sure you would not like to . . . ?"

"I'm going to check on my room."

"Very well," says Cooper Léon, standing as well. The two men shake hands. "Felicitations again, Monsieur Vicar."

"Yes."

"I am very pleased to have seen you in Cannes," he calls as Vikar rushes from the lounge.

208.

Forty-five minutes later, Vikar is in his small suite on the fourth floor of the Carlton. It's eleven-thirty. From the small balcony onto which the suite's French doors open, the Mediterranean is to the left; getting underway along the waterfront are the many parties of the festival's closing night. Party yachts line the harbor. Vikar can't see the fireworks but can hear them.

207.

He lies on the bed in his unbuttoned shirt watching the TV. He flicks around the channels; the news is in French so he doesn't understand much. There's a story about an Italian president or prime minister who appears to have been assassinated. Grace Kelly's daughter is getting married; both are princesses now. The granddaughter of Charles Foster Kane has been sent to jail for being kidnapped, which Vikar didn't realize was a crime. The coffin and body of Charlie Chaplin have been recovered, not far from where they were stolen; Vikar didn't know they had been stolen. When were they stolen? Soon Vikar finds on the TV an old American black-and-white movie.

Vikar's award sits in a furious ball of mangled parchment and red ribbon on a table next to a basket of fruit, cheese and red wine. The suite is all white and reminds him of the room at the end of *2001: A Space Odyssey* that he saw his first afternoon in Los Angeles. In another corner of the all-white suite is a small writing table. Vikar is trying not to think about anything. When someone knocks at the door, he doesn't answer because he assumes it's Rondell and he doesn't want to talk to him.

The knocking continues and Vikar ignores it, until finally the door opens and she walks in.

206.

The younger woman from the lounge, with the dark curls and the long white coat, closes the door behind her. In the light she appears in her early thirties; she's tall, just under six feet. "*Bonsoir*, Vikar," she says, slipping off her long white coat that falls to the matching floor, and except for her jewelry and high heels, she's perfectly naked.

205.

Her face is pleasantly attractive, not beautiful, but her long body verges on the preposterous, the most extraordinary body Vikar has seen. He hasn't seen many naked female bodies in person but he's seen them in magazines and in the movies and he's never seen one like this. When she drops the coat, she doesn't pose. It barely occurs to him that she's not simply being straightforward but making a point of getting his name right.

204.

She takes a plum from the fruit basket and bites into it, then puts it back. She wipes the juice on her chin precisely with a single finger and picks up the bottle of wine. "May I?" she says, holding up the corkscrew.

Vikar says, "I can open it for you."

"*Merci*," she says, bringing the bottle over to the bed. Two wine glasses dangle lightly by their stems from her other fingers. She sits on the edge of the bed looking around as he works the corkscrew; in her nakedness she's entirely casual. "Do you like the hotel?"

Oh, mother, it has to have been the older blonde, Vikar assures himself. "Buñuel stayed here."

"*Oui, bien sûr*. Cary Grant stays here, Orson Welles. Olivier, Sophia Loren, Alain Delon. Mussolini was thrown out, I believe before the First World War, when he was a journalist."

"He slept on the floor as a revolutionary act."

"Mussolini?"

"Buñuel."

"*Non, chéri*," the woman says, "Buñuel slept on the floor because the bed was not comfortable enough for him." She looks around the suite. "It is a bit, what is the American? nose in the air," and she brings her finger to the tip of her nose and pushes it up. "After the First World War, it was a hospital. Blaise Cendrars was a patient."

"I like the poem about Little Jeanne and the train," Vikar says, distracted, sweat on his brow.

"I am impressed. Almost no Americans know of this poem."

"Is your name Christine?" Vikar blurts.

She shrugs, "Would you like it to be Christine?"

"No."

"Who is your favorite French actress? You may call me that." She looks at the TV.

"Falconetti," he says.

She's slightly taken aback. "I supposed you should say something predictable like Brigitte Bardot."

"I like Brigitte Bardot," he says.

"You are a man, you are allowed." She watches the movie on the TV. "When they asked Simone Signoret how she felt about her husband Yves Montand fucking Marilyn Monroe, Signoret replied, 'But it was *Marilyn Monroe.*' So I might have said as well, had you said Brigitte Bardot. But I am content you did not." She says to the movie on the TV, "I adore this part."

203.

In the movie on the TV, Jean Harlow, who's living in the jungle with Clark Gable, climbs out of a barrel of rain water.

"When they shot this," the woman says, "Harlow came out of the barrel with nothing on. It was her idea. Immediately the director seized all the film so the frames of Harlow naked could be removed from the film and destroyed."

"I saw where Jean Harlow is buried," says Vikar.

"Her husband murdered her," the woman says, "he was an associate of Irving Thalberg. He committed suicide while she was making this film. When he married Harlow he found he was impotent, perhaps he was impotent before but now he was married to the great, what would you say, sex god . . . sex *goddess*, and he was impotent. He beat her all the time and then . . . " she puts two fingers to her temple with her thumb as the trigger, " . . . boom, while she was making this picture with Gable who, *bien sûr*, was the great male sex god. Perhaps Harlow's husband believed she and Gable were sleeping together. He might have said, 'But it is *Clark Gable*' . . . but men do not know how to think in such a way. In fact Gable

and Harlow were not sleeping together at all, or not that anyone knows. She died four, five years later."

"How did her husband murder her if he already killed himself?"

"He beat her so much that her kidneys failed but took years
to do so, after he was gone." She turns to him; he's looking at
her body. She says, "Falconetti seems, what is the American? a
mouthful," and laughs at some private joke. "You could call
me Maria or Renée, I believe Falconetti went by both. Or perhaps you should call me Joan," she laughs again.

"Not that," he says.

"*Non,* I do not think so either." She sips her wine, "Besides
I am Jewish, a bad Jewish *oui* but still I do not think one can
be a Jewish Joan." She says, "I saw *Passion de Jeanne d'Arc*
only once, nine years ago . . . or some version of it."

"That's when I saw it."

"It was the greatest film I've ever seen and I do not think I
could stand to see it again."

"Did somebody send you?"

"Pardon?"

"Did somebody send you here tonight?" Of course it was
Rondell; it had to have been Rondell. So Cooper Léon must
have meant the older blonde.

"*Chéri,* what do you suppose? I am strolling the Croisette
and look up at this hotel and see a light in one window out of
hundreds and say the mystery tattoo-man Vikar is up there
alone and needs company?"

"But you weren't strolling the Croisette, you were in the
lounge."

"Then you noticed me."

"Then you weren't sent by the man I was sitting with?"

"It is not an interesting question, and the answer is neither
interesting nor difficult if you think about it. Can you imagine
what it was like to actually *act* in a film so powerful that no one

can stand to see it twice? No wonder it drove Falconetti mad, no wonder she never made anything else."

"Perhaps I'll call you Maria. The actress in *Last Tango in Paris* and *The Passenger* was named Maria."

She ponders it a moment. "I am not so much like her. But we can call me Maria anyway."

202.

She reaches over and rubs his bald head. "Monty," she says.

"Many people believe it's James Dean."

"*Pftt*," she says. Vikar has the feeling Maria says things like *pftt* and *chéri* because she believes he expects it.

"Do you live in Cannes?" If she actually lives in Cannes, then it must have been the older blonde.

"I live in Paris."

"Everyone in Cannes must know about movies."

She laughs. "You mean even the escorts in Cannes know about movies. Actually, not everyone in Cannes knows so much of movies, even at the festival. I know this because I meet quite a few. The young boys from the studios, the new ones, know nothing of movies, the new young producers know nothing of movies and even the actors know little of movies. I know more of movies than any of these people. The critics know something of movies, *bien sûr*, and the new young directors know."

"Have you been with famous directors?"

"Now *chéri*, would you want me to tell others that I had been with you?"

"It would be all right."

"That's sweet but others might not think so."

He tries to look at the clock discreetly.

"It is just past midnight," she says. "I have been engaged as your companion until your press conference at half past nine tomorrow morning. Unless you would prefer me to leave sooner. I can leave any time you prefer. For me it is the same, the donation is the same."

"The donation?" Vikar says.

"It has been taken care of."

"I hope it's a good donation."

"*Dix mille.*"

"How much is that?"

"Ten thousand."

"Ten thousand dollars?" he says.

"That would be very nice," she says, "*mais non.* Francs."

"How much is that?"

"Perhaps two thousand American dollars."

"That's still a good donation."

Lying on the bed, she turns her head upside down to look at him sitting behind her. She says, "Are you going to ask now why I do it?"

"Does everyone ask?"

"Actually, almost no one asks. The question is there but not asked."

"Why do you do it?"

"I do it only at Cannes, once a year, because I love cinema. I am . . . what is the American? 'moonlighting'? This is my sixth festival. Now why," she says back to the TV, "would Gable give up Harlow for Mary Astor?"

"Moonlighting?"

"It is another life, different from my real life."

"Like *Belle de Jour,*" he says.

"*Non,* not like *Belle de Jour,*" she says a bit impatiently. "In *Belle de Jour* Deneuve has no other life, that is why she sells herself to men, in order to have a life, any life, a life of the senses, a life that is not dead or suffocated. I have entirely another life."

"What do you do in your other life?"

"I am, what is the American?" still watching the movie, "a barrister? . . . or is that British? 'Attorney'?"

"You're a lawyer?"

"A lawyer," she nods.

"Really?"

"Then at the end," she says, "Gable goes back to Harlow because he does not want to take Mary Astor away from her husband, who is his business partner, so because he does not have the heart to break her husband's heart, he finds it easier to humiliate Mary Astor and break *her* heart so she will hate him and leave him. And he tells Harlow he is being noble for once and she is content with that even though he has given up Mary Astor not out of love for Harlow but out of love for his own nobility, his masculine code."

"Press conference?" Vikar says.

"Gable," she says, "should just forget the two women and fuck the partner, that is what he truly wants, that is what this film truly is about." She says, "Certainly this is a film made by *men*."

"What press conference?"

"At half past nine tomorrow morning."

"I don't want a press conference."

"At the Palais in the *grande salon*."

"No."

"Someone will take you, it is arranged."

"That's not my name, what they said tonight."

"*Exactement*. You can, what is the American? 'set the record straight.'"

Vikar considers this. "Set the record straight."

Maria rolls over and runs her hand over Vikar's belly. "Let us set something else straight."

"What do you think," Vikar blurts, "of the films of Irving Rapper?"

"No more cinema for a few minutes, *chéri*."

"I . . . ."

"*Chéri*. I know what you want."

201.

He knows where Jean Harlow is buried, or at least where they say she's buried, but perhaps like Jayne Mansfield she's buried somewhere else.

Is her tomb empty then, or is someone else buried there? Is everyone who comes to Hollywood so desperate to be Jean or Jayne or Marilyn that she would accept being Jean or Jayne or Marilyn in death if she couldn't be in life? Are the hills of Hollywood filled with the bodies of doubles, of imposters for legends? Do only dead blondes with large breasts have surrogates for their graves?

It has to have been the older blonde, Vikar feels certain, but as Maria takes him in her mouth, irrational notions skitter across his mind like centipedes. He closes his eyes and thinks of Soledad.

200.

Afterward she says, "Was that what you wanted?"

He stares at the ceiling and feels from across the balcony outside the breeze off the Mediterranean. "How did you know?"

"It is my talent to know," she says. She wipes her chin very precisely with one finger as she did the juice of the plum. "I like doing it that way. I prefer it to the fucking."

"Why?"

"Why not. One of those things not to regard so much. It makes me sexy."

"You mean it makes you feel sexy?"

"That is what I said, *non*?"

"I guess."

"This is over now," she says to the movie, "it is curious. When Harlow died, you know, she was the fiancée of William Powell, who once was married to Carole Lombard, who married Gable before *she* died so young, like Harlow. Both men outliving their great loves who died so young. There was a second version of this film . . . what is the American title?"

"Which one?"

"This one we just watched."

"*Red Dust*."

"There was a second version twenty years later, with a different title, a funny title, also with Gable, twenty years older, playing the same part as in the first. *Bien sûr* in cinema the men get to remain young even as they are old."

"I saw where Carole Lombard is buried. I saw where Clark Gable is buried."

"Ava Gardner and Grace Kelly were in the second version, with the funny title."

"I don't know where Ava Gardner is buried."

"She is still living."

"She is?"

"She has made several bad films of late. A few years ago a big shitty earthquake film."

"*Earthquake*."

"Are there four women less alike?"

"What four women?"

"Gardner and Kelly, Harlow and Astor? Change around all those women, put them in each other's parts, and the films would be completely different, *non*? Five if you count Garbo, who originally was supposed to play the Harlow part in the *Red Dust*, when John Gilbert was to play the Gable part, because you know Garbo and Gilbert were so popular together from the silent films. But Gable, he was the first true super-star—after cinema had sound? When he killed a man in an auto accident, the studio got someone else to, what is the American? 'take the fall'? Directors, they make the art, but stars make culture. My country has made too much of the directors. I cannot remember in the second version if Ava Gardner plays the Harlow part and Grace Kelly the Mary Astor part, or the other way around."

"It's the way you said first."

"What is the funny title?"

"*Mogambo*. Grace Kelly is a princess now."

"*Oui, chéri*," Maria says, changing the TV channel with the remote control, "she is forty kilometers down the coast if you want to go visit her. Watching the *Mabom*—"

"*Mogambo*."

"Watching that second one, you think the same as in the first, why would Gable give up Ava Gardner for Grace Kelly? *Mais bien sûr* Gable and Kelly were fucking when they made the film, so how can one argue." Searching the channels, she comes upon a porn film of two people fucking who don't look very much like Clark Gable and Grace Kelly. "It is strange that no one seems to make a great film about sex."

"*Last Tango*," says Vikar. "*Realm of the Senses. Emmanuelle.*"

"*Emmanuelle* is shit," Maria scoffs. "In *Dernier Tango* Brando is great but the film? The Japanese are interesting because about sex they are even more *perturbé*—crazy, nuts—than Americans. But I mean a film that makes audiences sexy."

"You mean that makes them feel sexy?"

"That is what I said, *non*?"

"I guess."

"That . . . turns them on? is the expression? As a porn but also *dramatique*. In America you have this idea that anything about sex is acceptable only if it absolutely is not, under any circumstances, sexy. It would be the same to say that a comedy is acceptable only if it absolutely is not funny. The Americans are too romantic to make such a film. They are in love with shame."

"The French are romantic."

Maria dismisses this with the flick of her fingers. "*Quelle mythe!* No one ever said in a French film, 'We'll always have Paris.' Can you imagine Bogart fucking Bergman with a cube of butter on the Champs-Elysées as the Nazis march in?" For a few minutes they watch the two people having sex on TV. "The pornographer? He is concerned with what the characters do, while the artist, the artist is concerned with who the characters are. For the pornographer, sex is . . . *spectacle humain sans* consequence. It is as they say: you do not pay me—well, not *you*, in your case—the man does not pay me for the sex, he pays me to leave afterward. For the lack of consequence."

Vikar says, "He pays you to leave?"

"This is what Brando believes will save him in *Dernier Tango*," says Maria, "sex without consequence."

"You are paid to leave?"

She changes the channel. "That is what destroys him, because there is no sex without consequence."

"Perhaps *Last Tango in Paris* isn't just about sex."

"*Chéri*," she laughs, "*sex* is never just about sex."

199.

"*Mon dieu*," she says to the TV. For the first time, her French sounds like she means it.

"Positively the same dame!" says Vikar.

"This film!" Maria says with the first delight Vikar has heard from her. On TV, Barbara Stanwyck says to Henry Fonda, "Why, Hopsi, you belong in a cage," and begins stroking the befuddled Fonda's hair. Maria curls up behind

Vikar and begins stroking his bald head. "Preston Sturges invented a kiss-proof lipstick," she says.

"When?"

"Before he began writing plays and cinema, before he became a director. He invented things."

"He invented lipstick?"

"Kiss-proof lipstick."

"I don't know what that is."

"He should have made a film about that. Perhaps he did not see the humor in it."

"The humor?"

"I heard a bizarre story," she laughs, pointing at the TV, "about someone who went to see this because he had been told it was *not* a comedy. He sat through the entire film wondering why everyone was laughing."

Vikar is silent.

"This is the brilliance of Sturges, that someone could sit through one of his films under the impression it is a tragedy."

"I own this movie," he says.

"You own it?"

"I own a print of it, and prints of other movies."

"You own a print of this film?"

"Many. Perhaps more than a hundred now. I keep getting more."

"How do you get these films?"

He considers his response. "I steal them. Some of them. Some of them I've been allowed to steal. Can you say you actually stole something when you were allowed to steal it?"

"Do you watch these films you stole?"

"I don't have a projector."

"So it is just to have them? Like your own theater but you cannot watch them?"

"Sometimes," he says, "I believe I stole them for another reason I don't know yet." Together they watch *The Lady Eve* in silence and then she says, "You should sleep. You have your press conference."

"I don't want a press conference."

"It is not for you, it is for the press and your company. Well, it is for you, too."

"That's not my name and I don't know what to say."

"*That* is what you say. '*That* was not my name, *this* is my name, I wish to discuss it no more.' By the time you leave France, everyone will know your true name."

"Setting the record straight," says Vikar.

"Do you want me to leave?"

Vikar frowns. "Were you paid to leave?"

"Forget about that, *chéri*. I will stay or go as you like."

"I would like you to stay."

"As you like then," she says, and turns off the TV.

Before he falls asleep, he says, "I don't know where Falconetti is buried."

"She is not buried," comes the answer in the dark, "she was cremated. Fitting, *non*, for someone who played Joan of Arc?"

198.

Two hours later, Vikar wakes suddenly and turns on the lamp next to the bed.

He staggers over to the small writing table in the corner of the suite and grabs a small pad of paper and pen. He sits on the bed next to the lamp. "Do you want me to leave now?" Maria murmurs half asleep from her pillow.

He doesn't answer, absorbed in his transcription.

She raises her head long enough to look. "What are you doing?"

"I'm sorry to wake you," he says.

"*Qu'est-ce c'est?*" says Maria.

"For a long time now," Vikar answers, "ever since I saw my first movie, I've had this dream. Every time, there's an ancient writing." He shows Maria the pad of paper on which he's transcribed the ancient scrawl. "I've seen it many times, and this time when I woke I could still see it in my head."

She glances at the paper. "It is Hebrew," she says, plopping her head back down on the pillow.

Vikar looks at it. "Are you sure?"

"I do not know what it says," she answers into the pillow, "I cannot read it and I do not understand it. But I know it is Hebrew."

197.

Vikar arrives at the press conference in the Palais' *grande salon* the next morning a little before ten o'clock. Because he has no other clothes, he still wears his black tux pants and open white shirt. He's greeted by the same barrage of flash bulbs as on the Red Steps the night before; already Mitch Rondell and a translator are seated onstage behind a gold-clothed table with a bank of microphones. Lining the edge of the stage before the table is a row of small potted greens that seem out of place, and behind the stage hangs a large crimson banner that reads FESTIVAL DE CANNES. Rondell says to Vikar, "You're late."

196.

Vikar says, "I don't want a press conference." Four hundred seats are filled and as many reporters stand around the room and at the back.

"Monsieur, we will begin now?" the translator on the other side of Vikar says, and then says something into the microphone in French. The new onslaught of camera flashes is accompanied by an outburst of exclamations in other languages. The translator raises his hands as though trying to impose order, which only provokes a new wave of questions.

195.

One rises from the din. "Monsieur asks," the translator relays to Vikar, "what is your reaction to the special award to you, and . . . ." pausing to follow the question with another, " . . . what is your response to those who disagree with it?"

"I'm setting the record straight," says Vikar. "My name is Vikar, with a k. That other name is not mine. I wish to discuss it no more."

Only when it's clear to the translator that Vikar is finished does he translate what Vikar has said. He turns to Vikar. "But about the question asked?"

"By the time I leave France, everyone will know my true name," Vikar says into the microphone. "I'm setting the record straight."

A momentary silence is followed by more questions. "Uh, it is asked," says the translator, "what is your *philosophe*—philosophy—of *mise-en-scène*?"

"What?"

"*Mise-en-scène.*"

"I don't have any philosophy like that." Vikar turns to Rondell. "Should I tell them about how all time is in the movie?"

Rondell seems dazed. He doesn't answer, nervously chewing his lip as other questions explode around them. Gleaning one from the racket, the translator asks, "How do you feel about the attention from the festival, and how do you feel about the journalists and all their questions?"

"Mussolini was a journalist," Vikar says.

This doesn't seem to need translation. There's a stir among the crowd. "What do you think," the slightly agitated translator interprets another question, "of the other films that won prizes . . . ?"

"I believe everyone in Cannes knows of cinema," says Vikar. "I met a nice woman last night who knows more of cinema than anyone. I believe the monkey movie sounds like a very good movie though I didn't see it. I believe Italians like to make movies about bicycles and shoes."

The translator stares at Vikar as though a challenging mathematical equation has formed on his forehead. He translates what Vikar has said, which seems to inspire more confusion out among the lights; Vikar is happy to hear a question in English. "What do you think"—he can't actually see the questioner—"about the American film industry's new preoccupation with expensive escapism, such as outer-space movies and blockbusters about monster sharks and comic-book supermen who fly?" The translator seems relieved not to have to translate to Vikar, but he translates the question into French for the other reporters.

"I want to see the flying superman one," says Vikar. His thoughts drift back to a night at the beach years before. "It has a girl I know, the crazy one with the tits."

There's a smattering of laughter but mainly more confusion. Vikar can make out in the next question something about "place in the sun." Slightly shell-shocked, the translator says, "How do you feel about *A Place in the Sun*?"

"I believe it's a very good movie."

Another question. "Monsieur asks," says the translator, "what are your favorite films?"

"I believe *The Lady Eve* is a very good movie. I believe *Belle de Jour* is a very good movie. I believe *Now, Voyager* is a very good movie. I believe *The Battle of Algiers* is a very good movie. I believe *Written on the Wind* is a very good movie. I believe *The Devil is a Woman* is a very good movie. I believe *Detour* is a very good movie, and *Kiss Me Deadly*. I believe *Splendor in the Grass* and *Strangers When We Meet* and *Pretty Poison* are very good movies, and the actresses in them are very attractive. I believe *The Third Man* and *The Shop Around the Corner* are sublime movies that existed before they were made. I believe the movie about the car keys is very good. I believe the movie where the attractive Japanese actress says 'Beast needs beast' is very good. I believe *My Darling Clementine* is a very good movie. I believe *The Searchers* is a wicked bad-ass movie whenever my man the Duke is on screen, evil white racist honky pigfucker though he may be. *Emmanuelle* is shit, though *Emmanuelle 2*, *Emmanuelle '77* and *Goodbye, Emmanuelle* may be very good movies. I believe *The Long Goodbye* is a very good movie."

Someone in English calls out, "Are you going to direct a film of your own?"

"There's a book. It's called *Là-Bas*," says Vikar. "I've read it many times."

"This is a somewhat notorious book in France," the translator says. "They want to know why an American filmmaker would make into a film this book."

"Americans are in love with shame," Vikar says. "Can you imagine Bogart fucking Bergman with a cube of butter on the Champs-Elysées? This movie will be"—a small pandemonium now seems to surge from the back of the salon—"about the right hand of Joan of Arc who became the greatest child killer of all time, next to God. This movie will expose the child-killer God in all His profiles. It will set the record straight on God." It's unclear to Vikar whether the translator actually has finished translating before the press conference appears to collapse into chaos. As the shouts and demands wash over them, Vikar turns to Rondell, whose face is buried in his hands. "Do you think," says Vikar, "they understood the part about my name?"

194.

That evening in his suite at the Carlton, the phone rings. "God love you, vicar," comes the voice on the other end, "don't you know all that business about saving the movie in the editing room is just one of the great urban legends of film? Nobody ever really saves the movie in the editing room. That's one of the excuses they have for taking movies away from directors, that they can save the fucking thing in the editing room. Now you've gone and actually saved a movie in the editing room and there will be no end to it. You've created a lot of trouble."

193.

Vikar says, "I'm sorry."

"It's a joke, vicar," Viking Man says, after the usual transatlantic lag. Vikar hasn't heard from or spoken to Viking Man in three years. "Well, sort of, anyway. The trades over here are all trying to figure out whether anyone ever has gotten an award at Cannes for editing, or montage or *mise-en-scène* or whatever fancy word they're using."

"I heard one of those words this morning. There was a press conference."

"Yeah, that's the other thing they're all a-twitter about here."

"It was only this morning."

"News travels fast, vicar."

"They called me by the wrong name. I had to set the record straight."

"You set the record straight all right."

"It's important that in Hollywood they're straight on the name."

"I think in Hollywood what they're straight on at the moment, vicar, is that you're a lunatic. But then they just don't know you like I do, and I suppose it could be worse—a lunatic means no one can figure out what you might do next, and since it might be something phenomenal and they don't want to miss out on it, it can make them irritable in a potentially productive way."

"We'll make it work for us."

"I'm not sure you should have said that thing about John Wayne."

"Perhaps you're right."

"I have to take exception there, vicar."

"I'm sure you're right."

"I mean, the man is dying. Vicar, you still there?"

"Can you hear me?"

"There you are . . . hey, vicar, listen—"

"Have you seen Zazi and Soledad?" Their voices cross.

"How's that?"

"Zazi and Soledad?"

"Last I heard she was in New York on your movie there . . ."

"No . . . ."

" . . . thought that's what I heard. What?"

"I need to find them."

"When are you coming back?"

"Tomorrow."

"We'll get together and drink tequila, amigo, scope out the local wenches who become more creatures of the Devil's seed with every passing day. But listen." A pause. "Vicar?"

Vikar has a momentary impulse to tell Viking Man how his film about the Berber chieftain wound up in a film about the death of the assassin the Generalissimo.

"Give Dot a call sometime. I know she would love to hear from you. She's got to be peeing in her rubber panties about this Cannes thing."

192.

Back in Los Angeles, Vikar no longer has room in his apartment on its secret boulevard for all the movies he's stolen. With the money from *Your Pale Blue Eyes*, he rents a house further west in the Hollywood Hills, which he could barely see from room 939 of the Roosevelt Hotel nine years before, if he had known to look for it.

191.

It's an old house for Los Angeles, dating back to the thirties. It cascades down the side of the hill in three levels, the large windows on the top level staring out at a panorama of trees and little houses and little cars driving up winding roads that seem to drop off in midair. As on a fjord of galvanized stardust, the house sits on the edge of the city, overlooking a vast shadowless sundial.

190.

The top floor of the house, at street level, is the living room with the kitchen. It's shaped like a half moon, walled in white brick with a wooden floor and fireplace, circled by the large bare windows with window seats. On the second level below are two bedrooms; Vikar's has a window facing east. The one large room at the foot of the stairs, on the third and bottom floor, becomes the film library, with a small console for editing and enlarging stills. Large canisters line all four walls, except where a small window faces south.

In the distance to the southeast, Vikar can see downtown. Directly below the house and the hill, occasionally blurting into view between the knolls and gullies, is Sunset Boulevard, now an asphalt timeline with not simply geographical address-es but temporal ones, from the classic forties, when glamour ran like silver sewage, to the utopian sixties, when hippies rampaged the gutters, to the anarchic present at the boulevard's far eastern end where a Sound grows, not unlike what Vikar heard in the Bowery.

189.

Vikar goes to see a new movie by Buñuel. It's a remake of Von Sternberg's *The Devil is a Woman* and takes place near Soledad's hometown of Seville. At first Vikar believes the movie is about a middle-aged widower in love with two women who share the same name, until he realizes, halfway through, that in fact two different actresses are playing one and the same woman. Buñuel knows about the profiles, Vikar realizes. He has taken it farther than anyone, actually showing each profile as played by an entirely different person. In one incarnation the woman dances flamenco, as Soledad did when she was a small girl.

188.

He doesn't install a telephone, as much by design as indifference. "Give Dot a call sometime," Vikar hears Viking Man in his sleep one night, and when he wakes, he knows it's too late.

187.

"All of us are too fucking late, vicar," Viking Man says quietly, a week later, "once someone is gone." Subdued, he smokes his cigar in the bar of the Hyatt on the Strip below Vikar's house, across from the Sunset Tower where Vikar used to look for a light in George Stevens' window. The two sit at a small round corner cocktail table as young girls flit around in tiny cellophane dresses waiting for rock stars to appear. "Who thinks he did all he could, once someone is gone?"

"I should have called," Vikar says.

A shot of Cuervo Gold sits on the small cocktail table before Viking Man. Vikar drinks a vodka tonic like Dotty first ordered for him at Nickodell's. "You see the thing that ran in *Variety*?"

"Yes."

"Not much," says Viking Man. "It's a cliché to say it doesn't seem like much of a life when it comes down to an inch and a half in *Variety*, but that's more than most of us get." He puts out the cigar. "I mean, she worked on *A Place in the Sun*. Never was a George Stevens man myself, but still."

186.

Vikar says, "I didn't understand about the note." Viking Man doesn't answer. "The part in *Variety* about the note."

Viking Man nods.

"Did you understand about the note?"

"Well, vicar," says Viking Man and stops, suspended for a moment, "just briefly, as a matter of fact, I saw the note, such as it was. Barely a note at all, really, some half-baked haiku on a cocktail napkin about sore throats and broken hearts—isn't it just like Dot to leave a 'suicide note' on a cocktail napkin, to be read in a bar?"

"She was in love with an actor once."

"Whose daughter died of strep . . . yeah, I know that story. That poor bastard had a shitstorm of a life, his last five or six years. The fucking patron saint of Hollywood martyrs."

"God kills children in many ways," says Vikar.

"She wasn't a child."

"I meant the little girl with the sore throat."

"Does not caring if you wake up the next morning constitute suicide?"

"Sometimes God has help. A mother leaves her daughter in a car."

"Vicar, are we having the same conversation?"

"Where is she now?"

"Hollywood Memorial, there behind Paramount. I tried to get word to you."

"I know. I don't have a telephone."

"That constitutes aberrant behavior in Hollywood. They take away your Hollywood passport if you don't have a telephone."

"Cecil B. De Mille is buried there. Jayne Mansfield." Vikar says, "I believe I may have killed a man there once."

"Did this homicidal spree take place recently?"

"Three or four years ago. Perhaps five."

"Jayne Mansfield isn't buried there. She has a tombstone there, but she's buried in Pennsylvania."

"I'm from Pennsylvania."

"I see your movie opens next week."

"It's not really my movie."

"I gather the DGA sorted out the credit. Friedkin must have had an aneurysm," Viking Man chortles. "You going to direct that French novel of yours?"

"I don't know."

"You might make more headway with a telephone. Just tempestuous wild-hair-up-the-ass speculation on my part."

"It's about God's greatest disciple, the right hand of Joan of Arc."

"I imagine Hollywood gets a hard-on thinking about that."

"I don't know."

"I thought Siamese-twin sisters," shrugs Viking Man, "was the stupidest idea in the history of cinema, so what do I know? But I would move if it's something you want to do, vicar. Get yourself a phone and then get yourself an agent. Because it's all changing, and not in our favor. We've run it into the ground. That egomaniacal wop in the Philippines is spending thirty million or whatever it is on a Vietnam movie no one understands, and that includes me and I wrote the bastard, or thought I did, with all apologies to Conrad, and you have that hermaphrodite up in Montana trying to follow up *his* Vietnam movie with some prairie *Gone With the Wind* or whatever it is he thinks he's making. Oil companies own the studios now, vicar. Schmuck though Louis B. Mayer may have been, he knew the difference between movies and unleaded."

"If God makes us bury our children," says Vikar, "who makes us bury our parents?"

"We do that on our own."

185.

Seen from the bus, the shimmering black limos on La Cienega reflect the city as pieces of a jigsaw night rearranging themselves. *I am the passenger*, the radio plays, *I ride and I ride*, and it isn't the soundtrack for an Antonioni movie but Vikar's life, and he doesn't even know it's by the same man who sang the song about the dog.

184.

In the waning days of winter, Vikar sits on the top floor of his house watching a serviceman install a telephone on his kitchen wall, next to a cork bulletin board. The man finishes, walks out the front door, and ninety seconds later the phone rings. Vikar runs after the serviceman to take the phone out, just as the truck is pulling away.

The truck disappears down the road that eventually empties onto Sunset Boulevard in one direction and Laurel Canyon in the other. Vikar watches it the whole way and then walks back into the house where the ringing has stopped. He looks at the phone and it begins ringing again.

183.

He picks up the phone on the ninth ring. "Hello."

"Hello?" The woman on the other end is about to hang up.

"Yes."

"Is this Mr. Vikar Jerome?"

"Yes."

"Mr. Jerome, my name is Molly Fairbanks. How are you?"

"I'm all right."

"May I call you Vikar?"

"Yes."

"Vikar, I'm with Creative Artists." Vikar doesn't say anything. "CAA. We're a talent agency. Have you heard of us?"

"I don't know."

She laughs. "Well, we're still a little new, but we're doing very well. Do you have a moment to talk?"

"All right."

"Congratulations, first of all."

"Thank you." He says, "For what?"

There's a pause. "The nomination."

"Oh. Thank you," Vikar says. "What nomination?"

"This is Vikar Jerome the motion-picture editor, is that correct?"

"I've edited motion pictures."

"You edited *Your Pale Blue Eyes*, is that correct?"

"Yes."

"Have you been answering your phone, Vikar? Or read any newspapers?"

"I just got the phone."

"You mean you just had a telephone installed?"

"Yes."

"You just had a telephone installed this morning?"

"I couldn't catch the phone man as he was driving away. I would have had him take it out, if I could have caught him."

"Have you heard of the Academy Awards?"

"Of course."

"The nominations were yesterday."

"Oh."

"Your picture received two, including for editing." She says, "That's you."

"Oh." He says, "Will they make me go like they made me go to Cannes?"

"Did you like Cannes?"

"No. But I met a nice woman who knew a lot about cinema."

"I see."

"I believe she wasn't the woman who used to be a man. She knew what I wanted."

There's another pause. "I see. Do you want to go to the Academy Awards?"

"No."

"Well, then, I think you don't have to if you don't want to."

"They might try to make me."

"Would you be relieved or disappointed if I told you that you probably won't win?"

"Relieved."

"Well, there you are. But as I understand it, there's a project you've been wanting to direct, and if that's the case, then this is a good time to pursue that."

"The company hasn't called me."

"Well, they've been going through some changes."

"I haven't had a telephone, either."

"There's that as well."

"Perhaps the company doesn't want to make the movie."

"They may be more interested, Vikar, if other studios are interested. Studios tend to be like that. Also, these days distributors are trying to figure out just how involved they want to be on the production side of things. The business has gotten a little unsettled the last few years." That was a word, "unsettled," that Rondell used. "But as to this project, I believe you had some sort of informal understanding with UA, is that correct?"

"Yes."

"Normally, informal understandings don't mean a great deal in this business. But you've just been nominated for the Academy Award."

"I probably won't win."

"No, but the nomination is not a small thing and there's a general feeling that, if not for you, UA might not have had a releasable picture, let alone an Academy Award nominee."

"They booed in Cannes."

"I know, and the reviews here were a little mixed too, but the good reviews were very good, and strange as it may sound, being booed at Cannes is not always bad, if you're booed for the right reasons. Or maybe I mean the wrong reasons. Sometimes when people don't like a picture for the right reasons, it makes other people want to see the picture, and studios appreciate that. They booed *L'Avventura* at Cannes, too."

Vikar likes the way she talks. She sounds young and friend-ly, and he completely understands everything she says. He wonders if she's related to Douglas Fairbanks and Mary Pickford. "I completely understand everything you say."

"I don't want to press you, but I can make inquiries for you among the various studios and production companies and rep-resent you in trying to get this off the ground."

"Thank you."

"I would go to UA first and to Mitch Rondell, who's started his own independent company and is no longer working for UA in the same capacity, although they maintain a partnership."

"It sounds confusing," Vikar says.

"He's in L.A. now."

"Is he on vacation?"

"He's living with someone and has moved his work here."

"I haven't heard from him."

"Your situation with the telephone, maybe."

"Maybe."

She says, "I'm sure he would have called otherwise."

182.

We bury our parents on our own, said Viking Man, and one afternoon Vikar picks up the telephone and dials the entire number and doesn't hang up until it rings on the other end. He has no idea if his father or mother are alive or dead. He puts the phone back before anyone answers. This is why I should have the phone taken out.

He came to Los Angeles as a Traveler hurtling through space toward infinity, vestiges of childhood falling away like dimensions.

One morning he walks down the hill to Sunset and takes the bus heading west. It continues along the boulevard through Beverly Hills to UCLA. Vikar crosses the street and through the film school and into the Structure Garden; slightly overwhelmed, he finally stumbles into the campus art gallery which directs him elsewhere. For an hour he wanders from one school to the other until he winds up in a large flat black building everyone calls the Waffle that looks more to Vikar like the monolith in *2001: A Space Odyssey*, except bigger and with windows. On the eighth floor is the School for the Study of Biblical Languages.

181.

The man in the office behind the desk doesn't look like a professor of Biblical languages. He's in his early forties and wears a black T-shirt and his head is shaved; looking at Vikar, he says, "I have to get me one of those."

Vikar puts his hand on his head like he does sometimes, as if he's just finding it. "Elizabeth Taylor and Montgomery Clift," he nods, "*A Place in the Sun.* Are you Professor Cohen?"

"Cohn, without the e."

"I'm Vikar, with a k."

"Vikar with a k," he says, putting things in a briefcase, "what can I do for you?"

Vikar takes from his back pocket a piece of paper and unfolds it on the desk.

180.

Standing up behind the desk, the professor looks at the paper and frowns. "May I?" he says, picking it up and examining it more closely. "Can I ask where you got this?"

"I would rather not tell you yet," Vikar says. "I didn't do anything wrong."

"I'm sure you didn't. It just would help me to know where you got it."

"I don't believe it would help you. Do you know what it says?"

"Not really. It's a kind of Hebraic."

"Does that mean it's Hebrew?"

"Yeah . . . . " The professor sits back down in his chair still looking at the piece of paper from the Carlton Hotel. "It's like, there's Chaucer's English and late twentieth-century American English. They're the same language but they're not."

"So, it's an old language."

"It's a very old language, maybe pre-Aramaic. Carrying out the analogy, it's not Chaucer, it's, I don't know, early Celtic Dark Ages, for all I know about the Celtic Dark Ages, which should teach me not to make analogies. It may be the oldest form of Hebraic I've seen, but at this point I can't even be sure about that. Can you leave it with me?" Vikar hesitates. "Let me make a xerox."

"All right."

Making the xerox, the professor examines Vikar's head again. "What movie did you say again?"

"*A Place in the Sun.*"

He nods and rubs his own head. "I'm thinking maybe Dylan in *Don't Look Back.*"

179.

Your Pale Blue Eyes loses the Academy Award for editing. Vikar regrets not attending when he learns the presenter—though he would not have been the one presented to—is Kim Novak, with whom he cheated on Elizabeth Taylor long ago.

178.

Variety, May 25, 1979: "NEW YORK—Following protracted negotiations, Mirron Productions has signed Academy Award-nominated editor Vikar Jerome to direct *God's Worst Nightmare,* based on the 19th-century French novel *Là-Bas*, for possible release in fall 1980 by United Artists.

"Jerome received an Oscar nod this year for his work on UA's *Your Pale Blue Eyes*, under the supervision of Mitchell Rondell, who recently left his position as a production executive at UA to launch Mirron. Insiders say the budget of *God's Worst Nightmare* has been set at $3.75 million, with the stipulation that a lead with box-office draw is attached.

"'At that cost,' says one unnamed participant in brokering the deal, 'which may not be blockbuster but isn't paltry for a feature by a first-time director, UA must be planning to spend close to a million on a star—maybe not a Redford or Eastwood or Nicholson, who are out of that price range, but someone of the next rank.' Names mentioned include Robert De Niro, Richard Dreyfuss and Kris Kristofferson (provided a speedy completion of UA's *Heaven's Gate*, which began shooting in Montana last month).

"Written by Belgian author J. K. Huysmans, *Là-Bas* (Down There) is the story of a writer who becomes obsessed with the possibly historical figure of Gilles de Rais, a trusted lieutenant of Joan of Arc who may have massacred hundreds or even thousands of children. Over the course of the writer's investigations, he becomes involved with a mysterious, perhaps demonic woman. It's not clear whether Huysmans' story will be updated for *God's Worst Nightmare* or remain a period piece.

"Mirron's announcement is taking some by surprise in the industry, where there are concerns about the experience and even stability of the untested director, particularly following behavior at last year's Cannes festival—where *Your Pale Blue*

Eyes received a special jury award—that varying reports characterized as 'unhinged' and 'retarded.'

"Responds Molly Fairbanks, Jerome's agent at CAA: 'Everyone understands Vikar Jerome is an unusual individual but also an original, perhaps singular talent.' Denying rumors that Mirron and UA resisted the deal until other companies such as the newly formed Orion indicated interest, Rondell personally issued a statement expressing 'extraordinary enthusiasm and passion' for the project and calling Jerome 'potentially the most interesting American director since Scorsese, if not Welles.' When contacted about Jerome's alleged eccentricities, Rondell answered, 'We'll make them work for us.'

"Rondell offered no comment on widely circulating stories of contingency plans that include a back-up director such as Alan Pakula, William Friedkin or John Milius."

177.

From the windows on the top level of his house, he believes he sees her on the hillside below. The first time, she's near the bottom where the road that eventually leads to him begins to wind its way upward. He believes he sees her standing there looking up and then the next moment she's gone; the next time he sees her, at dusk several days later, she's moved up the hill but stands motionless as before. It's like *Last Year at Marienbad* where people are statues on a vast terrace, except Soledad plays all the statues, posed against chaparral. Each time Vikar believes he sees her, she moves up the hill a little further, advancing in frozen *Marienbad* poses.

176.

By the time the Sound has seeped west to all the Los Angeles clubs—the Whisky and the Roxy on the Strip, the Masque in a cellar off a sidestreet in Hollywood and Al's Bar downtown, Madame Wong's and the Hong Kong Café in Chinatown—it's grown in desperation with the sunlight, having swallowed itself alive as the city in which it now lives has swallowed itself. At the Starwood on the corner of Santa Monica and Crescent Heights, Vikar hears a local band that plays songs about riding the bus in Los Angeles. They have a blond rock-abilly guitarist and the lead vocalists are a married couple: *A thousand kids*, they sing, *bury their parents*; and as though he's tracking down De Rais, child killer of the Middle Ages, Vikar wanders from room to room among the children of the Starwood, searching the Punk Ages for pedocidal monsters, hurling himself into audiences and slam-dancing to ward the monsters off, dancing so maniacally as to clear the floor. Soon he's alone in the middle of the room, the band to one side, everyone else centrifugally compelled to the perimeters. On two occasions he's removed by security guards, mild carnage in his wake.

175.

Mitch Rondell says, "That's not half bad." Vikar is sitting with him in an office in Culver City; it's more than a year since Cannes, when the last thing Rondell said to him was, "You're late," before fleeing the press conference that followed. Vikar isn't entirely clear whether he's actually proposed updating *Là-Bas* to a punk milieu, but Rondell goes on, "It's an interesting idea. I think we do need to nail down a screenwriter ASAP, then have a story conference and hash out the possibilities, so you can convey your vision of the picture. Of course, most America hates this punk shit."

Rondell strikes Vikar as less cordial than before. Vikar wishes Molly Fairbanks was here; he likes the way she talks and completely understands everything she says, except when he doesn't, such as recently. "You're not writing the script," she tried to explain in their last conversation, "so although the deal memo stipulates the property belongs to you, we need to get you a story credit even if the Writers Guild squawks . . . . " Vikar isn't certain what this means. Molly also talks faster than she used to. "We don't want to get into a situation where Mirron or UA can take away the project later." There seems to be some urgency on everyone's part to "get a star attached," Molly says, "and they're expecting someone in the eight-hundred-thousand range, which is why the budget is set at what it is, including your one-eighty-five K as director . . . . " This last part Vikar finds particularly incomprehensible.

"So it makes a difference," Rondell says now, "if this is a contemporary or period piece. If it's contemporary, a Richard Dreyfuss, for instance, might make sense, but not if it's set in the nineteenth century. And, uh," he swivels his chair away from Vikar slightly, "the role of the woman—"

"Hyacinthe."

"Hyacinthe. It's not a leading role but an important one, wouldn't you say?"

"Yes."

"Maybe she's a figment of the main character's dreams, maybe not."

"Maybe not."

"Comes to him in the middle of the night, an erotic presence . . . she needs to make the right sort of impression. Wouldn't you say?"

"Yes."

"An erotic presence."

"Yes, you said that."

Swiveling the chair away from Vikar further: "What would you think of Soledad Palladin?"

174.

"What?" says Vikar.

"Soledad Palladin? From New Y—?"

"I know who—"

"I don't think nudity or explicit sexuality would be a problem. I mean, only if you see it as an integral part of the picture, of course."

Cylinders click into place, like the night he found Zazi sleeping in the car on Thirty-Fourth Street. "You know where she is."

Rondell moves his head from side to side, in a way that's neither a nod nor shake. "It's an idea. But this is what casting directors are for."

"What about Zazi?"

Rondell is confused. "Zazi?"

"Do you know if she's all right?"

"It was just an idea." Rondell waves it away.

"You know where they are."

"They're fine. You're getting off track here."

"I'm getting off track?"

"The picture . . . . "

"You said, 'What about Soledad.'"

"Vikar, forget it."

"I just want to know the little girl is all right."

"She's getting to be not so little," Rondell says irritably, "except a little too smart beyond her years. She's with friends. She's with her father."

173.

Vikar takes the Sunset bus as far east as it will go, then walks north to Chinatown's central plaza not far from Philippe's where, barely an hour in Los Angeles a decade before, he swatted a hippie with a lunch tray.

The night-black central plaza is gashed with neon, and the opium dens and gambling joints of the early twentieth century have given way to the punk clubs. In Madame Wong's off Gin Sing Way, when she touches his arm between the Alley Cats' set and the Germs', he doesn't recognize her. "It's me," she says.

"You're not supposed to be here," he finally answers.

"That's what you said the last time, at CBGB's."

"You're nine."

"I haven't been nine in almost five years," Zazi says. "Do I look nine? I've been trying to find you."

172.

He says, "How did you know I would be here?"

"I didn't," she says. "But word is out, and it was a matter of time before you and I wound up in the same place."

"What word? You shouldn't be drinking that."

"The word about the freak with James Dean on his head."

"Nobody knows me," he says.

"Are you serious? Everybody knows you. I just missed you at the Masque last week."

"It's not James Dean. I've been looking for you as well."

"Really?"

"For your black Mustang."

"Mom doesn't have that anymore. That never made it back from New York. Now Mom has the Jag that Mitch gave her."

"Rondell gave her a car?"

"You didn't know about Mom and Mitch?"

After a moment Vikar says, "Is he your father?"

Even in the dark, something of her seems to wither a bit. "God, no," she says. Recovering her teenage poise she says, "First he completely cut her out of that movie you were working on, then offered to 'take care' of her when we had no place else to go. Very smooth. She's been living with him awhile." She adds emphatically, "*I* don't live there."

"Where do you live?"

"I like to think Jim Morrison is my dad. But probably not."

The band comes on. The last thing he says that either of them can hear is, "Do you want to go to a movie?"

171.

Vikar finally meets Molly Fairbanks in person for dinner at Martoni's on Cahuenga, along with the prospective screenwriter. Molly is in her early thirties, a slightly less pretty and less pixilated Diane Keaton; in person, she's a bit shyer than on the telephone. The screenwriter is the grandson of a famous French filmmaker who made a lost silent epic more than half a century before about the French Revolution. The young writer wears an eye patch that he moves from one eye to the other; the waiter doesn't know whether to look at the writer's eye patch or Vikar's head. The writer says even less than Vikar but does seem to have read *Là-Bas*. Molly does most of the talking while Vikar drinks cappuccinos heavily dosed with kahlúa.

170.

In the car afterward, driving Vikar back to his house as he stares out the window at a Los Angeles he almost never sees from a vantage point lower than a bus, and which now seems to him less suspended in space than floating on a billowing dark sea, Molly says, "Mitch should have been there, I don't know why he wasn't but it doesn't matter. The good thing is you don't have to deal with the pre-production crap setting up a picture that you might if you were trying to make it independently, Mirron will work some of that out with UA though I would think you'd want to be involved in some of these decisions, your choice of D.P., for instance, there's this guy over in Europe who's shot some of the new pictures coming out of Germany, *Kings of the Road*, *American Friend*, you might take a look at what he's doing, it's lyrical while still being raw and having some intensity, what do I mean to say—?"

"Punk," says Vikar.

"—well, yes, that's one word for it I guess, it might be perfect for what we're doing, on our end the priorities are to get a workable script, who knows at this point if this writer can pull it off but I thought it made sense for you two to meet tonight, and then to work with the casting director finding the right lead who's willing to work with a first-time director, UA wants a star, it's part of what they're spending the three-point-seven-five on, Clint and Jack and Redford you can't afford and they aren't right for it anyway, too American, Newman is too old and it's not widely known but McQueen is sick, Pacino is about two hundred thousand out of our price range and Dreyfuss is impossible to work with even when he's not around the bend on coke, De Niro would be great and at the moment may even be affordable but has projects lined up for as far as the eye can see, just went into a boxing picture with Scorsese that's really Bobby's baby and even if we were willing to wait he won't be affordable by the time we get to him, a Depardieu seems obvious but less so if we update the story and UA won't think he's bankable as far as American audiences are concerned, and it's also probably not too soon to start thinking about the female lead," Molly pauses for a moment as if suddenly realizing she's wandered into dangerous territory but it's too late so she forges ahead, "even though she's not really a lead but there's this one actress coming up now with a name out of a Dickens novel who's everywhere in everything, she was in *Julia* and Woody's new one and was in the Cimino and now is making this divorce picture with Dustin Hoffman where everyone says she's phenomenal and going to win the Academy Award—though for our thing she might be a little, I don't know, cerebral? maybe not quite, I don't know, erotic enough? Vikar?"

At the corner of Sunset and Clark, a throng of kids waits outside the Whisky. The marquee reads

X

DEVO

BLASTERS

and Vikar opens the car door. "I'll get out here," he says. "Thank you for the ride."

169.

One evening Vikar meets Zazi at the Fine Arts on Wilshire Boulevard just west of La Cienega to see *A Place in the Sun*, which premiered at the same theater nearly thirty years before.

The line circles the theater and up the side street. Inside, every seat is full. Vikar buys popcorn and Cokes and talks to Zazi with more excitement about the movie they're going to see than about his own movie. He doesn't ask about her mother or Rondell. She carries a guitar case; when someone takes the seat next to her, she holds the case between her legs. Vikar asks if she plays guitar and she says it's a bass. He doesn't know the difference between a guitar and a bass guitar.

The movie begins and when Montgomery Clift says, "I've loved you since the first moment I saw you. I guess maybe I loved you before I saw you," and Elizabeth Taylor answers, "Tell mama. Tell mama all," the audience laughs, including Zazi. Since it's not in Vikar's DNA to feel rage toward Zazi, devastation is his only option. "I guess it's O.K.," Zazi says afterward, "sometimes it seemed kind of silly. And what's with that ending? Did he mean to kill the pregnant chick or not? And if he didn't, why does he seem so, you know, blissed out at the end, when he's going to be executed? It sort of doesn't make sense—not that it has to make sense, I guess. But." She shrugs. "He seemed kind of gay, too," she tosses it off, and then, to the crestfallen look on Vikar's face, "sorry."

"It's all right," Vikar answers hollowly. But they don't talk about movies anymore.

168.

On the radio, an English band sings about Montgomery Clift.

> *I see a car smashed at night*
> *Cut the applause and dim the light*
> *Monty's face broken on a wheel*
> *Is he alive? Can he still feel?*

and listening to the song, Vikar stands before the windows on the top floor of his house staring out at the night, his reflection in the glass, Elizabeth Taylor and Montgomery Clift floating above the city in the golden glow of the house lamp. The city tumbles out at his feet, a grand catacomb of neurons. Vikar turns his head from side to side, from profile to profile in the reflection: which profile was it that Monty broke on the steering wheel? Was it the profile that revealed his light, or the profile that revealed his dark? If Vikar were in the editing room choosing one over the other, would he choose Monty's beauty over his truth, if in fact it was the profile of truth that was shattered? And if the profile of truth happened in fact also to be the profile that was still beautiful, still unbroken, what did the light lose to no longer have the dark?

167.

Variety, June 3, 1980: "LOS ANGELES—Principal photography is set to begin this summer on *God's Worst Nightmare*, it was announced today by Mirron Productions.

"Starring Harvey Keitel and based on a 19th-century French novel that reportedly has been updated to a local punk milieu by screenwriter Michel Sarre, *God's Worst Nightmare* marks the directorial debut of Academy Award-nominated editor Vikar Jerome (*Your Pale Blue Eyes*).

"The Mirron announcement follows a year of delays on the project due to script and casting problems. Outsiders note that, today's announcement aside, a more precise starting date has not been set, indicating the possibility of still unresolved issues particularly in the face of next month's pending SAG strike. Mirron has scheduled the picture for release in May 1981 and competition at next spring's 34th Cannes film festival, coinciding with wide domestic and overseas distribution by United Artists."

166.

Vikar sees a movie about New York. The narrator talks about how it's his city and always will be. To a crescendo of romantic music, fireworks explode above the park and the buildings that line it. Vikar doesn't remember fireworks exploding over the park when he lived in New York, although he had a suite that overlooked the park for months. He doesn't remember New York so gleaming or the contrasts of light and dark so beautiful. He remembers the city as shades of gray. This is a science-fiction New York, Vikar realizes, a fantasy New York of people who are not very practical about the real world, unlike Hollywood. Perhaps there's a movie about Los Angeles where fireworks explode to a crescendo above the Hollywood Sign, but Vikar has never seen it.

165.

A week later, Vikar is still thinking about the New York movie at a pre-pro meeting in the Thalberg Building on the Columbia lot. Two worried-looking associate producers, a slightly pinched costume designer and several faceless production assistants, as well as a production designer with long hair who wears an open leather vest, sit around a conference table with Vikar and Molly Fairbanks. Mitch Rondell is not there. In these meetings, Vikar says nothing and Molly functions in Rondell's place as a kind of production coordinator and translator of Vikar's wishes, or what she supposes to be Vikar's wishes.

164.

The conversation turns from one subject to the next. "The punk-club set looks great," one of the production assistants flatters the production designer, "I don't know if you've seen it," not certain whether she should be saying this to Vikar or Molly.

"Is our D.P. here yet?" asks the production designer.

"Do we have a D.P. yet?" tentatively asks the other assistant.

"Robby Müller," says Molly.

"Who's Robby Müller?" the production designer says.

"He's the best cinematographer to come out of Germany since Von Sternberg," Molly says forcefully, "and he's ready to fly in from Berlin when we're ready for him. It would be nice," she adds, "if that's before he gets locked in on another Wim Wenders picture."

"Who's Wim Wenders?"

"Wasn't," asks an assistant, "Von Sternberg a director?"

"I meant whoever shot Von Sternberg's pictures," says Molly.

"We've got a small window in terms of Harvey's schedule," says the associate producer. "He's got a Nic Roeg project on tap and Tony Richardson after that."

"We're not pay-or-play with him," someone else says, "are we?" Vikar wonders how it is he can love the movies so much and still not understand anything anyone in Hollywood says.

"No," Molly answers, "but that's not to say he can't decide to do something else if this takes too long."

"Well," says the production designer, "a completed script would be nice too. As long as we're talking about things that would be nice."

163.

"Not to get too ahead of ourselves," says the associate producer, "but as long as we're waiting anyway, should we be thinking in terms of who's going to score, who's going to edit . . . ?"

"Vik is editing," Molly answers, "it's in the deal memo. As for the script, I spoke to Michel this morning. We're almost there with the script."

"Are you sure that's what he said?" the production designer snorts. "He stutters." All the Los Angeles movies, Vikar believes, still gazing at the commissary outside, are about fathers who have sex with their daughters and friends who betray friends and men and women strangling each other with phone cords. "Well," the production designer continues, "the set is ready, so we can at least start, if need be, go ahead and shoot the club scenes, keep the continuity straight—"

"Fuck continuity," says Vikar.

Silence falls over the meeting. This is the first thing that anyone in any meeting has heard Vikar say.

"The scenes of a movie," Vikar says, "can be shot out of sequence not because it's more convenient, but because all the scenes of a movie are really happening at the same time. No scene really leads to the next, all scenes lead to each other. No scene is really shot out of order. It's a false concern that a scene must anticipate another scene that follows, even if it's not been shot yet, or that a scene must reflect a scene that precedes it, even if it's not been shot yet, because all scenes anticipate and reflect each other. Scenes reflect what has not yet happened, scenes anticipate what has already happened." Vikar rises from his chair. Los Angeles is the City of the Real, whose stories are as old as time, where people go to hide from God, unlike the more hopeful, childlike people of New York. "Scenes that have not yet happened," he explains to those around the table, "have." New York makes sense to Vikar now—as he leaves the room, everyone staring after him—in a way it never did when he was there.

162.

The soundstage on the Columbia lot looks like a punk club as envisioned by somebody who's never been in one. It glistens, an Asian fantasia like the bordello of Von Sternberg's *Shanghai Gesture*, several slabs of wall replaced with mirrors. Lights and scaffolding line the walls; on the ground, two laid dolly tracks meet at a vortex. Grips, gaffers and various production personnel wander in and out.

"It's very nice," Vikar says to the production designer.

"Thank you," answers the production designer with the long hair and leather vest.

"No," Vikar says, "it's *very nice*." He tries not to be too vexing. The two men stand in the middle of the set looking at each other.

Comprehension visits the production designer. "You mean it's *too* nice," he says, seething. "What about all those places in Chinatown? Aren't those punk clubs?"

"Have you ever been inside them?"

"I didn't realize we're into an authenticity thing here."

"Please take out the mirrors."

"The audience needs something to look at. A little dazzle."

"Dazzle?" Vikar stares into one of the mirrors and has a notion that disappears from his mind before he can grasp it; but that night, at home, once again he's staring out the windows of his living room, turning his head again and peering at his reflection in the glass, when again the notion flits across his brain. It returns as he stands before the bathroom mirror shaving, trying to negotiate the tattooed teardrop beneath his left eye, which always bleeds whenever he nicks it:

161.

that what he's always believed was his left side in fact is his right, and that what he's always believed was his right side is his left. That what he's always believed was his true side in fact is his false. That what he's believed was his good side in fact is his evil, what he's believed was the Monty lobe of his tattooed brain in fact is the Liz.

160.

Molly is on the phone. "The strike is on," she says wearily, "the actors have walked. This is what video has wrought. Everyone wants more money and the hell of it is they're right, but the Mitch Rondells of the world won't see it that way." She says, "I wish I could tell you it will be over next week, but I have a feeling it may be more like two or three months."

"It's all right."

"I must say you sound remarkably sanguine."

"Yes, I'm sanguine."

"I almost wish you were less so. Are you sure your head is in this?"

"No," Vikar says, hanging up. On the cork bulletin board next to the telephone, he's tacked the original copy of the ancient writing from his dream in Cannes. After he phones Professor Cohn to no answer, he walks down the long hill to Sunset and takes the bus back to UCLA.

159.

Standing in the office doorway and looking at the professor's head, Vikar puts a hand on his own and says, "You didn't do it."

"Vikar with a k," the professor says. Today he's wearing a loose pull-over shirt with long sleeves. He puts his hand on his head too and for a moment the two men stand staring at each other holding their heads. The professor says, "It's a big step. I'm still thinking *Don't Look Back*. But maybe the space-child or whatever he is from *2001*."

"Perhaps it's a she."

"I never thought of that."

"This building reminds me of *2001*."

"Except with windows. I've been trying to call you."

"I didn't give you my phone number."

"No you did not. You're not listed, either."

"I tried calling you as well."

"Vikar with a k, do you please want to tell me," Professor Cohn holds up the xerox of the ancient writing, "where you got this?"

"I dreamed it," Vikar says. When the other man doesn't answer, Vikar says, "That's why I didn't tell you."

"When did you have this dream?"

"I first had it fifteen years ago."

"You first had it? So you've had it since."

"Many times."

"Do you mind my asking about your background?"

"My background?"

"Do you mind my asking?"

"Ten years ago I took a bus from Pennsylvania to Hollywood."

"Further back. For instance, what religion were you raised in?"

"Christian Reform."

"What's that?"

"Calvinist."

"Have you traveled in the Middle East?"

"I've been to Spain."

"Farther than that."

"I've been to Cannes."

"You've not traveled in the old Biblical countries. Israel, Jordan, Lebanon, Syria—"

"Is that from those places?" Vikar says to the xerox in the professor's hand.

"I'll spare you the circuitous route it's taken," Cohn waves the xerox, "among twenty or so experts, from one to the next—to the extent anyone is an expert when it comes to something like this."

"Does that mean you found out what it means?"

"It means 'faith before love, blood before tears,' or something in that ball park."

"Oh."

"Not very illuminating, is it?"

"No."

"Here's the illuminating part. Do you know the story of Isaac?"

Vikar says nothing.

"God decides to test Abraham by telling him to take his son Isaac to—"

"I know the story."

"—a mountain top and kill him, as proof of the father's devotion to—"

"Stop."

"—God, which Abraham is about to do when God stops—"

"Stop." Imagining lodging two pencils in the professor's head, one in each ear, Vikar steps back from the desk.

"O.K.," Cohn says calmly.

Vikar breathes heavily. "What does this have to do with the writing?"

"*Faith before love, blood before tears.* It was the inscription on the handle of Abraham's blade—either a knife or axe, depending on which version of the story—that he took to the mountain top."

"Why am I dreaming it?"

"I have no idea. I suppose it's possible Someone is trying to tell you something, though for a Biblical language scholar I tend to be skeptical on that score, maybe more than I should. Maybe it's all God's joke. Maybe the whole business with Isaac was God's joke—what a Kidder, huh? Do you know what 'Isaac' means in ancient Hebrew?"

"No."

"It means 'laugh.' Likelier, though, is that somewhere, somehow, this," holding up the writing, "is something you've seen—I mean other than in a dream. But Vikar with a k? If you figure it out, feel free to clue in the rest of us. Me and about twenty other skeptics I know."

158.

She sleeps to the bells, having plotted murder. She tosses and turns, monstrousness swirling beneath the beauty, monstrousness that is at odds with all the pain and loneliness the audience would come to know of her later. In this scene in this movie—her breakthrough, on her way to becoming the most famous movie star of all time—she knows the bells mean that the man she believed she murdered still lives. Stirred by the bells, she struggles for consciousness. Somewhere between existence and oblivion, Marilyn dreams us as surely as we dreamed her; and now in the dark, watching *Niagara*, knowing of her what everyone knows, of what she will come to, Vikar can only hope she never wakes.

In another movie a man is born completely deformed, with an enormous deformed head, at the beginning of the Age of Machines. It's as if the man's skull and flesh have been ground out by the epoch's new gears. Beauty swirls beneath the monstrousness; there is no right or wrong profile, no light or dark one, because the elephant man has no profile at all. At the end of the movie, when he literally collapses beneath the weight of his deformity, the soul takes flight from the body, and in the final moments, whispering to the dying man out of a fantastic Cocteau-ether, is the memory of his mother, beckoning him with the words, "Nothing ever dies."

157.

The movie about the elephant man is the only one Vikar can remember crying at, and like an erection that he hides by riding the bus into the night, he wants to hide his crying under the cover of darkness; so as the credits roll, he remains in his seat.

The theater is a little more than half full. As Vikar sits in the dark of the silvery credits, he sees a lone woman rise from several rows in front of him, over on the other side of the theater. She begins making her way up the aisle. One of her wrists is wrapped in her hair in that way Vikar has seen before. He doesn't move or say anything, he sits in the dark until she's passed, and he thinks she's gone and the credits are almost finished when he feels two arms circle him from behind, as if she knew he was there all along, she knew he was sitting there behind her before he knew she was there in front of him; and now her hair brushes his bare head. Her tears mix with his so he can't be sure whose run down his face.

"*Bárbaro* Church Builder," he can hear the sadness in her whisper, "promise if anything happens to me, you will watch after my girl."

"All right," he says in the dark.

"Promise."

"I promise," and then

156.

she's

155.

gone—as though she knew she would be—with the one-in-the-morning phone call two weeks later; and even before Zazi's sobs on the other end of the line Vikar knows, the way he knew about Dotty: *I should have taken out the phone*, but that wouldn't bring her back.

154.

He tries returning Zazi's call but doesn't have a number, and there's no residential listing for Mitchell Rondell.

153.

He takes a two-in-the-morning bus to Hollywood Memorial and stumbles up and down knolls of dead grass looking first for Dotty's grave, then Jayne Mansfield's proxy grave where Soledad was ravished by the dark, and where the dark then swallowed up ravished and ravisher alike, without the world's slightest acknowledgment. One does not need a song on his lips to kill someone.

152.

She has gone in the way of Hollywood tradition, custom-painted Jaguar the color of sangria spectacularly flipping one of Sunset Boulevard's curves while snaking west into Bel-Air—a moment suspended between the romantic tragedy of accident and the existential glamour of suicide. But what's incontestable is that moment two weeks before when she came up behind Vikar in the darkened theater and her sullen beauty counted for nothing, and she wrapped her arms around his neck and whispered into his ear final instructions, a last will and testament as to the only thing in her world that had value anymore.

151.

In the Hollywood tradition as well, for about a week and a half Soledad Palladin becomes more famous dead than she was alive, if not for the right reasons; but in Hollywood there are no right or wrong reasons for being famous. A small cult is born, flourishes, dies out. Accompanying Soledad's resurgent lesbian-vampire oeuvre are the tabloid tales—the snorted H, the nocturnal collection of anonymous lovers two, three, four at a time in episodes that often went violently wrong—as well as the grisly rumors about the accident itself: what was dismembered, decapitated, impaled. Had the heroin gotten out of hand? Was she fleeing a heated argument with Rondell when he returned unexpectedly to find her in bed with another woman? There's also speculation as to whether she was Buñuel's daughter; the consensus concludes against it, even as it wants to believe it.

150.

If there's an actual interment, it's private as far as Vikar knows. As in his suite in New York following their affair and the discovery of Zazi in the Mustang, Vikar doesn't move from his couch. The telephone rings but he doesn't answer, gazing at the sky out his living room windows until, a couple of afternoons later, there's a knock on the door.

149.

Letting himself in, Viking Man says, "Vicar?"

"Yes," Vikar says from the couch.

"You O.K.?"

"Yes."

"You don't seem O.K."

Vikar stares at the sky.

"Hell, vicar. She was a fuck-up."

"Stop."

"You going to the service?"

"What service?"

148.

Viking Man says, "There's a memorial service at Rondell's house."

"What about Zazi?"

"What about her?"

"Is she all right?"

"As all right as she can be, so far as I know. I think she and Sol had a complicated fucking relationship, to say the least, but you would know better than I . . . . "

"I don't . . . . "

" . . . the kid was raising the mother when she wasn't raising herself . . . now half the time she runs wild in the city, nobody knows where she is or what she's doing, twelve years old or . . . . "

"Fourteen," Vikar says, "almost fifteen . . . . "

"No one can keep up with her."

"Me neither."

"Nothing reminds you of time's passage like a kid."

"No."

"Would hate to see her get so fucked up too, forgive me for saying it. But she's always been smarter than her mom, even if," Viking Man snorts, "she does wear a ring in her nose now."

"Oh."

"I've started calling her Zulu." Viking Man sighs. "You want to go with me to this service or not?"

"No."

147.

But after Viking Man leaves, Vikar stirs from the couch and dresses and starts up the labyrinthine path that leads to Sunset Drive, which he then follows to the canyon top. Mitch Rondell's house on Lookout Mountain is all glass and pylon and tension cable, its decks and patios dropping off into Laurel Canyon; by the time Vikar gets there, the memorial is nearly over. The crowd is a mix of Eurotrash, unfamiliar faces, former UA associates of Rondell's whom Vikar recognizes. Molly Fairbanks stands alongside the room and waves sympathetically to Vikar but doesn't come over; there are remnants of the old Nichols Beach gang. Margie Ruth in black, whom he hasn't seen in years, embraces him. "Hey, superman," she smiles sadly, "the 'crazy one with the tits,' huh?"

The white carpet of Rondell's house reminds Vikar of his suite at the Carlton in Cannes, where Maria's white coat dropped to the floor. At the back, Rondell wears black and a sense of oppression, distractedly mumbling to the stream of condolences. Vikar catches his eye and then goes out onto the deck.

146.

He circles around the back of the house and finds her leaning against a post, gazing out at the sea that hides ten miles behind the haze. She's wearing black jeans and a man's black shirt, her hair dyed black, and from a distance she might appear unmoved by the occasion, until he gets closer; her eyeliner is smeared. He says nothing about her cigarette.

She turns and looks at him, drops the cigarette and steps on it. "Figured you weren't coming," she says.

"I'm sorry," Vikar says.

Zazi shrugs. "She was running out the clock as a scumball's accessory."

"Stop."

"I know," she says, "it's a cliché, the damaged Hollywood thing. The precociously bitter teenager thing."

"When did you get the ring?"

She touches her nose. "Couple months ago. I'm working up to the tattooed head," she nods at him, "maybe now that I won't have to fight with Mom about it—that would have been the deal breaker, though I'm not sure what my end of the deal was supposed to be or what deal was getting broken . . . maybe," she pulls back her dyed black hair with her hands, "well, all along I've been thinking Lora Logic," Vikar doesn't know who that is or what movie she's in, "but I guess it's one

of those things you should be sure about if you're going to tattoo it to your head, though if it's a mistake I suppose you can
just grow your hair back, anyway I haven't seen you around,
how's your movie coming, don't you start shooting next week
or something—?" and suddenly the outburst drops off into
space like the house drops off into the city.

"Are you all right?" Vikar says, and Zazi throws herself into
his chest crying.

145.

She composes herself and says, "Can I stay at your place,
Vikar? I'll sleep on the couch or the floor. But please don't
leave me here."

"There's an extra room," he says, "you don't have to sleep
on the floor."

"Can we leave now? None of this," says Zazi, waving at the
people in the house behind her, "is really about Mom anyway."

"All right."

Vikar and Zazi walk through the house and reach the front
door before Rondell, at the other end of the room, says,
"Isadora?"

It's been so long since Vikar heard her called this that at
first he isn't sure who Rondell means.

"Isadora?" Rondell crosses the room and the talking
around them fades. "What are you doing?"

"She's coming with me," says Vikar.

"Vikar?" says Rondell, inches from the other man. "I'm
speaking to Zazi. Isadora, where do you think you're going?"

"That's not my name," Zazi says.

"She's coming with me," Vikar says.

"Vikar, don't say that again. Zazi?" and Rondell grabs the
girl by the arm.

144.

Later there will be some discussion between De Palma and Schrader as to the cinematic nature of the moment, and as to the exact sound, perhaps for the purpose of how to replicate it in a sound edit; there's agreement about the crunching. No one disputes the sound of crunching. With the same hand that once smashed a car window with an eleven-year-old behind it, Vikar shatters one profile of Rondell or another—lately he's become confused about the profiles—and in any case, what's also indisputable is the bloody streak across the white carpet. No one argues about the cinematic nature of that, either. Rondell sprawls across the floor in the center of the room with blood running from his nose, everyone watching passively except Molly, who looks at Vikar ashen, as if two years of some determined and focused effort have just disappeared in an instant. Vikar walks over to deliver a swift kick to Rondell's other profile. "Whoa there, Shane," someone pulls Vikar back, and Vikar turns to land another blow but sees it's Viking Man. He turns back to Rondell on the floor. "She's coming with me," he says.

143.

Zazi walks over to Rondell, who lies in a daze; she leans over and whispers something in his ear. She looks him in the eye and whispers it again, as though to make sure it's registered. Then she strides from the house and Vikar follows.

142.

"That's not my name, what he called me," she says. By the time they're out to the street, Viking Man has run after them.

"Vicar," he says, "you got a ride?"

"I walked here," Vikar says.

"Let me give you a ride." Viking Man indicates a Toyota with a surfboard on top. "I don't think it makes sense to wait for the cops."

"They won't come," Zazi says.

"The police never come," agrees Vikar.

"You fucked him up pretty good," Viking Man says.

"He's not," Zazi answers calmly, "going to call the police."

141.

The last time Vikar saw his father was the night the divinity student mortified the review committee with the model church that had no door. He returned home to find the house dark: "Oh, Mother?" he called to no answer. At the top of the darkened stairs, at the edge of the bed where he lay as a small boy the night his father came into his room, Vikar now found his father sitting and holding a long knife. It gleamed in the light of the tiny lamp that stood on the night stand for as long as Vikar could remember. "Where's Mother?" said Vikar, and turned and went into his mother's room; the closet and drawers were cleaned out. He went back into his own room, and his father, face distorted and wet, looked at his son with the newly shaved head as though the son had become exactly what the father always knew and feared. The father turned the blade over and over in the palm of his hand, contemplating its destiny. But the blade was not for Vikar's mother, and it was not for Vikar; and that was the moment Vikar hated God most.

140.

Zazi comes to live in Vikar's house. She takes the spare bedroom on the second level; her window faces the side of the hill, so there's not much of a view. In the mornings, Vikar cooks Zazi the Basque Breakfast that he used to eat in the middle of the night in Madrid, eggs and potatoes and chopped tomatoes out of a skillet. The first night she says to him, "Does this mean you're not going to get to make your movie?" and Vikar, staring out at the city and at his reflection in the windows, turning his head from side to side and from profile to profile, says, "I don't know how to direct a movie anyway. I did once before, in Spain, and it didn't look so much like Buñuel."

139.

Vikar wonders what he'll do if the police come to try and take Zazi away. But as Zazi said, the police don't come: *If I had been singing when I hit him, they would have come. I would have sung the song from the radio about Montgomery Clift.*

138.

Zazi is gone the next day when Vikar rises, like the time she slept in his suite at the Sherry-Netherland and all that was left in the morning was a blanket draped over the end of the couch. She returns that afternoon and is putting a Marianne Faithfull poster up in her bedroom when Vikar, standing in the doorway, says, "Did he do anything to you?" The guitar case that Zazi brought with her to the Fine Arts to see *A Place in the Sun* stands upright in the corner.

She finishes with the poster and steps back to survey the result. "Is it O.K. if I put up a poster or two?"

"You can put up what you want."

"No, he didn't do anything to me," she says, "but I'm old enough to know the look in guys' eyes." She chews her lip for a moment. "I'm still a virgin," she says.

"So am I," says Vikar.

137.

Vikar goes to see a mid-sixties movie about an ex-race-car driver who teaches blind children until two hit men come to kill him. The ex-race-car driver/teacher is played by the director who told Vikar the story about hating *A Place in the Sun* and seeing it eight times in a row before realizing he loved it. In this film, the hit men are sent by a dark crime lord who slaps around his girlfriend; when Vikar leaves the theater, darkness has fallen and he wanders across the street into a paperback store where a television shows the same dark crime lord in another movie—until Vikar realizes it's not a movie but the news, and that the crime lord has been elected President of the United States.

Zazi comes and goes at all hours. She receives strange telephone calls, and sometimes strange cars pick her up at the house. Vikar has no idea how he's supposed to take care of her; he doesn't know what to ask or insist upon. "Shouldn't you go to school?" he says to her one afternoon after she's been out all night. Sitting in the kitchen eating a tuna sandwich, she nods slowly. "I don't," she says, even though she's nodding, "want to go to school." She says, "I'm learning more from being in a band."

"How long have you been in a band?"

"About eight months. I'm the weak link—the others have

all played awhile. The Starwood gave us the small room one night last week and Rhino may let us play their store some afternoon." She says, "It's your fault. I never would have seen Lora Logic and Poly Styrene at CBGB's if you hadn't taken Mom there."

He says, "I promised her I would take care of you."

She stops chewing the sandwich. "What?"

"I promised your mother I—"

"When?"

Vikar thinks. "Five or six weeks ago."

"Five or six weeks ago?" She says, "You saw Mom five or six weeks ago? When were you going to mention this?"

"I'm mentioning it now."

"A little late maybe?"

He considers this. "I don't believe so."

With deliberation, almost methodically, Zazi throws the plate and the tuna sandwich at the kitchen wall. Just missing the cork bulletin board and the phone—where the plate breaks into pieces and leaves the wall mottled with tuna—she stalks from the house.

136.

She returns a few hours later and finds him down in the film library on the bottom level of the house. "Sorry," she says. "You let me come live here and I'm acting like a teenager."

"You are a teenager," says Vikar.

"I just didn't know you had been seeing Mom."

"I wasn't seeing her. It was at a movie. She came over afterward and said take care of you."

"Just like that?"

"Yes."

"Like she knew, huh?"

"Yes."

"She said to take care of me."

"Take care of my girl if something happens, she said."

For a moment Zazi doesn't move, gazing at her feet. When Vikar steps toward her, she raises one hand and he stops; for a while the two don't speak. Finally she says, "So let's go to another movie sometime."

135.

Vikar doesn't really want to go with Zazi to the movies again, but one night the following week they meet at the Nuart in West Los Angeles. Afterward, as they're walking to the bus down Santa Monica Boulevard beneath the overpass of the 405, with the roar of the freeway above them, he says, "It's all right if you didn't like it."

"Actually I liked it a lot," she says, "except one thing. I really liked the main guy, the one who runs the bar . . . that Bogart guy, right?"

"Yes."

"And actually the whole cast was really great and it was funny in places, some good lines that I've heard before . . . did all those lines come from other places, or did they come from this movie first?"

"They came from this one first."

"I didn't get the political stuff. All the stuff about the good French and bad French. But it was all pretty cool—except for this one thing."

"What?"

"'Someday you'll understand that.'"

"What?"

"He says, 'Someday you'll understand that.' There at the end, when the Bogart guy is telling her why she can't stay with him, he gives this big speech about how their problems aren't worth beans and they have to do what's right and her place is with her husband because he's fighting the Nazis and it's important—and then he says, 'Someday you'll understand that' . . . and that was kind of infuriating, if you want to know the truth. Because if you want to know the truth, she's the one who's understood it all along. It's why she left him to begin with, why she's spent the whole movie trying to explain it to him, trying to get *him* to understand—and now he's telling *her*? It's bullshit, it comes off as, what's the word? sanctimonious, and Bogart, he seems a lot of things, he feels sorry for himself a lot and he's bitter . . . but sanctimonious? That didn't seem like him. He doesn't seem like a guy who puts up with that kind of bullshit. So I just don't think he would have said that. He would have said, 'Finally *I* understand.' Or something like that."

"It's one line," Vikar says.

"But it's an important line. In a way, the whole movie comes down to that line."

134.

There's a contradiction between the way things happen like a movie yet don't feel like a movie. The things in life that are like movies have profiles as well, the profile of how they happen and the profile of how they feel. When the stranger emerges from the shadows of the 405 with the gun, Zazi lets out a small scream; out of fear for the girl, Vikar resists the inclination to reach over and gouge out the stranger's eyes behind the stocking over his head. It's not clear at first whether this is a burglary or an act of random violence.

The three are motionless, there in plain sight on Santa Monica Boulevard for everyone to see and no one to bother about. It's dark, but headlights rip across them, with nothing said until finally, from behind the stranger's mask, Vikar and Zazi hear "Damn! *Place in the Sun!*" and the stranger pulls the mask off.

133.

Even in daylight Vikar isn't sure he would have recognized him, but of course the other man recognizes Vikar. "*Place in the Sun,*" he says again, "it's me."

"*The Christine Jorgensen Story,*" Vikar says, pointing at the man, and then, when he sees the look on the man's face, "I'm just vexing you. *My Darling Clementine. Now, Voyager.*"

132.

The burglar laughs, "Yeah, you are vexing me. *Christine Jorgensen Story*, shit. Remember that?"

"It's been—"

"—five, six years?"

"Ten," Vikar says, "eleven."

"No! Well, yeah, maybe. Anyway, let's not go into that whole Christine Jorgensen thing."

"Your hair is shorter."

"Yeah, and you're still a stone freak," the burglar says, waving his gun at Vikar's head, "so we won't go into the hair either, or the way you hit me that night and tied up my ass."

"You stole my television."

"I did," the burglar says, "what can I say? No point denying it—it didn't get up and walk away by itself, did it?"

"No."

"Who's the little girl?"

"She's fourteen. She's . . . . "

"A niece," Zazi says.

"Dig the nose ring. Say, what are you walking around here for, anyway?" the burglar says. "It's dangerous to be walking around a place like this. You could get dusted."

"Yes," Vikar says, looking at the gun.

"What? Oh, yeah," the burglar looks at the gun too and laughs, "well, like I'm tellin' ya."

131.

Vikar says, "Perhaps you shouldn't use a gun around kids."

It's difficult to hear over the roar of the traffic. "Now, see," the burglar says, "I've given that some thought." Sometimes when a car passes on Santa Monica Boulevard, someone inside turns to look. "On the face of things," the burglar continues, "it would seem as you say. But the way I figure it, if I rob someone who has a kid, they're less likely to try and get all Dirty Harry on me, you hear what I'm saying? It keeps things cool when there's a kid."

"So what you're telling us," Zazi says, "is that it's for their own good that you rob people with kids."

"Now, darling, I hear you taking a tone with me," the burglar says, "but that's exactly what I'm telling you. Chalk it up as one of life's little paradoxes. You still living in the same place?"

"No," Vikar says, "I moved." He says, "I'm not going to tell you where or you'll come rob it."

"There you go, son," the burglar laughs, "you're probably right. Seen any movies lately?"

"We just saw *Casablanca*. Zazi had never seen it."

"Wow, seeing *Casablanca* for the first time, imagine that. One of the fundaments of a cinematic education there, little girl. Round up the usual suspects. I came for the waters. I was misinformed. I stick my neck out for nobody. I think this is the beginning of a beautiful friendship. I'm shocked, shocked that there's gambling going on. Here's looking at you. We'll always have Paris. Play it, Sam, you played it for her, now you can play it for me."

"Someday you'll understand that," Zazi says.

"Huh?"

"Another line from the movie."

"I don't remember that one. Who said that? You sure you have the right picture? Check it out," the burglar says to Zazi, his words sometimes lost in the sound of the freeway, "my man Bogart, he was a whole different cat than anyone had seen in movies up to that point. Cagney was complicated but Bogart was *neurotic*. You don't get from Gable to Brando without going through Bogart, you hear what I'm saying?"

"I know where Gable and Bogart are buried," Vikar says, then, remembering Jayne Mansfield, "at least I believe I do. When Gable killed a man in an auto accident, the studio got someone else to take the fall."

"Course," says the burglar, "everyone now knows they had no idea at the time they were making any kind of classic. When it got the Oscar, everyone was shocked—figured the Oscar folks dropped the ball, like they were slumming or something to give it to something they thought was barely better than a B-picture. As it turns out, other than maybe *Lawrence of Arabia* that was the only time the Oscars *did* get it right, except they should have laid one on my man Humphrey while they were at it."

"He was nominated for an Oscar," Zazi says.

"But he didn't get it, little girl."

"No. *He* was nominated." She points at Vikar. Vikar didn't know she knew.

"Who?" The burglar looks at Vikar, stunned.

"It wasn't for best actor," says Vikar.

"What was it for?"

"Editing," says Zazi.

Vikar says, "I didn't win."

"Man, are you shitting me? You were nominated for an Oscar?" The burglar stomps his feet with excitement. "I've never known anyone who was nominated for an Oscar! Put it there!" He changes gun hands and puts out the free hand and Vikar slaps it. "For what movie?"

"It was called *Your Pale Blue Eyes*."

"Yeah, I saw that picture. Didn't understand a goddamned thing about it. But then I've never been nominated for an Oscar, so fuck me, right? What won?"

"Uh," thinks Vikar.

"*The Deer Hunter*," says Zazi. Vikar looks at her.

"Oh, well, that was the big picture that year, jack," says the burglar. "You weren't going to win against that."

"I'm certain you're right."

"So you're working in movies now?"

"I don't know anymore."

"You didn't work on *The Shining*, did you?"

"No."

"You see *The Shining*?"

"I don't understand comedies."

"You're getting vexatious on me again, right? Don't answer, I don't even want to know. That *Shining* movie scared the shit out of me. What have you seen lately? I mean besides the golden oldies like *Casablanca*."

"*The Elephant Man*."

"I don't want to see any movie like that, man."

"I believe it's a very good movie."

"I'm sure it's fine entertainment. I'm sure it's a motherfucking peak in the topography of cinematic history, but I'm not seeing any movie like that. Hard enough being born a black man in this world without seeing movies about people born elephants."

"I never thought of it that way."

"You see Scorsese's new one?"

"No."

"Oh, man," says the burglar, who starts walking in circles there on the sidewalk as though the very thought has thrown him into a tailspin, "well, you got to see that one, that's all I can say. It's like Tosca wrote an opera about boxing or something. Check it out, what you got here is the confusion of white folks thinking they're all civilized and shit—arias playing overhead—while the real white *thang*, which is beating the shit out of folks, by which I mean white folks reaching down into their souls for what they really are, you hear what I'm saying? compared to what they want to be? which is the ferocious animal thing De Niro is because that's what white America needs, its raging bulls trying to keep the black panther down both in and out of the ring if you can feature that . . . anyway, what I'm getting at . . . uh . . . and De Niro! Watch out! He's White American Death in our time, jack, until he gets the shit beat out of him by Sugar Ray, who's a brother, of course . . . so you got the whole white terror of black power, you got that whole white American jive up against the anti-jive, white America just too fucking mixed up, can't work out whether to embrace the myth or anti-myth—"

Vikar says, "Are you going to rob us now?"

"Uh." The burglar stops his circling and ponders this. "Man, how much do you have on you? I'm not going to take your credit cards or anything like that."

"I don't have any credit cards." Vikar takes out his cash. "A hundred and thirty-eight dollars."

The burglar seems slightly anguished. "Maybe you could give me the thirty-eight? I'm pretty strapped, I—" He stops. "No, you know what? Fuck that. If you hadn't let me go that night, my ass would have been on ice most of the last ten years."

"Take the hundred," Vikar says.

"No, son, can't do it." Vikar holds out the hundred; head raised, a slight tone of hurt in his voice, the burglar says, "You're messing with my self-dignity now."

"I'm sorry."

"Well, O.K.," before Vikar can put the money away, "if you're sure."

"I'm sure."

"For a freaky white man, you're O.K."

"Perhaps you shouldn't use the gun around kids anymore."

"I'll reexamine that policy," the burglar agrees, although he doesn't put the gun away. Rather he waves it goodbye to Vikar and Zazi before vanishing back into the shadows of the 405. "And kudos on that nomination, man."

130.

Sometimes Vikar hears Zazi crying behind her closed bedroom door. He stands at the door ten, fifteen minutes, wondering what to do, before finally turning away.

129.

The panorama of the city below Vikar's house is swallowed up by the inky cloud of his past, until there's nothing left of the city that he came to more than ten years before. Shaken loose by a temporal tremor, the house drifts unmoored in the dark. Zazi comes and goes unpredictably; in her room she practices to records by the Doors, who never had a bass player and could have, she feels certain, used one.

128.

One afternoon Zazi says, "What's this?" On the cork bulletin board next to the phone is tacked the original copy of the ancient writing from Vikar's dream, as he copied it that night in Cannes.

"It's nothing," he says.

"It's nothing?"

"No."

She studies the writing. "What does it mean?"

"Nothing."

"It means nothing?"

"No."

"Who wrote it?"

"I did."

"Well, then it must mean something."

"No."

"Well, where did it come from? It must have come from somewhere. It's tacked to the board." She takes it down to look at it more closely. "Didn't you tack it here?"

He says, "Yes." He puts out his hand. "Here."

She doesn't give it to him. "Well, you wrote it and you tacked it up."

"Here."

"So it must mean something. Is it Latin or Greek or something?"

"It's from a dream."

"From a dream? You dreamed this?"

"Here."

"You dreamed this and wrote it down and tacked it up?"

"It doesn't mean anything. Here," and he snatches it from her hand violently enough to make her jump. He turns, stops for a moment but then continues down the stairs, wadding the paper in his hand.

127.

Hours later, Vikar comes upstairs to find Zazi sitting in the living room, watching television and smoking a cigarette. She says, "Do you mind if I watch this by myself?" He assumes she's angry about earlier that day. "All right," he says. Turning back, he sees *A Place in the Sun* on the TV.

126.

Now and then in the early morning when it's still dark, Vikar wakes to the sound of Zazi's guitar. The next morning when he gets up, she's still sitting on the edge of her bed practicing. "Didn't you sleep?" he says.

"You know what's weird about that movie?" Zazi says.

"Which movie?"

"That *Place in the Sun* movie."

"What?"

She sets the guitar aside and leans back against the wall. "The truth is, I've never liked movies much. I think maybe because of Mom, I just never wanted to have anything to do with them. I'm into music."

"We don't have to go to the movies."

"No, I wanted to because, you know, the earliest memory I have as a kid?"

"Yes."

"Guess."

"The Houdini House in Laurel Canyon."

"That house belonged to Houdini?"

"Yes."

"Houdini the magician guy?"

"He wasn't living there then." Vikar says, "When you saw me there."

"I can't say it isn't a bit hazy, but you were like a fantastical creature or something, from some story my Mom might have read to me. And I liked living there in the canyon with the Zappas and all those crazy people, though at the time, of course, I didn't know they were crazy—they were nice to me. Whereas that movie crowd at the beach, they didn't pay me any attention at all, which I didn't mind so much, but still." She shrugs. "So going to the movies with you is different. You know, like there's a difference between a movie life and a Hollywood life, and the Hollywood life was what my Mom had, and the Hollywood ending that goes with it, I guess."

"Montgomery Clift's life had a Hollywood ending as well."

"The thing is, that movie last night is a completely different movie when you watch it by yourself. Why is that? Movies are supposed to be watched with other people, aren't they? Isn't that part of the point of movies—you know, one of those social ritual things, with everyone watching? It never occurred to me a movie might be different when you don't watch it with any-one else. And *that* movie," she says, "that's one fucked-up—"

"Stop," says Vikar.

"—movie, but not in a completely bad way. That's a movie you see alone and it gets into you—I've been up all night. I said it was silly when we saw it together, but that was way off. There's nothing *silly* about that movie. Twisted and deeply fucked up, yeah—"

"Stop."

"—but silly, no. Too twisted *not* to be private, you know? I mean, five hundred or a thousand people or however many it is in a theater—what are they going to do with a movie like that? There's too much common sense floating around the room, and what you have to do with a movie like that is give up your common sense, which is easier to do when it's just you alone. It just seems . . . radical, any movie that, like, *demands your privacy*, because it's, you know . . . a movie like that makes common sense *completely beside the point*, and you're one on one with it, in the living room by yourself rather than the theater with all those people, and watching it is like being naked and you can't be naked like that with strangers, you can't even stand the idea of it, and you know that after you're finished with it, much more with a movie like that than any stupid horror flick, some deep dark shit is going to be waiting at the bottom of the stairs . . . so I just couldn't sleep. That movie's like a ghost. Watch it alone and you become the thing or person it haunts. Last night, the movie became mine and no one else's. Not even yours, Vikar." She says, "It may be the greatest thing I've ever seen. It may almost be as great as the X album or 'Aerosol Burns' or *Germfree Adolescents.*"

125.

Vikar says, "Once Cassavetes told me about seeing *A Place in the Sun* when it came out. He hated it so much that he went back and saw it the next day and then every day for a week, until he realized he loved it."

"Who's Cassavetes?"

"He is to movies what the Sound is to music."

"Isn't that weird when that happens?" says Zazi. "It's like the first time I heard the second Pere Ubu album and thought it just blew completely, I thought anyone who liked it must be stupid and full of shit—and then for about a year it was practically the only album I listened to. It was the only album that made any sense at all. So why does that happen? The music hasn't changed. The movie hasn't changed. It's still the same exact movie, but it's like it sets something in motion, some understanding you didn't know you could understand, it's like a virus that had to get inside you and take hold and maybe you shrug it off—but when you don't, it kills you in a way, not necessarily in a bad way because maybe it kills something that's been holding you down or back, because when you hear a really really great record or see a really great movie, you feel alive in a way you didn't before, everything looks different, like what they say when you're in love or something—though I wouldn't know—but everything is new and it gets into your dreams."

"Yes," says Vikar, "someone dies when the movies get into your dreams."

124.

"Maybe not the absolute pinnacle of Hawks' work," Viking Man says, "that would be *Red River*, of course, but nonetheless a brilliant distillation of themes that Hawks understands to his core."

Vikar, Viking Man and Zazi are watching a Western on television one night.

"In some ways," Viking Man continues, "if *Red River* is his masterpiece, then *Rio Bravo*," indicating the TV, "is Hawks at his most quintessential, although of all directors Hawks may most defy the very notion of quintessence, inspired renaissance man of film that he was. If nothing else, you might say this is existential in its exploration of courage and professionalism even at its most futile, practically Hemingwayesque in its understanding of masculinity's values and rituals, and Hawks knew Hem of course, having directed *To Have and Have Not*. Dean Martin has always been completely underrated in this—this was around the time he was doing first-rate work in *Some Came Running*, *The Young Lions* . . . for a guy who cultivated, maybe a little too well, his image as a fuck-up . . . sorry, Zulu . . . ."

"I'm shocked, shocked that there's bad language going on in this house," says Zazi.

"The opening scene, where Dino fishes the coin out of the spittoon, with all the piss and phlegm, is silent, you may have noticed, all action, everything expressed in action. Someone once called it a kind of American kabuki, and Angie Dickinson is the modern incarnation of the definitive Hawks woman."

Half an hour passes in silence, and it's during a scene when John Wayne goes to visit Angie Dickinson up in her hotel room that Zazi says, "I hate to disturb the rapture with an emperor's-new-clothes-like moment, but this really isn't a very good movie."

For a moment Viking Man is speechless. "Zulu," he finally gathers his wits to respond, "the genius of *Rio Bravo* is in its unprepossessing tone, the leisurely unfolding of familiar motifs in narrative and character interplay."

"Oh, is that it?" Zazi says. "I thought it was basically wankers on parade. A kind of, you know, pointless exercise in guyness. Really, don't you have to have a dick to—"

"Stop," says Vikar.

"—to even *pretend* this is a good movie? A testosterone level somewhere north of growing hair on your back?"

"They learn young, don't they, vicar?" Viking Man snarls. He gets up to leave. "The woman is fifteen years old—or," he says to Zazi, "however old you are—and she's already busting our balls."

"Perhaps this is one of those movies you hate now and you'll wind up loving," Vikar says to Zazi.

"But that's it, I don't hate it. I don't feel anything about it one way or the other. You *know* this isn't *A Place in the Sun*, Vik. I mean, you said yourself," she says to Viking Man, "that basically what makes this movie so fucking—"

"Stop."

"—great is its *comfort* level. There is no comfort level in *A Place in the Sun*. No movie worth hating or loving has a comfort level."

"Well," Viking Man says, "you've wrecked it, Zulu." He actually sounds annoyed. "You've gone and fucking wrecked Howard Hawks' *Rio Bravo*. When did you turn into Pauline Fucking Kael? Remind me not to see *Red River* with you."

"Is it Hemingwayesque in its understanding of masculine values and rituals?" says Zazi.

"Montgomery Clift is in *Red River*," says Vikar.

"Then I might actually want to see it," says Zazi.

"Not with me," says Viking Man, and storms out of the house.

"Jeez, I'm sorry," Zazi calls after him.

123.

Out at the car with the ever present surfboard, Viking Man says, "Ah, hell, she's just a smart-ass teenager, vicar. I know that."

"She used to not like movies at all," Vikar says. "Because of her mother."

Opening the door, Viking Man pauses for a moment before he says, "You've sort of dropped out of the world."

"Yes."

"I guess your Joan of Arc project is dead, huh?"

"It wasn't actually about Joan of Arc." Vikar says, "Perhaps they've given it to another director."

"How's that?"

"I believed," Vikar says, "perhaps they had given it to you."

"What are you talking about?" Viking Man says, shocked. "First of all, I don't want to direct a movie about Joan of Arc—"

"It wasn't actually about—"

"—and second of all, Mitch Rondell hates me."

"He always called you the 'madman.'"

"But third, haven't you heard? Aren't you even reading the trades?"

"No."

"UA's gone under. Or been sold to someone, or something. Mirron is dead, Rondell is going over to CAA to be an agent. The movie business has bigger problems than you these days, vicar. That hermaphrodite cowboy up in Montana ran it all into the ground with his cowboy *Gone With the Wind*. Most expensive movie of all time and it was pulled after one screening in New York—just a colossal stink bomb in terms of money and press. Of course it's one of those things where everyone talks about what a shame it is when secretly they're in the throes of joy. In principle I'm all for whatever anarchy can be wrought upon the studios, but the truth is UA was the best of them, Rondell notwithstanding, and in the long run something like this, well, it's just not that great for movies in general. The hell of it? The hermaphrodite's movie is really not bad. It's rather good. Not forty-million-dollars-and-a-hundred-miles-of-film good—a hundred miles, vicar!—but good as a thing unto itself. No one can see that now, of course—all they see is all that money and a director who thought he was Erich Fucking von Stroheim. In twenty-five years, when Vincent Canby is an asterisk in film history, they'll see the movie as a thing unto itself."

"What are you doing now?"

"Fantasy heroes, vicar! Comic-book characters! That's the movies now in a scrotum sac—glorified afternoon-serials and cute little robots. Who's to say it's right or wrong? Maybe this is the age we need new myths. I don't know," resignation creeping into his voice after the futile effort to hold it back, "once we all thought we were going to make grand movies. Me and Francis and Marty and Paul and Hal and Brian and the others, even George and Steven. But then George and Steven fucked it up, and it's not that they've made bad movies, you could almost wrap your mind around that. It's that they've made really good versions of bad movies, while the hermaphrodite cowboy went and made what everyone figures is a really bad version of a good movie, though what he *really* made is a pretty good version of a grand movie, which is the sort of ambiguity that confuses the fuck out of everyone, including me. Anyway this thing I'm doing now is my *Alexander Turgenev*, vicar, with a little Genghis Khan tossed in—we've got Max Von Sydow and James Earl Jones and a whole Nietzschean slant, and the main character is this barbarian-type in animal furs with horns on his head as played by this preposterous Austrian body-builder so muscle-bound he literally can't hold the sword, but he *is* getting blown on a semi-regular basis by one of the Kennedy women, rumor has it."

"*Bárbaro*," Vikar says, more to himself.

"Are you getting blown on a semi-regular basis by one of the Kennedy women, vicar?"

"No."

"Me neither. So what do we know. By the new millennium I'm sure Hollywood will be done with comic-book characters and we'll be making real movies again. Right?"

Vikar doesn't answer.

"Because God loves the Movies, like He loves the Bomb."

"God doesn't love the Movies."

"Sure He does. Or He wouldn't have shown us how to make them."

"He didn't show us how to make them."

"Well, if He didn't, who did?"

"No one showed us how to make them," says Vikar. "The Movies have always been here. The Movies were here before God. Time is round like a reel of film. God hates the Movies because the Movies are the evidence of what He's done."

"O.K., vicar," Viking Man says wearily, "I just got my ass kicked by a preternaturally worldly fifteen-year-old, or however old she is, so I don't need to get into it with you too. Listen, when you decide to re-enter the world of the marginally sane, let me know. Come edit my comic-book movie for me."

122.

Often Vikar hears Zazi up all night watching television. "You should go to bed sometimes," he tells her.

"I don't sleep anyway," she says. "I've been having these dreams."

"What kind of dreams?"

"Hey, Vik, you can keep your dreams to yourself and I'll keep mine to myself. O.K.?"

121.

Vikar goes to see a movie by a Polish director, starring the woman who was Victor Hugo's daughter in the movie where she follows her soldier-love to Nova Scotia. In this movie Victor Hugo's daughter is in modern-day Berlin giving birth to a monstrous creature who then becomes her lover, and whom she'll protect against any other lover, husband, soldier or god. As in Nova Scotia, everything she is or has been, everything she believes or has believed, has collapsed for her into the form of her demonlover and child; since Vikar came to Los Angeles, all the children in all the movies are born monsters, born elephants, possessed by the Devil, *are* the Devil.

120.

Vikar hears on the radio that Natalie Wood, for whom the beautiful woman tattooed on his head has so often been mistaken, and whom he saw in a movie where she was in a bathtub possessed, has drowned, as though God reached down to her in her bath and grabbed her by her wet hair, and pushed her under the water and held her there.

119.

Zazi's band gets a semi-regular gig at the Whisky as a kind of unofficial house band, so sometimes Vikar descends from his house, disappearing down into the inky cloud that swathes the hills, and finds himself back in the realm of hours and days and years where he used to live. When the band comes on, Vikar launches himself into the slam dancing with a ferocity that clears the floor, until he finds himself sprawling at the foot of the stage just below where Zazi plays. He's removed from the premises in a chrysalis of spit and blood. Wandering up the Strip toward where George Stevens used to live in the Sunset Tower, he feels like a tourist; he no longer lives here: there are no fireworks above the trees, and it's no one's city and never will be.

118.

He wakes in the morning to Zazi standing in the doorway of his bedroom, watching him. "The band, Vik," she says, "is supposed to cause the commotion, not you." She's been edgy lately from the lack of sleep; Vikar doesn't answer. "As I remember it, you were this notorious in New York, too."

"Something comes over me," he says, "the Sound comes over me."

"We've talked to the club about letting you in again. So if you decide you want to come hear us again, maybe you can let the Sound come over you a little less." She says, "In the meantime, we're not playing tonight, and there's this movie at Royce Hall I thought I'd check out."

117.

On the UCLA campus at Royce Hall, the printed announcement says that the silent film is to be accompanied on the Wurlitzer organ by the same man who Vikar heard play years before at the silent-movie theater on Fairfax. Before the screening begins, someone announces to the crowd that the accompanist will not be playing after all, adding that in fact the film's director always had intended the film to be shown and watched in silence. "This is the first movie I ever saw in Los Angeles," Vikar tells Zazi. Composed almost entirely in close-ups, the inquisition and execution of Joan as played by Maria Falconetti is all the more unbearable for the quiet; the audience can barely bring itself to applaud afterwards.

116.

Shaken, Zazi finally says on the bus home, "That wasn't even a movie. I don't know what it was. It was a . . . *sighting* or something."

"No wonder it drove her mad," says Vikar. "No wonder she never made anything else."

"You know what's strange? This is going to sound strange, O.K.?"

"All right."

"I mean crazy-strange. Like, you-won't-believe-it strange."

"All right."

"But not that long ago, I dreamed this movie."

"You did?"

"I mean, this same movie. How can that be?"

Vikar doesn't answer.

"Of course I didn't know it was a movie. When I dreamed it, I didn't even know the woman was Joan of Arc. I mean, I'm not even sure I understand who Joan of Arc was. But I dreamed it, just like I saw it tonight, you know? scene for scene, I mean . . . is that like the weirdest thing? It was so vivid I even wrote it down when I woke up. Have you ever had a dream and then seen a movie of it?"

Vikar says nothing.

"I knew you wouldn't believe it."

115.

That night Vikar's dream returns more powerfully than it ever has. He's so close he can almost touch the rock, and can almost see the face of the altar's designated sacrifice. The white of the script glows so hot it almost burns him, and he reads it rather than just knows it: *Faith before love, blood before tears.*

After not reading a newspaper for months, Vikar scours the obituaries every day until it appears, and there's even a picture of Chauncey from younger days, and a mention of his last scheduled engagement at a UCLA screening which he missed, as though the director of the film reached from the grave to silence the musician and protect his movie's ministerial hush.

114.

He arrives at the Whisky early to catch Zazi's band, beating the rest of the crowd. The doorman eyes him warily, and as Vikar enters the club, another security man taps him on the shoulder. "Be cool," he says. Vikar suppresses a compulsion to take the man's finger and snap it back; he envisions the man falling to his knees in shock. Vikar positions himself at the edge of the Whisky's stage and waits, until finally the lights dim slightly and the crowd behind him cheers, and Zazi's band walks out.

Zazi's band walks out—and stops in place. Not a chord has been strummed nor a cymbal tapped. The band stands onstage staring at the crowd; and Vikar turns to look.

There behind him is a sea of shaved heads, every one tattooed. There are no other Elizabeth Taylors or Montgomery Clifts from *A Place in the Sun*. But there are three or four Nosferatus, one or two Anita Ekbergs frolicking in the Trevi Fountain from *La Dolce Vita*, half a dozen Bogarts from *Casablanca* or *The Maltese Falcon* or *The Big Sleep* and another half dozen Belmondos doing his impression of Bogart in *Breathless*, surprisingly more Louise Brookses from *Pandora's Box* than the one or two obligatory Marilyns from *Seven Year Itch* and Brandos from *The Wild One* and James Deans from *Rebel Without a Cause*, and many Alexes from *A Clockwork Orange* and even more Travis Bickles from *Taxi Driver*. If Max and Travis Bickle themselves were there, each would have a tattoo of the other. They're all behind Vikar watching him, as though he's the general of an army, leading the children in revolt against gods and fathers.

113.

One night when Zazi is recording with her band at a studio in Hollywood on Cherokee, Vikar goes to the Nuart to see a "Forbidden Films" double bill. The first film is a Japanese movie about a young model who arrives one day at an art gallery showing an exhibition of bondage photos for which she's posed. There she sees a man running his hands over a sculpture of her; feeling as though his hands are on her own body, she flees the gallery. Later she makes an appointment with a blind masseur, whose touch the woman is startled to find she recognizes: "I have eyes in my fingers," he announces; and before he chloroforms her into unconsciousness, she rips the dark glasses from his face to recognize him as the man from the gallery. When she comes to, she's in a strange warehouse, cavernous as a cathedral. On the walls are the sculptures of eyes, noses, mouths, torsos, arms and legs, and as she scurries among the shadows to elude her abductor, she scrambles over monumental replications of reclining female bodies, lurking in the valley of monumental breasts, darting in the ravine of monumental thighs. Imprisoned in the blind man's studio where he sculpts a statue of her, eventually she becomes blinded herself by the endless darkness; seducing her captor, she becomes not just the model of his art but the art itself, the blind sculptor lopping off real arms, real limbs. Over and over he says, *I have eyes in my fingers.*

112.

The second movie on the double bill is a porn film. It's not like any porn film Vikar has seen, or like any other kind of film: a woman in a psychiatric ward is having sexual hallucinations and surreal sexual experiences; in one scene she has sex with two jacks-in-the-box, in another she's in the Arabian desert at night being taken by two men, one at each end of her, while a low muttering continues unabated as the only soundtrack. In another scene she's a slave of the Devil in a Hell of smoke and burning coals. Another female slave chained to the rocks exhorts the Devil on as he violates the star of the movie in a number of ways. He has a two-pronged pitchfork, one prong larger than the other, which he can insert in two orifices at the same time. As the Devil has her, in the background is the endless clashing and surging of machinery and people crying out.

111.

It's while watching the porn film that Vikar sees it: it flashes by in the wink of an eye, and if he hadn't seen it hundreds of times over the years he wouldn't see it at all, or he might suppose he's imagining it; but he's not imagining it. As powerfully as he dreamed it the night after seeing the movie at Royce Hall, he sees it now, there on the screen, and this time he knows it isn't a dream.

110.

Sometime in the sleepless night he hears Zazi return home, and after he's heard her door shut, and after the first light over Laurel Canyon comes through his window, he rises from bed. He walks down to the Strip and waits forty-five minutes for a bus to pick him up and take him west through Bel-Air, past UCLA, cutting up past the veterans' cemetery where he transfers to an express bus on Wilshire that heads north to the Valley through the Sepulveda Pass. At Ventura and Van Nuys Boulevards, waiting for a third bus, he buys a box of glazed doughnuts and a quart of milk, and sits at the bus stop waiting.

109.

He catches a third bus heading west on Ventura. Eight miles later he changes again to another heading north on Highway 27 that cuts from the sea through Topanga Canyon. He takes this final bus to Chatsworth in the far northwestern badlands of L.A. County and gets off among the rocks and train tracks not far from Corriganville, where many Westerns have been shot. It's taken him four hours to make the trip. He wanders up and down the Chatsworth roads asking directions until he finds what he's looking for on De Soto, a plain industrial building with no windows and a single glass door.

108.

In the small lobby of the building beyond the glass door, the receptionist behind the counter takes one look at Vikar, jumps up from her chair and vanishes into a back room.

107.

The receptionist returns with another woman, who looks around fifty but may be younger. She has chopped peroxide blonde hair and enormous breasts beneath a tight t-shirt; a cigarette burns between her fingers. She reminds Vikar a bit of a female punk singer he once saw who performed wearing only shaving cream. "What do you want?" she says.

"Is this Caballero Films?" says Vikar.

"What do you want?"

"Did you make a movie called *Nightdreams*?"

"We can't help you," says the blonde.

"I want to buy a print of *Nightdreams*," says Vikar. The receptionist appears terrified and backs into the wall.

"Nobody can help you," says the blonde.

"I'll wait," Vikar says, "for someone who can help me."

106.

The woman regards Vikar and takes a puff on her cigarette. "I'll call the police," she says.

"The police never come in Los Angeles," Vikar advises her.

"Maybe *you're* the police."

"I'm not the police."

She takes another puff. "It's on video," she says, "why don't you rent it?"

"I don't want to rent it. Are you sure you don't have a print?"

"I'm sure."

Vikar isn't sure she's sure. "Do you have a cutting room?"

"Why?"

"If you can't sell me a print, can you rent me the use of the room?" He says, "I'll pay a hundred dollars an hour to rent your room and look at a print of the movie. I won't do anything to the print and I won't leave the building with it."

The woman glances at the receptionist. "A hundred an hour?"

"Yes."

"How long will it take?"

"Perhaps the rest of the day, if I start now."

"A hundred an hour for the rest of the day."

"Yes."

"We lock up at six."

"I hope before then that I find what I'm looking for."

105.

Vikar waits in the small lobby ten minutes until the woman with the cropped hair reappears and motions for him to follow. They cross the warehouse to a line of rooms on the other side. "You can use this," she says, opening the door to one.

"Thank you."

"A hundred up front. Every hour I'll come by and collect another hundred."

Vikar hands her two fifties.

She looks at the money and says, "In about an hour, a guy comes by selling sandwiches. There's a soda machine over by where we came in."

"Thank you."

"You must have a thing for this movie."

"I believe it's a very good movie."

"Yeah," she says, "a very good movie. I've never had any-one like a movie so much they wanted to look at the print. You're not going to jerk off or anything in here, are you?"

"What?"

"Just keep it in your pants, is all I care about."

104.

Inside the editing room, he's surprised to find a relatively sophisticated flatbed table, which is good for looking through more film quickly but not as good as a moviola for locating a particular frame. Several canisters sit on the table. He takes the film out and begins unspooling it, running it through the table's prism and searching.

103.

An hour passes. There's a knock on the door and the woman sticks her head in. "Got an extra sandwich here," she says, holding out a cellophane-wrapped sandwich.

"Thank you."

"Want a soda?"

"Thank you."

102.

The hours pass, then the afternoon, interrupted only by the hourly collection of another hundred dollars, until Vikar isn't sure he trusts his eyes anymore, when

101.

around five o'clock, frame by eight thousand frames into the film

100.

he finds it

there in the Hellfire sequence, all shimmering heat, the constant, relentless surging sound in the background of machinery grinding and people crying, like hydraulics bashing and engines being stoked, the clanging of metal to metal slightly muffled as though by a volcanic sea, and beyond the Devil's

shoulder is the dim naked figure of the slave chained to the molten walls of the underworld urging the Devil on, and the madwoman bending over before him as the Devil stands behind her, spearing his pleasure, saying things just barely more than sounds and groans, grunting meaningless proclamations over and

over and pulling out of her now and then for no other reason than to reveal a satanic cock, all to the same ongoing muffled industrial roar, and then, spliced wetly between the frames of the PornHell, so that any untrained eye not searching so intently would glide right over it and never see it or ever know it was there, he finds the single frame

> of the horizontal rock, out of its open
> chasm a sound roaring as though it's
> the crashing machines of the
> PornHell, as though another movie
> is trying to emerge through the
> rock's portal, and the glowing white
> writing across the top of the rock,
> and there, draped across the top of
> the rock, the still silhouetted figure

waiting; and Vikar reels, shoving himself back from the table. Although he can hardly stand it, he looks again

99.

and is overcome by a kind of panic. "Oh, mother," Vikar says out loud, or perhaps he doesn't say it out loud but just feels as though he does.

He catches his breath, regains his bearings. Then he removes an exacto-knife and a plastic baggie from his pocket. He locks the door of the editing room. He removes the single frame from the print, puts it in the baggie, puts the baggie back in his pocket. Then he splices the film back together.

98.

He walks quickly from the editing room, crosses the warehouse, passes the two women, pushes out through the glass exit and keeps walking.

97.

At some point he realizes he's walking the wrong way, away from the first of the four buses home. On the bus he has to make himself focus in order not to miss his connection. When he arrives home at ten-thirty, Zazi is waiting; he isn't through the front door before she's screaming at him, "Where have you been? Where did you go?" and then barricades herself in her room.

96.

He hears her crying in her bedroom as he has before, when he would stand at her door wondering what to do. When he opens the door, she's stopped crying but lies on her bed with her face in her pillow. "I would never abandon you," he says, and goes into his own room, closing the door behind him.

95.

Zazi is gone the next morning when Vikar wakes.

He takes from his pocket the baggie with the frame of film, half expecting it will have vanished with the morning.

94.

The curator at the UCLA film school says, "Of course you understand I can't let you take the print." He looks more like a banker, a short stout man with thinning hair and glasses.

"What if I use one of your editing rooms here?" Vikar says.

"What are you looking for anyway?"

"I'm not going to hurt the print."

"You're not Vikar Jerome the editor, are you?"

"Yes."

"The, uh . . . . " The curator nods at Vikar's head. "It's kind of a giveaway." He says, "The only editor ever to win a prize at Cannes."

"No one is sure of that."

"I heard you were directing something of your own."

"I don't know."

The curator looks around his cubicle as if someone else might be listening before he says, "If you weren't who you are, I wouldn't consider it. It's on loan from the Cinématèque in Paris."

"I promise I'll be careful."

"But . . . what are you looking for?"

93.

Vikar spends the rest of the day poring over the rare footage, and returns the following day.

92.

The curator says, "Did you find it?"

"No," says Vikar.

"Are you sure it's there?"

"I was certain."

"You do know, right," says the curator, "that this isn't the real movie?"

"What?"

"It's not the real movie. It's an alternate version."

"But I've seen this movie. It was the first movie I ever saw in Los Angeles."

"Whatever you saw or have ever seen was only a substitute," the curator answers. "The real movie vanished after it was finished in 1928. It probably had a single screening in Copenhagen, the director Carl Dreyer's home town, and it may have had a screening in Paris. Then it was burned in a fire, like Joan herself, goes one story. Suppressed by the French government—like Joan herself—goes another story. Lost, anyway. No one knows. So Dreyer assembled another version from outtakes and scraps of footage he had cut from the master copy. Can you imagine? The most powerful film of all time, and it's made from *leftovers*."

"God," Vikar says, "was destroying the evidence."

"So maybe what you're looking for was in the *real* movie."

"But this is the one I saw," Vikar says, pointing at the canisters on the curator's desk. "Where is the real film?"

"That's what I'm telling you. It doesn't exist."

"No," Vikar says, "it exists."

"Well, then, Mr. Jerome, you know something the rest of us don't."

91.

Zazi says, "Where are you going?"

"I'll be back soon."

"I don't understand."

"I promise I won't be gone long."

"Is this like a work thing or something?"

"It's like that."

"A movie thing?"

"It's like that." He says, "Come with me."

"When did this happen?" she says with evident anger. "All of a sudden you're leaving?"

He says, "When you say it, it sounds like a long time."

"I can't go with you. I have gigs, studio time," she says irritably. She throws up her hands. "Hey, I know I just threw myself into your life. So."

"I'm glad you did."

"I know it's because you promised Mom."

"That's not all."

"Whatever," she says, and gets up from the kitchen table. There's no tuna sandwich to throw. She vanishes down the stairs.

"I hate traveling," Vikar says to the empty living room. "It's always too far from Hollywood."

90.

In the Air France terminal, Vikar slumps to sleep just long enough to be awakened by the boarding announcement. Flying overnight, he always feels like he's not really going anywhere. He sleeps little of the eleven hours. For a reason he doesn't understand, he finds himself compelled to draw on a sketch pad he bought in the terminal, over and over from memory, a picture of the model church he built at Mather Divinity, which now seems long ago.

89.

At Orly the next afternoon, he realizes he's never gotten off an airplane when there wasn't a driver and car to take him where he was supposed to go. Outside the terminal he stands staring at the cabs for ten minutes before he flags one. "Paris," he says to the cab driver. The cab driver says something back and Vikar keeps saying, "Paris," and the cab driver keeps arguing with him, gesturing some incomprehension. Finally Vikar says,

"Cinématèque Française," and when the driver still doesn't understand, Vikar writes it down.

88.

It's six o'clock before the cab gets into the city. All the streets are round like film reels and all the cars drive in circles. Parked before a large palatial building, the driver says, "*Fermé, monsieur.*"

"Thank you," Vikar says, getting out of the cab.

"*Monsieur, c'est fermé.*"

"All right." From the sidewalk, Vikar pushes a fistful of American dollars at the driver through the cab window.

"*Non, pas de dollars americains,*" says the driver. "*Francs.*"

"Yes, thank you," says Vikar, waving the dollars. The driver snatches two twenties in exasperation and speeds off, and Vikar turns to circle the building, discovering to his surprise that it's closed.

87.

Vikar crosses the Trocadero, the Eiffel Tower looming before him. The remnants of an anti-nuclear demonstration line the fountains that tumble toward the Seine. As always, people stare at him until he draws from his coat pocket the cap that he once took to Spain and pulls it down over his head. He crosses the river and the long military field beyond the Eiffel Tower and finds a small hotel where he rents a room. He keeps the cap on. Everyone yells at him about his American dollars.

He's hungry and has dinner in a small brasserie near the hotel. He identifies what he wants to eat by pointing at the menu and a picture of a ham sandwich on long bread. He orders a vodka tonic; the garçon brings him straight vodka in a tall glass that Vikar drinks immediately, asking for another. On the table next to his, someone has left a small magazine called *Pariscope* in which Vikar finds a section that he recognizes as a listing of movies. He's never known of a city that showed so many movies.

86.

It seems like every two blocks is a movie theater. Vikar goes into a tiny one showing an American movie not far from the brasserie. The movie already has begun; the usher who leads Vikar to his seat in the dark lingers after he sits. The usher stands waiting for a full minute while Vikar watches the movie, before finally muttering something and leaving.

In the movie Travis Bickle, who once sat in the Nichols Beach house staring at Vikar and later became a raging boxer, now has become a thirties movie producer named Monroe Stahr. Vikar laughs loudly at the stupid name and people turn to look. This isn't a comedy, is it? he worries. When Travis Bickle pointed a bloody finger at his head in the form of a gun and cocked his thumb, he blew himself into the next life, a life already in the past: All movies reflect what has not yet happened, all movies anticipate what has already happened. Movies that have not yet happened, have. The movie that Vikar watches now is from a book by F. Scott Fitzgerald, the uncredited author of *The Women* with Joan Crawford. The print is the worst Vikar has seen since the first time he saw *The Passion of Joan of Arc* at the Vista, except this movie is more recent, and after a while he leaves as angrily as the usher he didn't tip.

85.

Back at his hotel room he's exhausted but can't sleep. In the middle of the night he walks around and around the small hotel's courtyard until the concierge comes out and yells at him; other guests in the hotel watch out their windows. Vikar leaves the hotel and, in the middle of the night, heads back to the Trocadero to wait seven hours until the Cinématèque opens.

84.

At a quarter past nine in the morning, fifteen minutes after the Cinématèque is supposed to have opened, Vikar pounds on the door at the top of the steps. Someone walks by and says to him, "*Fermé.*"

"What?" Vikar says. He looks at the sign that says *9h - 17h*.

"*Fermé*," the other person says again, and points at the sign below the hours where it says MARDI FERMÉ.

Vikar explodes and attacks the door until five minutes later it's smeared with blood from his hands.

83.

A punk couple with spiked sea-green hair wearing rings in many various appendages stops Vikar by the fountains of the Trocadero. They don't seem to notice his hands are bleeding. They keep pointing at his cap trying to say something, *chapeau* one keeps repeating, and they consult a little book until Vikar realizes they speak English. They're from London and want him to take off his cap; they saw him the previous day. If they hadn't been punks and spoken English, Vikar probably would have smashed their heads together. They tell him the Cinématèque is open the next day and of an American bookstore near Notre Dame where he might be able to spend the night.

82.

From a public phone booth he tries to call his house back in Los Angeles. None of the operators speaks English, and when he hears a phone ringing, no one answers and it doesn't sound like his and he can't tell if the operator has connected him or not. When he runs out of francs for the phone, he pounds the plastic enclosure around the phone in a futile attempt to shatter it; his hands begin bleeding again.

"I will cut a path of destruction across this heretic city that has many movies but where all the prints are horrible!" Vikar bellows at the corner where the boulevard St-Michel meets the river, though he realizes he can't really say for sure all the prints are horrible. Passersby stare at him. He goes into the café at the corner and is told to leave. He goes up the boulevard and at another café on St-Germain orders a tall vodka.

81.

The American bookstore across from Notre Dame is on the rue St-Jacques. Downstairs is where the books are sold but at the back of the store is a staircase that leads up to two rooms, including one with a desk and an old French typewriter, and another with two old sofas and floor pillows. Vikar sits upright on one of the sofas barely dozing, as though afraid he'll sleep through the next six days when the Cinématèque is open. He shakes himself awake to find a young woman perched on the edge of the sofa studying his head. She holds his cap in her hand. He doesn't remember taking it off.

80.

She says, "Who are they?"

"Elizabeth Taylor," he says. He wipes his eyes. "Montgomery Clift."

"Oh," she nods. He can't tell if this means anything to her or not. "My name is Pamela." She's in her mid-twenties, pleasantly attractive without being beautiful, her body invitingly round. "Where are you from?"

"Hollywood," says Vikar.

"I'm from Toronto." Without asking, she runs her fingers lightly along the pictures of his scalp.

79.

That night, under her blanket he says, "I can't." He stares at the ceiling.

She looks down at him. In the light through the window from the cathedral across the street, she can see he's hard. "Are you sure?" she says.

"Yes."

"It looks like you can."

"No."

"It's O.K.," she says. "We can just sleep."

"All right."

78.

But he doesn't sleep. In the early morning hours, he steals from Pamela's bedding and creeps down the stairs of the bookstore, stepping over cats, and unlatches the front door. He pushes open the grating enough to slip through, then heads for the river, descending to the quays and heading west, following the light of the dawn sun that slips up the Eiffel Tower.

77.

At a quarter past nine, he's walking the massive passages inside the Chaillot Palace, unsure where to go. When security guards come into sight, he turns and walks the other way. He wanders the Palace nearly an hour until standing before him is a small balding man in a dirty jacket with a scarf; all of his clothes seem dirty except the scarf, which gleams. The man looks at Vikar with a funny smile. Vikar touches his head to see if his cap is on. The man walks up to him, still smiling. "Can you imagine," he says in English with a French accent, "Bogart fucking Bergman with a cube of butter on the Champs-Elysées?"

76.

He laughs. "It is you, *oui?*" He points at Vikar's head, and slowly Vikar takes off his cap. "I knew it," the man claps his hands once, "I was there! At that press conference! Fantastic! *Quelle scandale!* The only man," he proclaims, "to win a prize at Cannes for montage."

"No one," Vikar says, "is sure of that."

"It is my honor," and the man grabs Vikar's hand to shake it.

"Do you . . . " Vikar has to think what to say, " . . . work for the Cinématèque?"

"I only have managed it these last few years, since the death of Monsieur Langlois." He holds Vikar's hand and examines it. "I saw the blood on the door this morning," he concludes with delight.

75.

"But I am afraid, monsieur," the man says half an hour later in the Cinématèque office, "what you search for in all likelihood does not exist. My country's record on this is shameful."

"I believed," Vikar says, "that since the alternate version came from here, perhaps the real version was here as well."

The small balding man with the gleaming scarf lights another cigarette. "I wish it were so," he says, "but if there were a real version then there would not be an alternate version, do you understand? The Cinématèque has had a tumultuous fifteen years or so—revolutions, government oppression, fires. So what I mean to say is that it is difficult to be completely confident anymore of anything that has to do with the Cinématèque. But we would know of this, I feel certain."

74.

Vikar says, "Where do I go next?"

The man shrugs. "You could try Berlin, I suppose. There are stories the film was in Berlin at one point. But the same stories claim the film burned in a fire there, as well. Always the fires with Joan."

Vikar is something between crestfallen and exhausted. He wavers where he stands.

"Monsieur Jerome, are you well?"

"I'm tired."

The man nods sympathetically. "It is a heroic quest."

"I don't know."

"In a film, if one is on a heroic quest, how would you, what do I want to say? get from one place to the next? In the film, I mean? What is the word . . . ?"

"Continuity."

"Continuity."

"Fuck continuity."

"*C'est ca*, monsieur! Bravo!" The man repeats it with relish. "Fuck continuity. Perhaps that is the way to conduct *this* heroic quest."

"I'll go to Berlin."

"Good luck, monsieur. Are you certain you're all right?"

"Yes."

As Vikar reaches the door, the man says, "You know, there is another rumor about the *Jeanne d'Arc*. Not so reliable, but . . . . "

"Yes."

"But fuck continuity, as you say!"

"Yes."

"It is that the real film actually circulated the mental institutions of Scandinavia."

"Mental institutions?"

"I know," the man shrugs, "it seems one more, what do you say? tall tale. A mad film, starring an actress who went mad making the film, playing to madmen. But that's the rumor, for what it is worth. The real film made the rounds of various hospitals and asylums in the late twenties. One of the dozen greatest movies ever made, a film that doesn't even exist anymore, circulating among the loony bins of Europe, seen only by madmen just as, of course," the man seems embarrassed by the metaphor, "the world itself was about to go mad."

"How would that have happened?"

"The rumor is that the film somehow was acquired by the head of an asylum, and he would show it to the patients. Or inmates, as it were."

"An asylum in Copenhagen?"

"That would make sense," the man nods, "since it was Dreyer's city. But no, not Copenhagen. Oslo."

73.

On the way back to Orly, Vikar momentarily feels bad that he never said goodbye to Pamela. At the airport, again he tries to call his house in Los Angeles. Is it the middle of the night in Los Angeles if it's noon in France? After waiting four hours, he boards the two-and-a-half hour flight to Oslo.

72.

On the drive from the airport into Oslo, when the cab driver asks where he wants to go Vikar shows the cab driver the picture he drew on the flight from Los Angeles, of the small doorless model he made at Mather Divinity. "Church?" says the cab driver.

"Not a church," Vikar says. "Hospital."

71.

Vikar spends the night in a city park. A hotel light blinks only a hundred meters away, but Vikar is tired of people he can't understand who yell at him about currency and walking around his room in circles. In the park is a tall columnlike sculpture carved with intertwined bodies of men and women.

In the morning, when he's startled by the sound of a cab horn, he can't be sure that he didn't fall asleep. He realizes the cab driver who drove him from the airport the night before is honking at him; when the driver gets out of the cab, Vikar suppresses an urge to attack him. He watches the driver confer with several other cab drivers also parked there, then the driver signals Vikar to go with one of them.

70.

The second cabbie drives to a hospital. Vikar looks at his drawing and at the building. "No," he says.

69.

The cabbie pries the drawing from Vikar's fingers gently, like he might if he were trying to take a bone from the mouth of a snarling dog. He runs into the hospital, leaving the cab running.

He returns ten minutes later, shifts into gear, and begins driving again. Oslo seems to have water seeping up everywhere; at one point the cabbie tells Vikar there are three hundred lakes. They drive forty-five minutes out of the city, and when the cabbie pulls up to the building, its steeple—with the crowned lion holding a gold axe—is perched on the edge of a fjord, overlooking a vast sundial swallowed by shadow.

68.

Vikar isn't thinking about what to do or how to do it. The building has an older and newer section, with the entrance in the new section, SYKEHUS over the main door. Vikar walks into the lobby of the asylum.

As Vikar enters, the check-in desk is to the right. Beyond that, in the lobby, is a large aquarium, as though the fjord has bubbled up through the floor to fill an inner window. Stray nurses and attendants wander by, but Vikar is struck by how empty it seems. He sees no patients.

Every time someone looks as though they might ask him something, Vikar turns and heads down another hallway. He doesn't want to commit violence. He has broken continuity; he won't accept the continuity of guards or attendants or doctors.

67.

In the middle of a large central annex to the hospital, Vikar stops.

He imagines, fifty-three years before, the patients gathered here, watching *The Passion of Joan of Arc* on a screen; he wonders what they made of it. He imagines, some twenty years before, Soledad strolling these halls, in a paper-thin hospital gown such as a lost young woman might wear stumbling along Pacific Coast Highway or sleeping outside a club in the Bowery. What would she have thought of *The Passion of Joan of Arc*, had she seen it? He thinks of Anna Karina as the prostitute in Godard's *Vivre sa Vie*, in the scene where she goes to the movies and sees *Passion of Joan of Arc* and weeps; he can imagine Soledad weeping, if she had been within these walls in 1928, as she wept at *The Elephant Man*. Had Joan coupled with God and carried His seed, would they have produced an elephant child, to then be sacrificed as proof of Joan's devotion? He closes his eyes and turns where he stands. *If anyone sees me, they'll only believe I'm another lunatic.*

He turns where he stands, eyes closed, in the moviehouse of his mind until he sees it—the rock, the writing, the gaping portal, the figure draped across the top—then opens his eyes and goes through the doorway before him.

66.

Not a single person speaks to him or asks what he's doing. He follows the image in his head until he reaches a line of white doors, some open. Beyond the open white doors he can see tables with straps, cables, electrodes; he closes his eyes and turns, and when he opens them he's looking not at a white door but a common custodial closet.

65.

The first sign is the old projector at the far back of the closet, beyond the brooms and mops, the detergents and sprays, the discarded junk of half a century, its dust of more than five decades undisturbed.

64.

They're in plain sight, yet anyone not looking would never see them.

63.

On a small stool, he can just reach them.

62.

He looks up and down the hallway, then carries the canisters into the room behind the nearest white door, closing the door behind him and locking it.

61.

He has no editing table. He has no viewer, only a small eye glass he's brought with him. He pries open the canisters and inside is an official document certifying that the enclosed motion picture has been approved, without cuts or changes, by the Danish censor; the date of the document is 1928. Why, approved by a Danish censor, it would now be in a Norwegian asylum, Vikar doesn't understand or think about. He unspools the film carefully on the electroshock table, terrified it will dissolve in his fingers, but it's in extraordinary condition, like a mummified body. *They would have strapped Joan to this table*, but he's no longer certain who "they" are, beyond the interrogating monks, or on whose side Joan was, Joan who was a child herself. He turns on the examination light overhead. Strapped on this table, Joan would have stared into this light.

302 - STEVE ERICKSON

60.

Like making a leap of faith, he guesses that it might be around the same place as in *Nightdreams*, some eight thousand frames in. What does it mean, he will wonder later, that it was this easy? *I have eyes in my fingers*, and he runs his fingers over the spools like a blind man reading braille, like closing his eyes out in the lobby and following the movie that's projected on his eyelids. He has no way to count the frames. He guesses by looking at the feet of film on the reel.

59.

It's almost the same frame of the same image: the same image buried in a 1982 porn movie made in Chatsworth, California, and buried here in a 1928 silent classic made in Europe, the image of a dream Vikar now has had for the better part of two decades, with the only difference being that in the newer film the image is a bit larger, as though over the century a camera draws ever closer.

58.

Not until he's finished and exits the room through the white door does someone finally approach him: the janitor, who says something in Norwegian that Vikar doesn't understand. Vikar puts the canisters in the janitor's arms. "Get these to the Cinématèque Française," he says and walks away, a single frame in a baggie under his cap, somewhere near Elizabeth's kiss.

57.

At the Oslo airport, the phone connection is poor. "I'm coming back," Vikar says.

Her voice crackles over the thousands of miles. "Sometimes I think I'm losing it, Vik," he hears her answer.

"I'm coming back."

"I have these dreams," she says.

56.

Am I just another who's abandoned her? Am I another of God's child-killers? At Heathrow he almost dozes through the announcement of his connecting flight; someone jostles him in time for him to jump from his chair and board the plane at the last moment. After that he doesn't sleep, and has lost track of how long it's been since he did.

55.

Vikar says to the curator, "Do you see this?"

The curator looks into the viewer, then picks up the celluloid itself and holds it to the light to view with a naked eye. "What is it?"

In Los Angeles, Vikar has taken a cab directly to the UCLA film school. "What do you believe it is?"

"Uh." The curator shrugs. "A cave of some kind? A big rock? Hard to tell. Is that writing of some sort?"

"Does it look like someone is lying on top of the rock?"

"Maybe." The curator shrugs again. "Sure, I guess so."

"What do you believe *this* is?" Vikar pulls off his cap and opens the baggie and takes out another frame of film.

The curator puts it in the viewer. "Same thing."

"Is it?"

"Yes. Well," now the curator moves from frame to frame on the viewer, "maybe one is a little closer than the other." He looks at Vikar. "I don't get it."

"They're from two different movies," says Vikar. "One is from a silent movie and one is from, uh . . . another kind of movie. A more recent movie."

"Are you sure?" The curator says, "Is this what you were looking for in the Dreyer?"

Vikar doesn't answer.

"You mean you found it in the Dreyer after all."

Vikar says, "The real Dreyer."

"The real Dreyer?" the curator says. "What are you talking about?" But Vikar already has turned, walking away. "Wait a minute," says the curator. "Mr. Jerome?" Vikar doesn't stop. "You mean you found the real *Joan of Arc*?" Vikar continues down the hall. "You found in a week what no one has found in half a century?" Vikar doesn't stop; the curator calls, holding up the two frames, "Don't you want these back?"

"I believe," Vikar answers, not turning, "there are more where those came from."

54.

From a phone booth outside the film school, he calls the house again. No one answers. The cab that's waited for him at UCLA takes him first to Rhino Records on Westwood and then to Vinyl Fetish on Melrose, among the thriftshops and warehouses, on the chance he might find her. He calls again from a phone booth at the corner of Melrose and Gardner.

53.

On the way home, Vikar has the cab stop at a small market on Sunset to pick up some groceries. When he gets to the house, Zazi still isn't there. He goes downstairs to her bedroom on the second level, knocks on the door, and opens it when there's no answer.

On the walls are posters of Marianne Faithfull, Lora Logic, the Stooges, the New York Dolls, Bowie, Exene Cervenka, Patti Smith, the Doors, Siouxsie and the Banshees. Vikar notes with passing interest that Siouxsie reminds him of Maria from Cannes, with straighter hair. There's a mockup of an EP cover, a picture of Zazi and the rest of the band on the front. RUBI-CONS it says across the top, then the title *Tick Tock*, on Slash Records.

Vikar begins searching around her bed, looking at scraps of paper, looking in the drawers of her dresser and a small table by the window. Only after all of his other searching does it occur to him to look through the spiral notebook that's in plain sight on the window table.

52.

man these dreams, he reads, *one after another, they dont seem to have anything to do w/ anything, I'm not even in them. what does that mean I'm not in my own dreams? maybe i should ask some of the guys in the band except i dont want to go into it or talk about it—*

51.

woman surrounded by monks in robes in a church, theyre hassling & questioning her, i get the feeling its like, another century or something But HERES THE WEIRD PART theyre asking questions in words i cant hear or understand—whats THAT about. then they tie her to a post & burn her & i wake up. fucking horrible

50.

Then Vikar finds this entry.

49.

o.k. i cant tell ANYONE about this. last night i dreamed about, i think it was hell, i mean the real hell (if there is a real hell) everythings hot & burning & i could hear people kind of screaming/moaning, Then this satanic kind of guy, i guess the devil maybe, hes putting this weird pitchfork inside this womans various places & theres this kind of industrial sound, machines in the background. like in the other dreams none of these people seem to have anything to do w/ me, the woman isnt me, it would almost be better if it were—am i a PERV or something? this doesnt seem like any kind of fantasy i ever have, wouldnt i know that? This is somebody elses fantasy, whats it doing in MY dream

48.

Now, before Zazi returns, Vikar reads the rest of the dream

journal. *i write these down when i wake & by the next
afternoon i dont remember anything about them at all, they've
vanished from my memory & all i know is what I've written.
even reading the dreams over, i don't remember them*

47.

*another religious sort of dream last night, a convent? in the
middle of the mountains high on a cliff, theres this one crazy
nun trying to push another out of a tall tower & winds up
falling off herself—down down down*

46.

*another steeple dream, no crazy nuns but this private-eye guy,
in love w/ this girl hes following who thinks shes like this
reincarnated chick, then she jumps off this old mission steeple
& he thinks shes dead, then he meets another girl who reminds
him of the FIRST & theres more but the main thing is the
private-eye is just really VERY FUCKED UP*

45.

*in this bordertown this really fat horrible cop in this sleazy
hotel stands over this blonde w/ pointed boobs, shes drugged or
something, hes pulling gloves onto his fat fingers*

44.

that Bogart guy from the flick i saw w/ Vik lives in this little

*cottage in love w/ this chick, hes a writer or something & flies
off the handle like he could kill anyone any minute & the cops
think maybe he has & the chick begins to wonder because every
now & then the writer gets nuts/violent (reminds me of Vik)*

43.

*this beautiful dark woman in sunglasses, so beautiful shes not
even real looking, sitting in a rowboat on a lake watching w/o
emotion this kid drowning in the water just a few feet from
her, hes calling out to her to save him but she just watches*

42.

*on a stone bridge crossing a moat outside a castle or maybe its
just a big estate, this hot blonde holding this scythe & its got
blood on it, shes wearing a black cape & completely nude
underneath. she's pretty hot i must admit*

41.

*is it the middle ages or something? this sadistic prince guy &
this fucked-up masquerade ball going on inside the castle walls
while everyone outside is dying*

40.

*guy w/ blood smeared all over him, hes just killed everyone to
save this prostitute whos like my age, he looks kind of punk w/
mohawk & army jacket—*

39.

this maze-like apt complex of the future where this private-eye wanders trying to find this dark woman, i don't understand what language theyre speaking—

38.

THE MOST FUCKED UP ONE OF ALL & i remember all of it in vivid detail & DONT WANT TO REMEMBER ANY OF IT. this asian model goes to this art gallery showing these bondage photos shes posed for & sees this blind guy running his hands over this sculpture of her, she runs away feeling like his hands are actually on her & then goes to get this massage & hes the masseur & says I have eyes in my fingers *& drugs & kidnaps her, takes her to this warehouse place full of huge sculptures of naked women, bodies, body parts & the model is trying to get away from this ASSHOLE, climbing up & down huge thighs, huge boobs, on the walls are eyes, noses, mouths, arms, legs. he sculpts a statue of her & she becomes blind too then she fucks him because shes trying to escape, then she becomes not just the model but the art itself & this fucker is cutting off her arms,* I have eyes in my fingers *he keeps saying, WHY AM I HAVING THIS DREAM*

37.

i think i must be going insane

36.

Vikar goes downstairs to the house's bottom level, into his film library with the moviola. He unpacks from the bags he bought at the small market on Sunset three quarts of Stoli and a quart of tonic, then begins pulling movies from his shelves. He doesn't have them all. He doesn't have *Taxi Driver* or Mosumura's *Môjuu*, about the blind sculptor, and he doesn't need *Nightdreams* or *The Passion of Joan of Arc*. But he does have Powell's *Black Narcissus*, Hitchcock's *Vertigo*, Welles' *Touch of Evil*, Ray's *In a Lonely Place*, Stahl's *Leave Her to Heaven*, Rollin's *Fascination*, Corman's *Masque of the Red Death*, and Godard's *Alphaville*, in which private-eye Eddie Constantine cries, "This isn't Alphaville, this is Zeroville!"

35.

He no longer has to pore over the celluloid. Having found the frame in the same place in the silent film and the porn film, now he knows where to look. Now it doesn't takes more than half an hour to find the frames. After he's gone over these movies he begins pulling out others, old and new, near and far-flung, celebrated and obscure.

34.

Sometimes from exhaustion Vikar collapses where he stands, waking himself when he hits the floor, pulling another reel from the shelves around him.

Where is Zazi? Has she fled, as she receives nocturnal bulletins from the subconscious of film, dreaming one scene after another from movies she's never heard of, let alone seen? Did

Vikar loom above her with an exacto-knife, sacrificing her to the pursuit of a divine secret? From the radio of her upstairs bedroom comes the soundtrack of a new Los Angeles noir, without hours or latitudes—Ornette Coleman's "Virgin Beauty," X's "Unheard Music," Duke Ellington's "Transbluency," strange female chants from Tuva, the movie scores of Soledad Palladin lesbian-vampire movies.

33.

Soon film unspools from one level of the house to the next. It's fixed to the walls, draped in strips, hanging from the rafters like webs. Vikar viciously chops up film as though the frame he's looking for is hidden not only from him but from the film itself, in its own flesh. Isn't this flesh his to cut as he chooses? To flop right profiles with lefts as he chooses, and left profiles with rights, to reverse the utopian and anarchic ends of the boulevard? Down through the history of movies, what Auteur has invaded every movie ever made in order to leave him a sign, each of which grows closer and clearer with every extrication and every enlargement? Little pieces of black celluloid litter the floor like granite, up and down the stairs. He runs his hands along the trail of enlarged stills: *I have eyes in my*

32.

fingers, and in every film he examines he finds it, and from every film he extricates the single frame; though he doesn't know it, he's become the medium of Film Id. He enlarges the frames and assembles them until their own film is complete, an altogether different film that draws closer and

31.

closer to the horizontal rock, its open chasm, the white writing and the figure lying across the top, until he's so close as to be able to reach out and

30.

touch her face.

29.

Oh, daughter.

28.

Zazi doesn't return. *I've become father to the sacrificial child.* In his delirium, he has lapses; he finds himself riding a bus into Hollywood with no recollection of how long he's been on it. There's a song from a source he can't identify or find

> *To the center of the city where all roads meet,*
> *waiting for you*
> *To the depths of the ocean where all hopes sink,*
> *searching for you*

and at some point he's in the Chinese Theatre. He has no idea if, outside, it's day or night.

27.

An L.A. private eye of the future executes robots who believe they're human *because they remember*. The movie takes place in a Los Angeles where everything is reset at zero. The future is reset at zero. Memory is reset at zero, prophecies are reset at zero. All latitudes and longitudes are reset at zero; everything that one believes about oneself is reset at zero. There's no sunlight in this Los Angeles; every day is reset at zero. There's no starchild in this movie because childhood has been reset at zero. In this Los Angeles, there is no Hollywood; in this movie, the Movies have been reset at zero . . . .

26.

. . . and somewhere in this movie he knows he's seen the frame of the sacrificial rock, he knows it's there just like in all the movies

25.

and the lights in the theater rise and Vikar stirs. He wonders if he fell asleep; he's now entered a fever where it's impossible to know anymore. He sits up in his seat, watches the people file up the aisles. Then his heart rises to his throat.

Coming up the other aisle of the huge Chinese Theatre, he sees him.

24.

Vikar is frozen, trying to think. It can't be him. I was sure he was dead, reset at zero like everything else; and what would he be doing here even if he were alive, all the way from Pennsylvania?

At first he can't decide what to do, but then Vikar jumps from his seat and runs into the lobby, only to see him again in the distance through the theater doors, outside among the throngs milling around the concrete footprints of stars. Vikar pushes his way outside.

23.

Outside, Vikar stands in front of the Chinese Theatre. People run into him as his eyes search up and down Hollywood Boulevard.

It couldn't have been him. Even if he were alive, is it possible he would have come to Los Angeles after all this time? Why would he have been in the theater? Did he know I was there? Vikar begins walking up and down the block until, to his astonishment, at the corner of Orange Avenue, he sees him crossing the street to the Roosevelt Hotel.

22.

The lobby hasn't changed since thirteen years before. Vikar strides past the front desk, through the sitting area with the bar beyond: "Sir?" says the concierge behind the front desk. Vikar wishes he were wearing his cap. The concierge calls again and again Vikar doesn't answer, taking two or three at a time the steps that lead to the elevators, slipping into one just as the door slides closed.

21.

Like a private eye eluding pursuit in the ongoing movie of Los Angeles, Vikar gets off at the seventh floor and takes the stairs the rest of the way to the ninth.

20.

On the ninth floor, he heads down the long hall. The door of suite 928 is half ajar. Vikar pushes it open slightly, steps inside.

19.

To the left, in the corner of the living room, are a sofa and chair. A small table sits in the middle of the living room, a small bar behind it. The man stands in the middle of the suite gazing out the window, and turns to look at Vikar; his eyes glance to Vikar's head and his mouth curls into a smile Vikar has seen a thousand times. "Hello!" the man says. "Come in."

18.

He says to Vikar, "Have a seat."

Vikar appraises the suite again, tentatively stepping into the living room and the rising lights of Hollywood through the window.

"Can I . . . get you something to drink?" the man says. "Vodka tonic?"

"All right."

"Have a seat?" the man says again.

"All right." Vikar lowers himself into the sofa in the middle of the living room. The man hands Vikar the vodka tonic but doesn't pour himself anything. He sits in the chair across from Vikar, smiles and nods; he leans forward and folds his hands, unblinking dark eyes on Vikar with a familiar intensity. Vikar says, "For some reason, from a distance I believed you were my father."

"Common mistake," the man laughs.

17.

The man says in his slightly high, cracked voice, "Well, of course, I know all about *you*." He gestures at Vikar's head and laughs again. "I guess I've known about you since . . . well, since before I knew you."

On anyone else, his smile might be a sneer. But it's without insolence; rather it's half serene, half ironic, the smile that rejects doom or accepts it—it's hard to be sure. It's the same smile with which he confronts John Wayne at the end of *Red River*, when Wayne says he's going to kill him. It's the same smile with which he refuses to be bullied by Burt Lancaster in *From Here to Eternity*, and then befriends him. It's the same smile when he sees Elizabeth Taylor for the last time at the end of *A Place in the Sun*, on his way to the gas chamber.

"Fathers, huh?" he says, his faraway gaze from under his predominant eyebrows floating over Vikar's face, before fixing on something somewhere just beyond him. "Nuts. Back home in Omaha, I didn't get on with mine, especially after the Crash . . . . " He shrugs, "He was a . . . *narrow* man. *Rigid* man. Sound familiar?"

"Yes."

"Of course," the man nods, "my Ma, uh, she wasn't exactly easy for him to live with. She wasn't easy for any of us to live with, with all the . . . lies . . . . But nobody ever lies about being lonely."

"I realize now," Vikar says, "how lonely my mother was."

"It helped in the acting, though—the thing with Pa. Never thought of motion pictures as a hiding place but . . . thought of my Pa when I went up against Wayne in *Red River*. Thought of him when I went up against Lancaster in *Eternity*. Pa and I, we patched things up after the accident . . . about the only thing after the accident that . . . got better."

"Your face," says Vikar.

The man touches his face. "Yeah."

"It's better now."

He nods. "It's better."

"I get the right profiles and left profiles mixed up."

"Another common mistake." He stares at Vikar. "You got trust in your eyes, like you were just born." He smiles the smile. "You know I was a twin?"

"No."

"Had a twin sister. So when you're a twin, you got *four* profiles in a way, right? Or maybe . . . one right profile cancels out the other left, and one left cancels out the other right . . . . "

"Was it bad?"

"How's that?"

"The accident. Did it hurt?"

"It was bad," he nods, "can't pretend it wasn't. Bad outside and . . . " he taps his head, " . . . inside. Pretty much lost half my face. Bessie Mae—that's what I call Elizabeth—she saved my life. Reached into my mouth and . . . pulled my teeth out of my throat, which is the only reason I didn't choke to death. I gave her the teeth later," he laughs, "as a sort of keepsake. The nose . . . never got fixed . . . jaw was cracked . . . all the nerves on the left side . . . . *Lots* of pills for the pain. A *lot* of drink. You know, I'll never forget the *gesture* of it, Elizabeth saving my life, but—" He laughs again. "I would have been Jimmy Dean if I'd died then. Hollywood is *full* of people who would trade their lives in a heartbeat just to be legends. Would have traded mine in a heartbeat not to go through the next nine years." He says matter-of-factly, "Before the accident, I always was arrogant about my face. Felt a little guilty about it too, I realize now. Went to enlist in the War, before they turned me down for dysentery, and I was scared not that I'd get killed but that . . . something would happen to my face. Got away with a lot, because of this face. So it figures," he smiles, "life would get me *there*."

16.

He smiles at Vikar's head. "*Fan*tastic. Never expected to be tattooed on somebody's head."

"I believe it's a very good movie," says Vikar.

"Never figured it would be the finest thing I did. Certainly didn't think so at the time. But then I didn't care for many of my pictures. The ones with Zinnemann I liked all right . . . *The Young Lions* with Marlon, that was maybe my best work. But the others . . . . " he shrugs, "*Red River* . . . . "

"I believe that's a very good movie as well."

"Nah, I didn't like it. They watered it down. Wayne was supposed to die at the end, but . . . . " He looks up at Vikar and smiles. "But funny how your perspective changes, right? Before *Place in the Sun*, George Stevens came back from the war feeling like everything he'd done before was . . . a *trifle*. Gave up directing to fight the war, and then he . . . was one of the first into the camps to see . . . all that. Dachau. Bergen-Belsen. Afterward, he thought motion pictures should change the world . . . or what was the point? Can't blame him. I probably would have agreed with him. I mean, Mister S, he just didn't know who to fight anymore . . . what did he want to make empty little musicals for, right? He was all set to make a comedy with Ingrid . . . biggest star in the world then . . . that was before the country got so worked up about . . . her . . . *private* life . . . then he had to fly to Paris to tell her, 'Can't do it.' A man doesn't go his own way, he's nothing. No more comedies, even if she *was* the biggest star in the world. Now, of course, with a little perspective, a person looks back and realizes, what in motion pictures can change the world more than Astaire and Rogers dancing?"

In his netherworld between sleep and wakefulness, it's difficult for Vikar to be certain whether he thinks about the question for a minute or five, or for an hour or a day or the rest of his life. In his mind he watches Fred Astaire and Ginger Rogers in George Stevens' *Swing Time*, dancing to "The Way You Look Tonight" that fades into "Never Gonna Dance." The floor gleams onyx, a black arch of stairs rises beneath a black backdrop of stars beyond the bandstand. Their dance is a melancholy goodbye—though of course in the end it's not goodbye—that drifts across the floor and up the arch, where Rogers slips from Astaire's arms into the white wings of the stage that glisten like an ice palace, and Astaire is left empty-armed, poised in mid-loss as the light settles into a kind of dusk that's only in the movies. "Nothing," answers Vikar.

15.

"Nothing," nods Monty. "*Nothing. Astaire and Rogers—fan*-tastic, even if Stevens did shoot so many takes that poor Ginger's feet bled. A man should be what he can *do* . . . but after the war he decided he had to make . . . well, you know," he shrugs again, "pictures about Jesus. Maybe you just can't make a good picture about Jesus."

"It's harder when God is the villain."

"Fathers and sons, right?"

"Yes."

Monty says, "Sometimes you know things before you know them."

"Once I made a model of a church before I saw it. Then when I finally saw it, it wasn't a church."

"That happens too. What you thought you knew all along turns out to be something else."

"It's like all along it was a sign for something."

"Uh huh."

"Sometimes I've seen things that were supposed to be there even when they aren't."

"The *Joan of Arc*," Monty nods. "Another vodka tonic?"

"No, thank you." Vikar says, "In a week, I found a movie no one else could find for fifty years."

"Doesn't that make sense?"

"There's a secret movie that's been hidden, one frame at a time, in all the movies ever made."

"Find it in mine?" Monty smiles at Vikar's head.

"That's funny. I didn't look in that one."

"Don't bother. It's there too."

"How did it get there? Who made it?"

"Doesn't it seem strange," Monty says, "that there are twenty-four frames per second of film? That in every second of film are the number of hours in a day?" He says, "What's it mean that every second of a film is a day in the life of a secret film that someone's been waiting for you to find in all the other films?"

"I don't know. Perhaps," Vikar says, "someone is showing me a way out of something."

"Or a way in."

"Am I possessed?"

Monty laughs.

"Am I possessed by the Movies?" says Vikar.

Monty laughs again. "Just because you love something doesn't mean it loves you back."

"Why me?"

"Is it just you?"

Vikar thinks. "No."

"Right."

"There's someone else."

"The girl," says Monty.

"She doesn't even like movies that much. She likes music."

"Maybe she doesn't choose."

"Lately she's had dreams of movies she's never seen. Movies she doesn't even know about."

"Maybe the Movies chose her, like they chose you."

"I miss Dotty."

"She misses you too."

"She once said movies are dreams."

"Maybe it's the other way around."

"What?"

"That Secret Movie? The one that's hidden frame by frame in all the other movies?"

"Yes."

"Maybe we're not dreaming it. Maybe it's dreaming us."

"I'm tired."

"I know."

"I haven't slept."

"I know."

"In days. Or . . ." Vikar can't think. "Longer. Since . . . ." Was it the porn movie, the last time he slept? Was it the night that Vikar and Zazi saw *The Passion of Joan of Arc* together? Was it before?

"Longer than that," says Monty.

"Yes."

"Since before you came to Hollywood."

"Yes."

"Since before you ever went to the movies."

"Yes."

"Since that night your father came into your room when you were a small boy."

Vikar nods. "Yes."

"You should sleep now," Monty says.

"Yes."

14.

In the past few nights, Zazi's dreams have suddenly stopped. It's as though they've been cut from the filmstrip of her sleep. When she gets home, she finds the front door wide open and celluloid in bits and pieces and loops strewn from the top level of the house down the stairs to the second level, past the bedrooms to the third. She knocks on the door to the film library. "Vik?" she calls.

13.

He hasn't returned by the time she goes to bed, and he's not home when she wakes the next morning. The door to the film library is locked, and she stands before it wondering if she should try to break it down like they do in movies. But she has a feeling it's not as easy as it looks in movies.

Like this movie she saw with Vikar where a small boy runs after the wounded gunfighter as he rides into the hills and graveyards, calling *Shane, come back! Mother wants you! I want you!*, she might now run down the street calling *Vik, come back! The Movies want you! I want you!* Zazi goes back up to the top level of the house, out the front door, and then slowly makes her way down the steep incline of the dirt hillside. At the base of the house, she's able to jump up and catch the edge of the small window to the library and to briefly pull herself up, just long enough to peer in before she can't hold on any longer. She drops to the hill and slides down, breaking the slide only by catching hold of some chaparral. "Shit," she says. Slowly she climbs back up the hill to the top. She's thinking to herself that, while the library appeared empty, she can't be positive Vikar isn't passed out on the floor, when she reaches the front door of the house and someone is waiting. For a moment, she thinks it's him.

12.

Viking Man stands in the open doorway studying the celluloid draped over lamps, curtains, the TV, down along the rail of the stairs. When he turns to her, she knows something is wrong. He takes the cigar from his mouth. "Zulu," he says quietly, "you need to come with me."

11.

In the lobby of the Roosevelt, the concierge behind the front desk says, "I'll get Mr. Cooper, the manager."

The manager, small, dark, well-dressed, appears immediately. He smiles sadly when he shakes Viking Man's hand and Zazi's.

10.

In suite 928 on the ninth floor, Vikar lies on the sofa. He might appear to be sleeping, but Zazi knows he isn't sleeping. The three stand in the middle of the suite looking at him. "I'm sorry," says the manager.

"What happened?" Viking Man finally says.

"I don't know," says the manager, with a slight accent. "There's no indication of anything untoward. He seems peaceful, I think. Don't you?"

"Yes," Viking Man says after a moment. "He seems peaceful."

"I have to call the police, of course. Probably I've caused myself some trouble not phoning them first, but." He shrugs. "He has no identification, so I thought I should tell someone who knew him."

"How did you know to call me?"

"Madrid."

"Madrid?"

"When he was working on your movie."

"You knew him in Madrid when he was working on my movie?"

"I knew him then. Another time too, in France. Not well, of course. But I knew he was a man of vision."

Viking Man says, "Who found him?"

"The concierge saw him come into the hotel and take the elevator up, and went looking for him."

"Who lives here?"

"Nobody. It's vacant now. But thirty years ago," the manager looks at Viking Man and Zazi, "it was Mr. Montgomery Clift's home."

"Say what?" says Viking Man.

"After making *A Place in the Sun*, when he was filming *From Here to Eternity*."

"Montgomery Clift?" says Zazi.

Viking Man takes an unlit cigar from his mouth. "He had presence, Monty, you have to give that to him. Held his own in *Red River* against the Duke." He says to Zazi, "Don't give me any of your 'male-wanker' feminist crap. Not right now, anyway."

"O.K."

"He never really had a place in the sun, Montgomery Clift," says the manager.

"God love him, neither did the vicar," says Viking Man, "unless he's there now."

9.

"That," Zazi says to Viking Man in the elevator, on the way back down to the Roosevelt lobby with the hotel manager, "sounded like something they would say in a movie." There is in her voice an edge she herself doesn't understand.

"And your point is what?" says Viking Man.

"Forget it."

"Did we sully the moment with something corny, Zulu? Sometimes people say things in movies not just because it's corny but because it's the true thing that people would say in life if it wasn't corny."

In the elevator, all the buttons on the floor panel light up. One by one, at every floor the elevator stops and the door slides open to no one.

"I've always heard," Viking Man says to the manager, "that the Roosevelt is haunted by the ghost of Montgomery Clift."

"Yes, but that," the manager smiles, indicating the lit buttons on the panel, "that's not Mr. Clift. That's Mr. Griffith."

8.

Back at the house Viking Man says, "You can't stay here, Zulu."

She stares out the windows that overlook the city. "Why not?

"Even if the cops don't show up, sooner or later Social Services will notice a kid is living here alone." Viking Man lights another cigar. "You don't surf, do you?"

She looks at him like he's asked if she's a cannibal, or has a *Brady Bunch* lunch box.

"No, I didn't suppose," he says. "Can't say I get in that many waves myself, anymore." He feels around in his pockets for a pen. "Got something to write on?"

"Over by the phone."

He writes a phone number on the pad by the phone, peels the number off. "Call me in a day or two, Zulu, or sooner if you need anything. Just to let me know what you're doing," and he sticks it on the cork bulletin board where Vikar kept the inscription of a dream.

7.

When Viking Man is gone, Zazi returns to the door of the film library on the house's bottom level, wondering if she should try breaking it down. Whatever corny things might get said in real life, she still has a feeling it's not as easy as it looks in the movies, knocking down a door, so rather than throwing herself at it, she gives it a good kick, and then another and another. Am I going to have to break into that stupid window, she thinks, where I almost fell down the hill? After one more futile kick, she takes hold of the knob to rattle it, anticipating the futility—except now the door isn't locked, and swings opens easily before her.

6.

Now she sees the havoc of the library that she couldn't see

from outside, in the few seconds she glanced through the window. Most of Vikar's five hundred or so movies have been pulled furiously from their places on the shelves, canisters ripped open and celluloid unspooled everywhere. What's more interesting, though, are the enlarged stills on the wall.

5.

Each is the same, except each is a bit closer than the next to some rock or small cave; and carved at the top of the rock, Zazi recognizes immediately the writing that Vikar tacked to the bulletin board upstairs, though there's still no way to know what it means.

4.

Someone is lying on top of the rock, and becomes clearer with each enlarged still.

3.

Zazi stands in the library as the minutes pass, and as the minutes pass she begins to hear the voices. Is someone upstairs? Is a radio on?

> *"You were such an apt pupil, weren't you,*
> *Madeleine? Such an apt pupil . . . . "*
> *"He was some kind of a man. What does it*
> *matter what you say about people . . . ?"*
> *"I was born when she kissed me.*

I died when she left me.
I lived a few days while she loved me . . . . "

but they're voices she knows, and growing closer to the stills on the wall, she presses her ear to each

and out of the door of the rock in each, beneath the form that lies across the top of the rock, Zazi hears come roaring out all of the dreams she's had

until she reaches the final still and, as she presses her ear to it, sees clearly the face before her: her mouth drops

2.

1.

: and then she woke. She woke and all the images in her head blew away; lying there on the rock, she looked up into the dark of the night sky. Then another darkness fell across her, and it was her father's shadow. She screamed.

She kept screaming as her father took her in his arms. "Oh, daughter," he said, "why do you scream?"

"Don't kill me," she said.

"Kill you?" For a moment, his voice was at once alarmed and hurt, but both immediately gave way to something softer. "I never would hurt you," he said.

Olive trees swayed in a canaan desert wind. She could hear the flock of sheep on the knoll below, and the donkeys. "God hasn't commanded you to kill me?" she said.

"You've had a bad dream," said her father. "No true loving

God would command such a thing of a father, and no true loving father would heed such a god."

She clutched her father, felt his warm beard and long hair against her. "It was a strange world I dreamed of, with people so strange and beautiful they were barely people at all."

The father picked up the daughter and carried her to the nearby cave where a campfire burned. The wind clicked as it blew, and with the passing clouds, the light of the full moon overhead fluttered twenty-fours times a second.

0.

But when she woke the next morning, she knew her father was dead, and she wondered whether it was because he had defied God or just because his time to die had come, a soul reset at zero.

She built the makings of a pyre, where fathers and daughters alike might go up in the smoke of holy fires. With great effort, she pulled his body to the place and set it on the pyre, and it was only in the light of the torch with which she was about to set the fire that she noticed it: there was, below his left eye, a red teardrop, caught in his beard, that she couldn't brush away. And when she took her father's blade and cut away some of the beard, she saw there was no brushing away the teardrop, that it was like stigmata stained to his flesh. Then she noticed the dark mark at the root of his hair that she never noticed before, and began to cut away with the blade more of his hair, that she might determine whether it was a mark made by God, or something no God could account for.

And there on the top of his head were faces like she had seen only in a dream, almost too beautiful to be recognized as people at all: the most beautiful woman and the most beautiful man in the world, she the female version of him, and he the male version of her.

ACKNOWLEDGMENTS

I would like to thank the John Simon Guggenheim Foundation for its generous support. Part of this novel originally appeared in different form in *McSweeney's Enchanted Chamber of Astonishing Stories*.

ABOUT THE AUTHOR

Steve Erickson is the author of several
novels, including *Tours of the Black Clock*,
Rubicon Beach, *The Sea Came in at
Midnight*, *Our Ecstatic Days* and *Arc d'X*.
His novels have been translated into ten
languages. Erickson is the editor of the lite-
rary magazine *Black Clock*, published by the
California Institute of the Arts, where he
teaches writing. He also is the film critic for
Los Angeles magazine and lives in Topanga
Canyon with his wife and son.

The Days of Abandonment
Elena Ferrante
Fiction - 192 pp - $14.95 - isbn 978-1-933372-00-6

"Stunning . . . The raging, torrential voice of the author is something rare."—*The New York Times*

"I could not put this novel down. Elena Ferrante will blow you away."—ALICE SEBOLD, author of *The Lovely Bones*

This gripping story tells of a woman's descent into devastating emptiness after being abandoned by her husband with two young children to care for.

www.europaeditions.com

Troubling Love
Elena Ferrante
Fiction - 144 pp - $14.95 - isbn 978-1-933372-16-7

"In tactile, beautifully restrained prose, Ferrante makes the domestic violence that tore [the protagonist's] household apart evident."—*Publishers Weekly*

"Ferrante has written the 'Great Neapolitan Novel.'"
—*Corriere della Sera*

Delia's takes a voyage of discovery through the chaotic streets and claustrophobic sitting rooms of contemporary Naples in search of the truth about her mother's untimely death.

Cooking with Fernet Branca
James Hamilton-Paterson
Fiction - 288 pp - $14.95 - isbn 978-1-933372-01-3

"Provokes the sort of indecorous involuntary laughter that has more in common with sneezing than chuckling. Imagine a British John Waters crossed with David Sedaris."—*The New York Times*

Gerald Samper has his own private Tuscan hilltop, where he whiles away his time working as a ghostwriter for celebrities and inventing wholly original culinary concoctions. His idyll is shattered by the arrival of Marta. A series of hilarious misunderstandings brings this odd couple into ever-closer proximity.

Old Filth
Jane Gardam
Fiction - 256 pp - $14.95 - isbn 978-1-933372-13-6

"This remarkable novel [...] will bring immense pleasure to readers who treasure fiction that is intelligent, witty, sophisticated and— a quality encountered all too rarely in contemporary culture— adult."—*The Washington Post*

The engrossing and moving account of the life of Sir Edward Feathers; from birth in colonial Malaya to Wales, where he is sent as a "Raj orphan," to Oxford, his career and marriage parallels much of the twentieth century's dramatic history.

Total Chaos
Jean-Claude Izzo
Fiction/Noir - 256 pp - $14.95 - isbn 978-1-933372-04-4

"Rich, ambitious and passionate . . . his sad, loving portrait of his native city is amazing."—*The Washington Post*

"Full of fascinating characters, tersely brought to life in a prose style that is (thanks to Howard Curtis's shrewd translation) traditionally dark and completely original."—*The Chicago Tribune*

The first installment in the Marseilles Trilogy.

Chourmo
Jean-Claude Izzo
Fiction/Noir - 256 pp - $14.95 - isbn 978-1-933372-17-4

"Like the best noir writers—and he is among the best—Izzo not only has a keen eye for detail but also digs deep into what makes men weep."—*Time Out New York*

Fabio Montale is dragged back into the mean streets of a violent, crime-infested Marseilles after the disappearance of his long-lost cousin's teenage son.

The Goodbye Kiss
Massimo Carlotto
Fiction/Noir - 192 pp - $14.95 - isbn 978-1-933372-05-1

"A nasty, explosive little tome warmly recommended to fans of James M. Cain for its casual amorality and truly astonishing speed."—*Kirkus Reviews*

An unscrupulous womanizer, as devoid of morals now as he once was full of idealistic fervor, returns to Italy, where he is wanted for a series of crimes. To avoid prison he sells out his old friends, turns his back on his former ideals and cuts deals with crooked cops. To earn himself the guise of respectability he is willing to go even further, maybe even as far as murder.

Death's Dark Abyss
Massimo Carlotto
Fiction/Noir - 192 pp - $14.95 - isbn 978-1-933372-18-1

"A narrative voice that in Lawrence Venuti's translation is cold and heartless—but, in a creepy way, fascinating."—*The New York Times*

A riveting drama of guilt, revenge, and justice, Massimo Carlotto's *Death's Dark Abyss* tells the story of two men and the savage crime that binds them. During a robbery, Raffaello Beggiato takes a young woman and her child hostage and later murders them. Beggiato is arrested, tried, and sentenced to life. The victims' father and husband, Silvano, plunges into a deepening abyss until the day the murderer seeks his pardon and he begins to plot his revenge.

Hangover Square
Patrick Hamilton
Fiction/Noir - 280 pp - $14.95 - isbn 978-1-933372-06-8

"Hamilton is a sort of urban Thomas Hardy: always a pleasure to read, and as social historian he is unparalleled."—NICK HORNBY

Adrift in the grimy pubs of London at the outbreak of World War II, George Harvey Bone is hopelessly infatuated with Netta, a cold, contemptuous small-time actress. George also suffers from occasional blackouts. During these moments one thing is horribly clear: he must murder Netta.

Boot Tracks
Matthew F. Jones
Fiction/Noir - 208 pp - $14.95 - isbn 978-1-933372-11-2

"More than just a very good crime thriller, this dark but illuminating novel shows us the psychopathology of the criminal mind . . . A nightmare thriller with the power to haunt."
—*Kirkus Reviews* (starred)

A commanding, stylishly written novel that tells the harrowing story of an assassination gone terribly wrong and the man and woman who are taking their last chance to find a safe place in a hostile world.

Love Burns
Edna Mazya
Fiction/Noir - 192 pp - $14.95 - isbn 978-1-933372-08-2

"This book, which has Woody Allen overtones, should be of great
interest to readers of black humor and psychological thrillers."
—*Library Journal* (starred)

Ilan, a middle-aged professor of astrophysics, discovers that his
young wife is having an affair. Terrified of losing her, he decides to
confront her lover instead. Their meeting ends in the latter's murder—the unlikely murder weapon being Ilan's pipe—and in desperation, Ilan disposes of the body in the fresh grave of his kinder-
garten teacher. But when the body is discovered, the mayhem
begins.

Departure Lounge
Chad Taylor
Fiction/Noir - 176 pp - $14.95 - isbn 978-1-933372-09-9

"Smart, original, surprising and just about as cool as a novel can get . . . Taylor can flat out write."—*The Washington Post*

A young woman mysteriously disappears. The lives of those she has left behind—family, acquaintances, and strangers intrigued by her disappearance—intersect to form a captivating latticework of coincidences and surprising twists of fate. Urban noir at its stylish and intelligent best.

Carte Blanche
Carlo Lucarelli
Fiction/Noir - 120 pp - $14.95 - isbn 978-1-933372-15-0

"This is Alan Furst country, to be sure."—*Booklist*

The house of cards built by Mussolini in the last months of World War II is collapsing, and Commissario De Luca faces a world mired in sadistic sex, dirty money, drugs and murder.

Dog Day
Alicia Giménez-Bartlett
Fiction/Noir - 208 pp - $14.95 - isbn 978-1-933372-14-3

"In Nicholas Caistor's smooth translation from the Spanish,
Giménez-Bartlett evokes pity, horror and laughter with equal adept-
ness. No wonder she won the Femenino Lumen prize in 1997 as
the best female writer in Spain."—*The Washington Post*

Delicado and her maladroit sidekick, Garzón, investigate the murder of a tramp whose only friend is a mongrel dog named Freaky.

www.europaeditions.com

The Big Question
Wolf Erlbruch
Children's Illustrated Fiction - 52 pp - $14.95 - isbn 978-1-933372-03-7

Named Best Book at the 2004 Children's Book Fair in Bologna.

"[*The Big Question*] offers more open-ended answers than the likes of Shel Silverstein's *Giving Tree* (1964) and is certain to leave even younger readers in a reflective mood."—*Kirkus Reviews*

A stunningly beautiful and poetic illustrated book for children that poses the biggest of all big questions: Why am I here?

The Butterfly Workshop
Wolf Erlbruch
Children's Illustrated Fiction - 40 pp - $14.95 - isbn 978-1-933372-12-9

Illustrated by the winner of the 2006 Hans Christian Andersen Award.

For children and adults alike: Odair, one of the Designers of All Things and grandson of the esteemed inventor of the rainbow, has been banished to the insect laboratory as punishment for his over-active imagination. But he still dreams of one day creating a cross between a bird and a flower.